SEVENTEEN

OR

THE BLOOD CITY TOMMY O'REILLY BENEFIT TOUR

To /

Dear Aunt Jean

Hope you have a lovely birthday,
and excellent Christmas! Look forward
to seeing you before too long.
Lots of love always

David

x x

DGBailey   Lutterworth, December 2021

SEVENTEEN

OR

THE BLOOD CITY TOMMY O'REILLY BENEFIT TOUR

DAVID G BAILEY

SilverWood

Published in 2021 by SilverWood Books

SilverWood Books Ltd
14 Small Street, Bristol, BS1 1DE, United Kingdom
www.silverwoodbooks.co.uk

ISBN 9781-80042-139-4 (hardback)
ISBN 978-1-80042-099-1 (paperback)
ISBN 978-1-80042-100-4 (ebook)

British Library Cataloguing in Publication Data
A CIP catalogue record for this book is
available from the British Library

Page design and typesetting by SilverWood Books

To Mum, who gave me a sixpenny soldier from Woolies every day…and so much more

Contents

1

The Swallow Keepers

Vic Swallow was chopping wood when he became aware of the approaching horsemen. To people of a certain world and time, the picture was of a squat, heavily muscled man with a cigarette dangling from his mouth, wiping sweat from his brow before continuing to work. To others of others, the sweaty shirt would be similar but the mounts would be motorbikes, the man would be younger and taller, wielding the axe to no apparent purpose. In Cibola, Vic had not yet worked up a sweat in his unbuttoned old 17th Cavalry tunic. He did not lack a wiry strength, retaining most of the slimness of his goalkeeping prime, which had led to much punning around 'Swallow dives' from the unimaginative Blood press corps.

'Put the cawfee on, Ian, we got visitors!' he hollered into the dark doorway of the wooden homestead, not really expecting any reply or compliance. If the sun was barely up yet, his twin was hardly likely to be.

Vic had no fear of riders approaching so openly. He had no living enemies and nothing worth stealing. One attraction of living way out on the Meseta Central, whose ever growing heart was the capital: you did not have to fear casual violence. Unless it was from your brother.

The four of them, two Knights and two Arab Pirates, slowed their horses to an unthreatening walk as they drew up in front of Vic, who took his time over splitting the last log before burying the axe in the block. He had instantly recognised the former captain and vice-captain of Blood City, but they no longer had any power of command over him.

'Morning, Victor. RFD 17 was all the address we had, a fair stretch from Blood.'

'You got that right, Sir Tristram.' Vic returned the formality of greeting to the older Knight, always a bit of a stiff, unbending bugger. There was now a physical stiffness about him too as he dismounted.

'Jakob you know, of course. His brother, Malabar. May have been after your time – had a few games between the sticks for us.'

Vic could see no family resemblance between the two Arabs, unless turbans and beards counted. Jakob O'Reilly fairly sprang out of the saddle. He had succeeded Sir Tristram as skipper of the City, also going on to captain the Pirates' international team with distinction. If Malabar had made any splash in the football world it had passed by Vic, who hardly followed the game after leaving his only club.

In his yellow robes, having failed to acknowledge Vic, let alone offer a by-your-leave, Malabar was taking the two Arab stallions towards the barn. The newer Knight was doing the same with the heavier horses on which he and Sir Tristram had come.

'Tristan, where's your manners? Say hello to Mr Swallow here. This is my whelp, Vic – fancies himself as a tricky inside forward.'

'I'm sorry, Dad. Mr Swallow.'

'Hi, kid. Why don't you let the Ayrab take all the horses? Being as he didn't have the decency to introduce hissen, I'm not inclined to let him into my house.'

Malabar did not turn at the comment, designedly loud enough for him to hear. Jakob's hand was at his belted scimitar as he replied, evenly enough, 'An Ayrab's as good as Westerner trash any dey of the weak, Swallow. My brother's got no language for you, but I can speak for him if need be. We've come a ways to talk – we can do it just as well here as indoors. You decide.'

'Prickly as ever, Jake. Come on in. Not often I see old teammates. You can meet my own brother – you may struggle just as much to get a civil word outa him.'

Perhaps Malabar had the right of it, staying outside in the cool barn with the animals. The twins' living quarters were a single room, with a single bed on either side, above which were small, grimy windows. There was a fireplace with a pot on it but no appetising smell of food, or drink brewing. Sprawled

11

on one cot was a soldier with his face to the wall, wearing only a pair of trousers with a yellow stripe down the outside of each leg. Vic pulled a knife from the rough surface of the table at the centre of the room and, already looking towards the grate, stabbed it into the sole of his brother's bare foot. He turned at the stifled gasp from Tristan, matching the yowl of the figure on the bed.

'What, lad, you think I should be more gentle? I'd sooner start blood from him than waste water chucking it at his head. Don't work anyways. You ever need tell me and my brother apart, just take us boots off, you'll find a pretty patchwork on the bottom of this 'un's feet.' Abruptly changing his tone, he addressed the woken man: 'You slackin' bastid, Ian, din't you hear me yelling?'

There was no reply from the Swallow now sitting on the edge of the cot, apparently oblivious to the blood welling between his toes before soaking into the dirt floor of the shack. He had his head in his hands, as if stopping his ears.

'We only needed to register one of these boys back in the dey'—Sir Tristram continued his son's instruction—'at least as far as looks were concerned. Like as two beans in a bait. Pretty different as goalkeepers, mind, in talent and temperament both.'

Ian Swallow looked at the Knights through bloodshot eyes. 'Don't tell me it's pre-seesun already. My deys of training hard just to warm the bench while others play are long past, Tram.'

'Training hard?' Jakob was not having it. 'You were more bone idle than Sir Septimus – lucky to be on the roster at all.

You'll be glad to hear you won't be needed this time round.'

'We only got the two mugs, so it'll have to be sharesie. What you mean, Jakob, this time around?'

'I'll let our captain tell you, Vic.'

'Wait on me while I cop a urination.' Ian hobbled to the door, where he paused to shield his eyes against the watery sun. 'We may be twins, but we ain't telepathic. I need to hear whatever you gonna tell him. We's pards as well as brothers, ain't that right?'

'He still a boozehound then,' Jakob stated bluntly as Ian found his way outside.

Vic seemed about to contest the point, then smiled. 'That he is.'

'Can he still hold a gun? Best sharpshooter in the 17th, that soldier once was, Tris,' said Sir Tristram. 'Or was it only from himself I heard that?'

'You might well of, but there's plenty as would of agreed with him. That may be about the only time his hands don't shiver and shake, but sure he can hold a gun still. Mostly to bring home our dinner, whether it's muntjac, meerkat or just jackrabbit.'

'Yeah, we'd starve if it was left to my older brother. *And* I was a better keeper than him too, new 'un, whatever they may say.' Ian rejoined the company with a meaty slap to the side of Vic's head, at which he appeared to take no more offence than had Ian to his stabbing.

'You could make impossible saves, I'll grant you that.' Jakob grew notably more animated whenever talk turned to football. 'What about that time you threw the ball into your

13

own net against Ajax, though? Only cost us the double. No thanks, Vic.' The Arab declined a mug of sludgy liquid.

'We won't be facing Ajax this time.' Sir Tristram steered the conversation to the purpose of their visit. 'You boys heard of the Torneo Sesquicentenario? The Seskie?'

'You must have,' Tristan interjected. 'Everyone's been talking about it in Blood for, like, mumfs, even United fans.'

'We don't get much news out here since the Injuns switched from smoke signals to satellite, boy, but I'm sure your dad will tell us what it's all about. Sorry we don't have a chalkboard here for like when you used to give us our tactics talks, Tram.'

'I only hope I won't be wasting my time like I was back then. The Seskie's a trophy to mark 150 yeers of the oldest club fixture in the world, which I don't need tell anyone here is Blood City v Young Faithfuls. Only they're not playing it just with the current teams. No, it's so-called Legends of Yesteryeer that'll be contesting the tournament.'

'People like Dad who played in that very first game.'

'That gag's wearing a little bare, son. As I've told you many times, I didn't make my debut until 117 yeers ago.'

'I was in that team too, boy. Not you, Ian – you was still tomcattin' around Casablanca. And you, Jake, didn't you come a bit later, replace that Army guy Reaney at right-back? What a team we had!'

'I was the one to wear the painted 2 shirt when the league began.' Jakob put him right.

'I agree about the team we had, Vic, and that's the one I've been charged with reuniting. By King Henry himself.'

'Henry Morgan,' Ian cut in scornfully. 'I can't believe he's letting us compete in that Seskie-whatever. Din't he already rewrite the Subbutay Registers to make like Morgan's Marauders was the second team ever formed? He would have quit the Faithfuls the honour of being first if he thought the football folk memory would stand for it.'

'He may have his reasons for not wanting the Marauders involved. For one thing, they're a Casablanca team, like the Yofas. He wants this match to catch the imagination of all in Cibola, not just one city.'

'So will it be two legs then?' Vic asked. 'Even Morroco sticks more to Blood than the coast, so there's no neutral territory for a single match.'

'I thought so myself at first. But Henry is king. It will be in Piedra, Zanzibar. A single match for the Seskie trophy, with extra time, then penalties, then a fight to the death between the two captains, if needed to get a result.'

'Wait a minnit, Dad, you didn't say anything about a fight to the death. You're joking, right?'

'No, Tris. That's only if 136 minnits and seventeen penalties each can't decide it. Very unlikely to happen.'

'But Dad…' He fell silent at his father's raised hand.

'You boys seem a bit surprised?' Sir Tristram looked at the dumbstruck Swallows.

'Zanzibar? Does that island even exist? Has anyone actually been there? Been there and come back, I should say.'

While Vic's tone was one of puzzled wonder, his brother was more forthright. '*Now* I understand why the current teams won't be going. In fear of their lives, I should think. That place

15

makes the Casablanca dockside look like the Embassy Quarter in Blood.'

'It need not trouble you, Ian. You will not have to face your fear and go. We will, in fact, be under the protection of my brother Tommy, for so long already Morgan's Grand Vizor in Zanzibar.'

Seeing that Ian was not going to respond either to the provocation or the information – other than with a smile suggesting that whatever Jakob may say he, Ian, knew better – Vic ventured a further question. 'Jakob, no offence, but are you blowing smoke up our butts? I mean, I knew Tommy personally, a legend, but I also mind the stories of when he went off to Zanzibar all them yeers ago. For every soldier said it was to develop the colony, another said he'd run foul of Old Henry, still new in his kingship then, and it was a kind of exile. Zanzibar is the Last Ground, the place we all end up when our casts are broken.'

'That's mobo-jobo Vic. I'm surprised at you. Zanzibar is a real place, an island not so far beyond the horizon from Casablanca.' Sir Tristram knew his job would be hard enough without letting footballers' superstitions complicate it further.

Jakob also wanted to answer Vic. 'The O'Reilly clan heard all the rumours back then, that it was only our strength of arms and importance in the Pirate horde that saved our pa-brother Tommy's life. Rumours that Morgan was jealous of the love the people had for him, people of all the four Houses, and would have him out of the way. All that's old news.

'I say now: Tommy O'Reilly remains the most powerful soldier in the Zuni Kingdom. Save the king,' he added grudgingly. 'I have heard Zanzibar now has a stadium that will not disgrace the Seskie, fit to rival the Theatre of Blood or the Casablanca Capitarium.'

'I'm not frit of the unknown, and whatever you may say, Jake, nor ain't my brother Ian. Still, it's a long way to go for a football match. What about the tut? The money, Tram, what about the money? We can't all live by the Knights' Code of Camelot, and we don't all have a birthright of Arab clan millions.'

'All expenses will be found. I daresay you will live better than you are now, and I believe there will be medals of gold for the winners. For us.'

As if exhausted by his brief spell upright, Ian Swallow was again lying on his cot, head propped against the back wall. He sipped from a small bottle, then crooked it protectively in his right elbow. 'Up to you, my dear brother, but all that depends on if you live to get your mitts on the money.'

'Always with the fear of death!' Jakob flared. 'Zanzibar and the road and sea to reach it are not without hazards. If they are too many for you, so be it. We are not here to beg. Remember, Tram, how I said we should have looked to Nkulu the Zulu to be our number 1. He has his own place in Blood City folklore.'

'Glad to hear you admit there could be some risk to everybody's hide from this tour, and innaresting you mention the Zulu.' Ian seemed more relaxed the more annoyed Jakob became. 'You big-shot internationals may not remember my nickname at the City? The Judge – because I spent so much time on the bench, ha bluddy ha.

'When I went out to take a whizz I was fixin' to shoot someone in with our horses, till I realised he must be with you folks. I thought he looked kinda familiar, and now my head's a bit clearer I sussed it was Malabar. You mind he don't take your place and money both, Vic, leave you all the training and graft but none of the glory. He's got family connections – we don't.'

'Is that right, Tram? Is that the way yawl thinking?' Vic frowned.

'The man's drunk at sunrise. Why would you listen to him?'

'It's all right, Jakob, I'll take this one. I know back in our dey it was mainly eleven against eleven – less than that if someone didn't show up, or there was a murder or two. It's a squad game now, and on matchdey it will be two squads of seventeen facing off. Two keepers are always included. I swear on this boy's life'—since when did he need to raise his arm to put a hand on Tristan's head? he wondered—'it's not about the money. I'm trying to recruit not eleven, but seventeen at least, to give us a squadron with the best chance of completing the mission successfully. The final squad, the seventeen, will all get the medals.'

'Dvaeba, you make it sound more like a war raid than a benefit match. So you sayin' the money's safe, but my place in the starting line-up may not be. Have I got that right?'

'That's about the measure of it, Vic.'

'And you won't be going to that other Pirate, Nkulu the Zulu? I already lost my place to him once sixty yeers ago. I can't see he was a BC legend anyway – brought his boy Mbulu up Ajax, din't he?'

'Maybe I'm too sentimental, but I tell you straight what I'm doing. I'm looking for the same first eleven as in my first few seesuns, the ones with the numbers painted on their backs over that red shirt. You were the number 1, sure as I was 4. That was a team, the team I knew best and, for all its faults, one I trust. This tour is about more than football, trust *me* on that.

'Whatever his football background, Malabar would be coming with us as Jakob's brother and pick, just as I *might* take this newbie of mine along for the ride. You don't need to come with us right now, but I need your word one way or another if you'll be with us in Blood, ready to go, this time next weak.'

'Hell, yeah. You were always good at the speeches, Tram, but tell you the truth you had me at the chance of getting between the sticks for the City again. You headin' back to Blood right now or will we break bread first?'

'No, soldier, thanks. We made an early start because we're heading up to Busted Jaw.'

'To the Injun ski and gaming resort, I imagine, not the township. Bit of R 'n' R for you boys?'

'We'll be spending the night there, but the main job is to try putting the left side of our defence in place – numbers 3 and 6. Always build from the back, like I said on our way here to get our goalie, right, Tris?'

Malabar was ready with their horses when the visitors left the cabin, accompanied outside only by Vic. He watched them disappear in the direction of the Mighty Morroco Mountains, hoping that his brother would not give him too much grief about his decision to hit the road. If he was already back asleep, he might wake with no memory of the recruiting officers' call.

Sir Tristram and Jakob O'Reilly rode far enough ahead of the other two to keep their conversation private – a poor deal for Tristan. A talkative and friendly boy, he was scarcely able to get a word from Malabar.

'I tell you Tram, I never liked either of the Swallows much, but todey I was tempted to kill the drinking one. I do not trust him.'

'Come on Jake, we've both played in defence long enough to know you can never trust a goalkeeper. I need your support as vice-captain all the way, right down to putting up with Ian on the tour.'

'What? I thought we made it clear only Victor was invited. My brother is no Yashin, but Malabar is perfectly adequate backup in goal. We don't need the other Swallow.'

'Not as a keeper, I agree. I've never known those two be separated for long, is all. If Ian does show up with Vic in Blood, I tell you now I may take him along. I suspect in his wild deys he might have gone across to Zanzibar a few times, before transit was officially restricted to Army only. We may need all the specialist help we can get.'

Sir Tristram had every intention of taking Ian if he turned up, for reasons he had not discussed with his vice. He had been forbidden to do so by King Henry himself. An extra crack gun might make a big difference in the non-footballing aspects of the tour Morgan had outlined secretly to his chosen skipper.

2

The Double-A Team

There was no tribal segregation in Blood, where the four Houses lived cheek by chap, if never in perfect harmony. The big divide was between the sports colony and the rest of the populace that watched sports. There were many more people in Casablanca, where the Pirates were the dominant House. In Blood, King Henry depended on the Army to keep order, though there was also a higher proportion of Knights and Westerners.

The Indians had provided the kings before Morgan: Frederick I and Frederick II, figures who had not sought to impose themselves on the general population in the way the massive, kilted Highlander had with his forward line of brothers. Militant Indians claimed they once formed the greater part of the people, founding the High City of Morroco under a more ancient name on which even they could not agree. It had been so long since the troop of incomers from the other side of the great range had taken over that city, without ambitions of further conquest, that it had become again a recognised part of Cibola, albeit one that tended to keep itself to itself.

Indians dislodged from what became Morroco formed another mountain settlement, not high enough to serve as a control and command post looking both ways, nor yet low enough to be overrun with overspill from Blood or the Meseta. The township's lower limit – on a track still wide enough for one wagon, if not quite two – was marked by an unauthentic totem pole. Animals and soldiers alternated on the way up to three times the height of Jakob on horseback. At the top was not a Zuni but a dog, black mouth open as in a yawn or a bay. A wooden clapboard sign was attached to a chain hanging from the two biggest bottom-row teeth. Only Tristan read its message:

Busted Jaw awaits you, if you come in war.
Bring your money, come in peace, welcome even more.

While not perhaps the saints of Cibolan popular history, the Fredericks had been soldiers of personal frugality and humility. Nevertheless, the public purse, managed by a committee of chieftains, had built them a palace complex. Morgan had little interest in taking this over, though he was naturally always comped the Royal Suite in the entertainment and health resort it had become.

Little Doe greeted them in the red shirt (number 3) and white shorts of Blood City's time-honoured kit, not as a particular sign of respect but because it was his uniform. Leading Indian players from the past could always make a living at the complex schmoozing guests, a better one than their fellows who worked in its kitchens, restaurants or as cleaners.

'How now, my friends.' A feather in his black, slicked-back hair, Little Doe sprang into the classic pose in which he had so often taken the field as Jakob's full-back partner: dagger raised behind his ear to thrust at their faces, shield stretched out before him strapped to his left forearm.

'Little Doe, how are you? My boy Tristan, Jakob's brother Malabar. If we can just wash off a little of the travel dust, we'd be glad to join you with the big chief whenever convenient.'

'Of course. But perhaps you could give me a general briefing beforehand. White Eagle was particularly insistent on hearing to what we owe the pleasure of your visit before we all sit down together.'

'I'll be glad to show our old friend that respect.'

Respect was important to White Eagle. Although never vice-captain of Blood City – that post had been created for Jakob O'Reilly – he was a recognised leader and support to Sir Tristram. Always on his dignity, at number 6 he formed half of the central defensive pairing with Pink Viking that had been one of City's major strengths. He was the only member of the team who could compare in height and heft to its giant Pirate number 5.

Sir Tristram was briefly disconcerted to find their dinner meeting might not be limited to their own group. It was served in the egalitarian Indian manner, on a long refectory table to which anyone was free to bring his plate. The cafeteria for the whole staff of the resort was a large upper-floor room with a view along one full-glass wall down into the gaming pit. Tonight was a quiet one, the sport ranging from chess through dominoes and cards to roulette; on other occasions space would be reserved for boxing, wrestling or more deadly combats involving anything from fighting cocks or dogs to soldiers.

In the event, nobody approached too closely or showed the slightest interest in their parley. Tristan, Sir Tristram, Jakob and a distinctly uncomfortable Malabar faced White Eagle with Little Doe to his left, as they had so often lined up on the pitch. To his right was another Indian, in yellow buckskins and a chieftain's headdress, who greeted Sir Tristram and Jakob with a brief nod.

'Now then, White Eagle,' Sir Tristram addressed the Indian directly opposite him, 'a pleasure to see you again after so many yeers. I always felt safe to venture forward knowing you were guarding the back gate.' White Eagle had been renowned for crossing the halfway line only once each match, to change ends at half-time.

'How so, Alfred Tristram. Those were famous deys.'

'It's good to see you too, Yellow Cloud. You're based here nowadey?'

The other Indian nodded again. He had been a prolific goalscoring right-winger for City and the Westerners, always looking to cut inside and unleash left-foot thunderbolts.

'May I assume that Little Doe already put you in the picture?'

White Eagle lifted his jug of chicha in both hands, tipped it slightly towards his guests, replied at last 'Indeed he did,' then took a long pull at it, disdaining the glass on the table by his right hand.

'Good.' Sir Tristram paused to savour the look of disgust on Tristan's face at his first mouthful of the white pulpy drink favoured by the Indians, which could vary in alcoholic strength from zero to falling-down drunk. He had forewarned Tristan about this – not the alcoholic content, which would be nil for the boy and the Arabs (Indians were scrupulous hosts), but its taste. He was pleased to see the lad master his features quickly. 'Maybe we can use this time to clear up any questions or concerns you may have, but not before I say we really hope you will both be coming along with us.'

'We love football – none more. Why do you speak of "both"? We are three.'

Sir Tristram went patiently over his 1-to-11, historic-team speech, secretly already prepared to allow Yellow Cloud, a handy rifleman, a place in their squad. He was under no illusions – it would give him problems as coach and captain, since the third Indian would be directly threatening the starting place on the right wing of one of Jakob's cousins, the Berserker Oscar.

It was always difficult to tell whether you had got your point across to White Eagle, whom Sir Tristram was prepared to acknowledge as very wise while privately suspecting at times to be very slow (speed was never an asset of his on the pitch either). Perhaps he, or at least the fly Little Doe, could make the calculation that the historic 1 to 11 was in their favour, if not so much that of Yellow Cloud. At any rate, the big chief plodded on.

'What is your latest knowledge of the situation in Zanzibar as regards security? I ask not for myself but for my newer brothers.' He let go of the chicha jug long enough to put his hands palm up on the table in the direction of the other two Indians. Little Doe nodded in enthusiastic support of his elder; Yellow Cloud made a point of looking away, distancing himself from any suggestion that *he* might need looking out for.

'My personal knowledge is not great. Through the O'Reilly clan we know we have the guarantee of safe passage from our old rival on the field, the Grand Vizor Tommy, maximum law on the island. The Cup Final we go to play – you will notice I do not call it an exhibition, much less a friendly – is sponsored by none other than King Henry himself. Even so, we shall travel as a squadron, with our weapons. In truth it was a question I wanted to ask you. I believe there are many Indians in Zanzibar.'

'We are the Erfolk, here first and once as populous as the grains of sand by the sea, in every part of Cibola. We are not coeval with the Cowboys, as the old verse would have it. Remember?

'The Westerners were first to rule
But would not live in peace.
The Army came to keep things cool
Hard men, for sale or lease.
The Knights were ever strong and true,
The flowers of the realm…'

26

White Eagle had closed his eyes to recite the doggerel, opening them to nod across the table at the compliment to the Knights. Perhaps thinking he had forgotten the rest, Tristan eagerly helped him out.

'The Pirates, rank and motley crew,
All others overwhelm.'

It was as well that Malabar was seated as far away as he could be from Tristan, for he rose to his feet, full plate over his head, before smashing it down onto the wooden table. Potato salad, curried goat and smoked salmon flew everywhere. 'That's a lie.' The Arab found his voice.

'Across the seas the Pirate crew,
Were called to take the helm.'

'But that's…' Tristan fell silent as his father gripped his wrist. Yellow Cloud was crouching forward as if ready to spring, palms flat on the table, glaring diagonally across it at Malabar. Little Doe had his war knife out, using it calmly to sweep the debris of plate and food from table to the floor behind him.

'My son does not lie,' Sir Tristram said, half-turned to his right towards the two Arabs. 'He is not quick-witted enough to produce the rhyme from his own head – it must be what they are singing in the shulyards. That does not make it right. If any offence was caused, I ask pardon of our teammates – and of our hosts.'

The cue was plain for Malabar to make his own apology, but he had returned to silence. He did resume the bench, sitting with arms folded as if to remove any possible doubt that he had finished his dinner.

White Eagle spoke on, as if nothing had interrupted his flow. 'The sea claims the sand over the yeers, but yes, we do still have a colony in the Last Ground. You can count on good support from our fanbase, the more so if our brother Yellow Cloud occupies his well-deserved place as number 7.'

Sir Tristram knew that Jakob O'Reilly was never so dangerous as when he was motionless and silent by an effort of will, as he clearly had been since his kinsman tossed the salad. He was relieved to hear Jakob speak now, though the Pirate's tone was impatient. 'Sir Tristram has already explained, clear enough to all who would listen, that if we look at newer generations others may also have a claim. Cowboys like Sinbad and Bull would be a good shout for many, so be careful what you wish for.'

'I hear Sir Tristram.' The Indian's voice was cold. 'As there can only be one king, so can there only be one captain. I am happy to leave team selection to our once and future leader. I would like to speak apart with him about the logistics of our trip and other matters that need not detain you.'

'You are welcome to do so. I do not stand on position.'

So it was that Tristan, to his delight and no little relief, found himself released from table and free to wander the massive hall below, with a pocketful of slot-machine tokens supplied by Little Doe. A similar offer was declined by the two Arabs, who said they would have a smoke outside before turning in. Tristan went to approach Malabar, not in fear but to say he was only repeating the verse as he had always heard it. It seemed a curious thing to get so excited over; many nastier rhymes circulated about the Pirates. Jakob forestalled him.

'Do not apologise, if that is what you have in mind. He will like you less for it. In future, leave singing in public to those we pay to do it. Now go forth and multiply those tokens the Indians gave you into ten times as much cold cash.' To Tristan's surprise, the great bearded ruffian gave him a wink and a smile.

'I thought you said it would be just the two of us,' Sir Tristram remarked mildly when Little Doe showed no sign of leaving the executive box to which they had risen in a private lift. The circular space had views of the open-air pitches, the wider outdoors and what might be every single room inside the complex, by way of banked TV screens.

'I grow forgetful, Alfred. Little Doe is increasingly my memory as well as my eyes and ears. Feel free to speak in his presence just as if we were alone.'

'It's not Doey's presence that exercises me. I just wonder who else I might be speaking to. Nobody forgets the Drake scandal.'

Sir Francis Drake was acknowledged as the greatest goalkeeper in Blood City's history. First choice for the Pirate international team, as a Cavalier he was expected to be a staunch supporter of King Henry, and perhaps he was. He was clearly under the influence of some drink or drug in the video of him making extremely disobliging comments about the king. The footage had been shot in Busted Jaw, where he was supposedly on retreat during a suspension.

Many thought Henry's sentence of cutting both Drake's legs off at the knee harsh. All Blood City fans were furious to lose a keeper at the peak of his powers. Others thought it an abuse of his admitted prerogatives by King Henry to maim such a prominent Pirate for a few ill-chosen words. The king chose his own words of retribution carefully.

'Drake was a great footballer and a personal friend. That is why he still lives. Consider all if you have such claims to mercy before you raise your voice in public against myself or any of the clan Morgan.'

Drake had of course thought he was speaking in private, not public, to a sympathetic ear. There may even have been a prompting voice in his own ear. People had already feared Morgan. Those with the wealth and status to visit the Busted Jaw complex gained a new respect for the reach of the Indians who owned and ran it after seeing the arrogant Cavalier literally brought to his knees. There were rumours he had been more insulting yet about the Fredericks, killing an Indian brave enough to take him to task for it, though the film of that part of his night out had not become public.

'Drake was a bully and a braggart.' White Eagle's tone was dismissive. 'You are a renowned Knight and a friend to the Indian people. If you are concerned, let me speak first.

'You are right that we have eyes over, and ears open. Football is our life. I know, from the many times we locked horns when he was still centre forward for the Marauders, it was once Henry Morgan's also. Now he naturally has other things on his mind. How is his health?'

'So much for you doing the talking.' Sir Tristram laughed. He was not to be tricked into any revelations by the sudden blunt question, for all he had been shocked at the deterioration in the king when he had received his briefing for this mission.

'We are none of us any newer. Since he had the heathered tussock cut from his stand, football has been out of the question, a grievous blow for any of us. He still holds the voice of command. Have you heard otherwise?'

'King Henry is deep as well as broad. We Indians are not part of his court, but we are the only House to have known kingship before his time. While our dear Fredericks could each have been lifted in one of Morgan's hands, it was not only his greater strength that told. He was cunning as a Crow. He has always been the sole focus of power, knowing how to remove others from the sunlight.'

'Are you talking of Tommy's so-called exile, because I—?'

'It was not only Tommy,' White Eagle steamrollered on. 'What of Hulk, Morgan's vice at the Marauders, then captain, head of the Vikings, Henry's comrade in arms so many yeers? You were surely not one of those who thought when he went to Morroco it was only to play for the Continentals? The Marauders – owned as well as managed by the Morgans, lest we forget – received an unheard-of transfer fee. Let's call it a king's ransom. Why not? Many thought Hulk would be king. He has never returned, not once. And neither has Tommy.'

'Take me with you.'

'We Indians believe in the kingdom, not the king. Morgan believes only in himself. If our second Frederick had been a great footballer, he might still be in power. Morgan chooses to commemorate not the kingdom of a thousand yeers, but a football match of a piffling 150, within our own memory, dear Alfred. He would not stage such an event without a motive related to his kingship. That is our belief.'

Sir Tristram was increasingly curious. 'I grant you King Henry may not enjoy the popularity of the Fredericks. If you will forgive me the observation, that is because, unlike them, he has dared to rule. He has had to be ruthless in maintaining himself in power, as he was in seizing it. His clan is nothing like as numerous as that of the Vikings or Arabs, not to mention your own peoples. Just six Highlander brothers, five footballers, at its foundation.'

'As you say, no House is as populous as the Indians, nor any with so little power. We make money, yes, but much of it goes in tribute to Henry. It is no accident that all Houses now lack great leaders. They have not been allowed to flourish.'

Sir Tristram felt that White Eagle was edging uncomfortably close to the nub of his own mission. He decided to take a gamble (where better than Busted Jaw to do so?). 'Congratulations on your intelligence. King Henry, who once on meeting an old friend or competitor would have wished only to get mortal, this time spoke of mortality. I do not mean to suggest he is near death – nothing of that kind,' he added hastily, having sensed a quickening of interest more from Little Doe than his stolid chief. 'You know that Bene has recently been on an extended mission to Morroco, while Rab Rory is seeking to make himself a favourite in Casablanca?'

'The smallest brother has always supposedly been

Henry's own favourite, and Casablanca the Pirates' preferred homeland, with the sea at their backs. I have always wondered why Morgan did not make it his capital.'

'I wondered that myself for the longest time. I took instruction. I now understand he is showing his military skill in this as throughout his life. It is far easier to sweep downwards in attack than toil upwards. If he were to lose the support of Blood, he would lose much.'

'If altitude is the strategic key, then would Morroco not make a better capital? Forgive me if I speak out of turn.' Little Doe quickly remembered his role as factotum to the older Indian after revealing a glimpse of his interest in wider matters.

'Too remote. Blood's centrality is also critical,' White Eagle snapped. 'That is why Morgan spends most of his time there, with Albert and Asparoukhov. Major players too, by the way.'

'I am with you on that. On the pitch it was always felt the wingers had more talent, but those two brothers were his inside forwards and may still be closer to Morgan. What is it they call them lately?'

'The Double-A Team.' Having started talking, Little Doe seemed unable to shut up, despite another frosty look from White Eagle. 'Is it true they are actually daggers drawn with each other, or that they remain united but in a plot against the king?'

'Whoa, Doey. You are on home territory. I would not speak of such matters even in Camelot, unless I were seated at the Table of Trust.'

'Little Doe, go fetch the lift.' White Eagle's patience was exhausted. 'I fully understand your reticence, Alfred.' The chief leaned towards him as the other Indian disappeared. 'Let us not talk more of a world where a king with fading powers might wish to cover all his bases with those closest to him. Where if Bene were to hold sway in the High Country, Rab Rory on the coast, then why not Albert or Asparoukhov in the Last Ground, leaving the other – more or less favoured, I would not like to guess – at the king's side in Blood.'

This was one of the times Sir Tristram thought White Eagle might be very wise.

3

The Seventeener

Sir Tristram's pleasure in Tristan's company was an unlooked-for bonus of taking him to the uplands as his squire, while his man of all business was acting for him in Blood. He had no intention of finding himself too far outnumbered in the squad by people of other Houses. Since City's origins were as a team of Knights, he had a pool to draw from. Bowlegs had summoned them for cakes and ale at the Whipping Inn, on the eve of the wider group's planned departure from the capital.

The captain had spoken personally to the two Camelot Knights, 8 and 10 in his historic team. Barrie Knight was now more famous as a cricketer than a footballer. The Young Faithfuls were said to have bought him, in the same deal as they acquired the deadly centre forward John Ivanhoe, primarily to lead their cricket selection as an all-rounder, matched in talent only by Pink Viking. Sir Septimus, a run-of-the-mill left-arm spinner, was among the most-capped Knights ever as a footballer, deceptively strong for all his slim build, and good in the air too.

The Whipping, occupying a whole side of the small square supposedly located at the dead centre of Blood, was used to celebrities. Barrie and Septimus, first to arrive, would have had to jostle at the bar for their tankards just like everyone else, had they not been well in with the establishment's unsalaried potman. Not as agile or svelte as in his goalkeeping deys, when he rejoiced in the nickname the Pouncing Ounce, Nkulu the Zulu had for a while enjoyed some popularity as an informal cabaret turn. Where he now wiped tables and emptied ashtrays he had once performed with his heavy cowhide whip, plucking soldiers' cigarettes from their lips with it and only occasionally leaving a face a bloody mess.

'In my dey the deboshes used to be on tour or after matches, not before we got under way.' Nkulu plonked the Knights' beers down at a table he had magicked for them. 'Have you seen Swallow? He was in here earlier. I was kidding him I'll be coming along with you. I'd be the only one my boy Mbulu wouldn't dare do the whipping out on. Fine lad he is. In charge of the whole transport fleet to the Last Ground now he is.'

'It's Knights only this evening. You know the old gang – direct them through the fug over here when they show up, will you?' The friends were both faintly embarrassed at all the fuss around the Seskie.

'I'm not waiting all night for Bowlegs and the others. What news of our friend John?' Sir Septimus asked Barrie, of the centre forward who had stood between them at so many kick-offs. 'Will he be joining us?'

'Your guess matches mine, Sep. We rarely meet, his football seesun normally ends just as the cricket one begins. He's like a god down there with the Yofas, so I reckon he might be hard to win back for us.'

'Is he the only holdout?'

'We'll know more when Sir Tristram gets back from Busted Jaw. We should see nearly the full squad tomorrow when he rejoins us for the whipping out. Cowboy is down in Casablanca like John, I think, and you know we're making a 200-varst detour to the Pink Palace on the way down.'

'All to massage Pink Viking's ego.'

'That's superstars for you.' Barrie instinctively maintained the knightly ideal of courtesy to all, speaking ill of none. In that spirit he brushed aside the thought he sometimes had that Septimus was a trifle envious of the big money he and John were supposed to have pulled in from their transfer to the Casablanca team. 'Here's Bowlegs now.'

'Ar, and bringing another low-born with him.'

The soldier Sir Septimus so sourly referred to was François – *Sir* François when he thought it would fly. He was not only bow-legged (Sir Tristram's man had his name as an archer, not from any bandiness) but one-armed, a common enough characteristic of fighting soldiers. He was a by-blow of Martin Coluna, the Young Faithfuls' original captain.

Their party that evening was soon completed by

Brittanus and Chutney. The former, a legionary like Septimus and equally useful with his head, had replaced Barrie in the first team and proved himself a more prolific goalscorer. Chutney always wore a full suit of armour, the visor of his helmet making a dull thud as he placed it on the table at his right hand. Despite the additional weight of metal he carried, he was more mobile than François, not only on the field but in his career, having done a useful job for a number of teams. They were both utility defenders, remaining close despite the competition that implied.

They were all best mates by the end of the evening, their table well attended by Nkulu. Barrie was offering to get him a place in their squad as he became the first to leave.

'I'll be here and ready for the call, Sir Barrie, thank you. You take care on the way home.' He showed him solicitously to the door.

Back at Whipping Square in good time for the three o'clock kick-off the next dey, Barrie was unprepared for the strong Army presence. It looked like a full detachment of German WW1ers, including the Army's classy and powerful number three batsman, one of the Rumplebums (his brother Fritz was an opener).

'What's happening, Walter? Not expecting any trouble, surely?'

'Hey, Barrie. Not any more, I hope. The big slave driver was threatening to blow his top about the murder. He's been reminded he's here to do a job. He may take his frustrations out on you poor lambs, so watch out.'

'What murder?'

'Sorry, assumed you knew. I heard you were here last night.'

So the Army had been noting names and faces from the previous evening. In the Cibola of Morgan's reign, innocence was never to be taken for granted, even if you were guilty of nothing. Knight answered carefully: 'I was. Ducked out early.'

'Good job he was black in a way, since there was hardly a face left to identify him.'

'You mean Nkulu? He was the only black...'

'There you go then, must be him. I didn't know the name – believe he worked at the Whipping. After midnight it got a bit raucous there, clients getting annoyed about having to wait for their bocks. Someone went outside to find out where the guy had got to with the new barrel. Found it stove in, just like his head. Smashed to a pulp, that was.'

'So they weren't rolling him for the beer. What was it all about?'

'Bit early to say, Barrie. People wouldn't be looking too closely, except the big fellow – Mbulu, similar name, probably it *was* his Farter – kicked up such a fuss. You know the number of killings in Blood every night of the yeer? Especially round dives like the Whipping.'

'Nkulu was a famous player. He deserved a better end.' Barrie continued through the crowd, to the long table set up in the street for the Blood City squad. Although now spared the need to argue with Sir Tristram a case for including Nkulu in their party, he felt the Zulu's death was not an auspicious start to their adventure.

The origins of whipping out were said to lie in Blood's earliest deys and wars. Some said the idea had been to flog

39

conscripts, shanghaied soldiers or slaves into shape and submission before sending them off to battle. Others maintained it had been voluntary, used by warriors to work up a frenzy against their foes, represented by the soldier with the whip, perhaps costumed appropriately. Some said the event used to end with him being torn to pieces by the mob, giving him no incentive to go gently on his victims.

Sir Tristram had not shared with Barrie that their own whipping out ceremony was King Henry's idea. 'You know, Tram, give the squad a sense of community before you go off. We're harking back to historic times with the Seskie – let's have a bit of living history to stir people's interest.'

Many of the crowd, he was well aware, had come not to cheer Blood City away on tour but to see blood flow. State punishments nowadey were so cruel and unusual they tended to be carried out behind closed doors, lest they provoke revulsion or revolution rather than shock and awe. It was out of the question to cancel, for all that Mbulu was deranged with grief and anger. Sir Tristram knew him from football. He had managed to have a word with him – had come up with a suggestion that briefly calmed the wild-eyed look of the giant fleetmaster.

The window for Mbulu to wield his weapon was between three and six, though the concept of time in Cibola was, like that of innocence, never an absolute. There was no shame in going to embrace the post so inebriated you needed it to stay upright. Leaving the maddened Zulu a couple more ours to calm down might also have appeared a wise counsel to some. Nevertheless, promptly at five to three Sir Tristram stood up to speak, to a whistle blown by Bowlegs. His Knights and Westerners were around him. Arabs had little use for socialising outside their own tribe, so he was not expecting Jakob and his soldiers till later.

'Bloodsmen: this is not itself an historic occasion, but it may be the beginning of one. I would not normally expect fans of Ajax, of Blood United, of Sun City'—no orator, Sir Tristram did not have the art to conduct the cheers, diminishing in volume at each name—'to stand shoulder to shoulder with us of the City in our quest to bring back the Sesquicentenario – the Seskie. Remember this, though. We are representing you all – all our capital's teams against the cities of the plain. We go to fight for all of Blood!

'These are violent times,' he continued when the roar of acclaim had quietened. 'Witness the brutal slaying, within feat of where I now stand, of Nkulu the Zulu. It is not my place to give his eulogy, despite I knew him well, as a custodian for both City and Ajax. His son Mbulu, Master of the King's Fleet, is scheduled to perform the honours todey. He will do his duty. In fact, I believe he may do it with the whip of his father.'

Sir Tristram was delighted by the applause. Mbulu was in an extremely volatile state, where any perceived slighting of himself or Nkulu might have goaded him into fiercer application of the lash. He had arrived toting a case the size of a big soldier's coffin, containing a full selection of the tools of his trade. In his present mood he might have been tempted to go for a more punitive one than his father's single-strand cowhide.

41

Mbulu, towering a head and more above the crowd, did not need a whip in his hand to be given plenty of space by the pole, which rose to more than double his height. If it had once been barky and rough, it had long been worn smooth by clutching hands and by bodies sliding down it. At summer fairs it sometimes served a less cruel purpose, greased for the challenge to climb it for prizes.

Bowlegs was acting as barker. Sir Tristram shucked his tunic off and linked his hands around the pole, careful to stand tall as befitted a Knight. He had never taken the lash before. It held no fear for him. Whether from deference on the giant Zulu's part or because he was only warming up, his blow to the City captain was a lazy flick, raising a welt but not drawing blood. He smiled to reassure Tristan that he was unhurt, touched by his firstborn's curious protectiveness towards him. Tristan had not taken at all well his father's final decision that he would not travel with the squad, so Sir Tristram was glad to see him, enthusiastic enough to bag himself a front-row view: the bloodlust of the new, he supposed, usually cured the first time their own blood spilled beyond the playing field.

There followed Barrie Knight, Sir Septimus (a little more zip in that one, perhaps in memory of a goal where the legionary had nutmegged Mbulu), Brittanus, François and Chutney, who drew laughs by fixing to stand with torso suited in armour. The crowd enjoyed the spectacle, soon filling the theatrical pause before Bowlegs announced each victim's name by chanting his own. Their cries were satisfied when at last Bowlegs' turn came, with feigned dread taking off his chain mail balaclava until suddenly Tristan was addressing the whipmaster from about the level of his belly button.

'I am sorry for your loss, Mbulu. I am ready for my go.'

The Zulu smiled for the first time that dey, then frowned in puzzlement as he realised the lad spoke in earnest. Sir Tristram, chatting with Barrie Knight, responded quickly when Mbulu looked to him for guidance.

'Come away, Tristan. This is not for children. We have spoken of this.'

'I am no child, Father. We have spoken of that too. While I honour and respect you, I swear I am ready to take off my jerkin right now to join your squad.' He gripped the bottom of the loose-fitting garment with its undershirt and began to raise them.

'Stop!' Sir Tristram bellowed. 'Will you defy me?'

'I honour and respect you, Father. For that reason, I will come with you; for that reason I will bare myself to the lash.'

Sir Tristram knew he meant it. 'You will not. For all you have shamed me, I will not see you flogged in public. At home is another matter. You will come – you have my word. Now away from my sight. Be here again by six or we leave without you. Mbulu, I take another stripe for my disobedient child. And lay it on this time, dvaeba, lay it on.'

Tristan did not risk provoking further by hanging around, though he winced as he heard the whip crack again behind him. The incident had subdued the crowd. Among the whisperers was Chutney to François. 'Did I just see that? Sir Tristram giving way when challenged by his own get?'

'Hush. The lad is showing some balls, credit to him. I was enlisted myself at that age.'

'Sure you were, and he might lose his balls like you lost your arm. I wonder if the old Indian will take the lash for his boys like Sir Tristram did.'

'There I will agree the skip did wrong. Spare the whip, spoil the whelp.'

White Eagle addressed Sir Tristram as they crossed on his way to the pole. 'I too honour and respect you, my captain. It was a noble thing you did. Sometimes the child knows when it is time before the father. We shall be proud to have another of your line on our journey.'

Wanting nothing so much as to tell the old fool to shut his running mouth, Sir Tristram instead thanked him with a bow. White Eagle's back was already bare in the traditional Indian style, as was Little Doe's. Yellow Cloud, forever furious with the world, hurled his tasselled jacket to the ground when his turn came. The Zulu caught him a good one.

The Cibolan 17th Cavalry had a difficult role among the Westerners, neither Cowboys nor Indians and lacking the numbers to serve as a balance of power between the two. Since arriving at the Whipping Square that afternoon, Vic Swallow had cut an isolated and largely silent figure amongst the teammates. He did have a few quiet words with his fellow member of the goalkeepers' guild as he took his turn at the pole. If they were of condolence, they did not move Mbulu to take it easier on Vic.

From Sir Septimus onwards, the Zulu had always drawn blood, so precisely opening the welt on Sir Tristram's second pass that the Knight looked to have been struck only once. Mbulu could not be accused of taking any pleasure in his labours, declining Barrie Knight's offer to join the City table to sit morosely on his coffin as the afternoon wore on. As conversation flagged amongst the footballers, a commotion in the doorway of the Golden Fleece across the way drew their attention.

'Say Vic, isn't that your brother?' Little Doe was seated between the keeper and a snoring White Eagle. 'I was just about to ask what old Ian is up to.'

'No good, most like.' Vic showed no surprise at the sight of his twin dusting himself down and picking up his cap from the street. A Little John Sherwooder was blocking any way back into the Fleece.

Before greeting the other Westerners Ian, literally cap in hand, mumbled a request to Sir Tristram to join their company for a drink. The Knight, at the centre of the table between Barrie and Septimus, with Bowlegs stationed behind his chair, had been almost as silent as Mbulu since Tristan had left the square. He nodded, with no more interest in the dishevelled Ian than if he had been the beggar he resembled.

'Who peed on *his* strawberries?' Ian straddled the bench opposite his twin, humble demeanour discarded. 'How you doing, Doey?'

'How, Ian. Vic didn't say you'd be joining us.'

'Didn't know. Thought he was minding the homestead.'

'That can mind itself just as well for a dey or two. Anyways, you'll be able to buy us a new shack when you come back with the king's shilling. You should have more chance of a place now the old Zulu ain't goin' along.'

'Shut your fool mouth, Ian. That soldier over there is

grieving his pa – who was never *gonna* be comin' along, far as I know.'

'Far as you know. That feller was fair dancin' a jig last night, sayin' how your Knight friends was goin' to bring him along. His dancin' deys are over now, right enough.'

'You were here last night, then?'

'Not I, pard,' Ian answered Little Doe at once. 'That's what I heard, that's all. I didn't hit the City till late but I already wore out my welcome, funnily enough 'bout the same time as my money, at the Fleece. Bein' as I only come up on the spur of the minnit, to say cheery-bye to my bro – you see how delighted he is at the gesture – I figured I should at least have a beer afore wishin' him dvidspeed.'

'You're not hoping to take this place Nkulu supposedly had fixed up then, you being an ex-City keeper yourself an' all?'

'None finer, Doey, but no, I made my feelings quite clear on *that* subject when Cap'n Tram come callin' to our place, you ask Vic if I didn't. Course, that Malabar might be *very* pleased – bit less competition for him from another Pirate. Where is that old boulder-hurling Ayrab?'

'He'll be along later with the others.'

'I bet he will, large as life an' twice as ugly. Say, is there any service here? Where's the potman to get me a brew? Oh, hush my mouth I hear you, what a sad and tactless comment.'

Once settled with a drink, Ian did not have much more to say to the Westerners, falling in rather with fellow bench-warmers and topers Chutney and François. He did, however, take the time to approach Mbulu with the same kind of care he had Sir Tristram. The giant accepted a drink from a flask offered by the cashiered cavalryman, and took to pacing round the pole as if chained to it when Ian had returned to the main party.

Tristan was back in the square by five. Barrie Knight suggested there was no need for him to bother his father at that point. Just before six, with no sign of the Arabs as yet, the captain ordered Bowlegs to go and check the tour bus was ready, perforce a few streets away since it was too big to enter the higgledy-piggledy alleys around the Whipping Square. 'Barrie will take the mic for Jakob and his men. In fact, give it to him now so he can announce you – I don't recall you taking your hit yet.'

Sir Tristram's smile was flinty, but it was a smile of sorts that cheered his man willingly enough to the whipping post, stirring up enthusiasm again in the bystanders who had watched Bowlegs usher many others to it earlier before slipping it himself in the confusion after Tristan stepped forward. He had only just left the square when Jakob O'Reilly led a strong contingent of Pirates, mainly Arabs, in from the other side. The WW1ers straightened themselves up. Jakob had a few words with Rumplebum before approaching the pole. His followers melted away into all corners of the square, like water trickling through pebbles, only three staying by him. Sir Tristram had risen from table to join Barrie and greet the Pirates at the stake.

'Sir Tristram.' Jakob nodded formally. 'I will offer the Zulu no word of consolation or condolence until he has whipped us out, lest he think we are courting favour. You know Oscar and Malabar, naturally. And our brother Schwartz?'

'Only by name, Jakob.' He nodded in his turn at the dwarf O'Reilly with a big reputation as a contract killer. He had never played for Blood City, but Sir Tristram decided he would not haggle with his vice about bringing a close family member along.

Jakob took the lash first, then Schwartz, then Oscar. The handsome, moustached Berserker took some time to disencumber his upper body of various layers of clothing, bandoliers, separate belts for swords and daggers, and a rifle slung over his shoulder.

The Zulu went at it with a will on the uncomplaining Arabs. As Malabar was silently disrobing, he held his father's whip aloft in both hands, before abruptly bringing it down to snap the wooden handle across his knee. He then bent to entwine the ruined weapon around the base of the pole.

Malabar took his place without paying the slightest attention to Mbulu, who was busy in his coffin. There was a gasp from the resurgent crowd when he pulled out an instrument of a different order. Baring his teeth, he brought down with full force between the O'Reilly's shoulder blades the dreaded Seventeener. Malabar did not cry out, but he sank to his knees, bleeding from neck to croup.

It could have been worse. The Seventeener had not been fully assembled, as it would have been for cases of state-sanctioned punishment. Each of its strands would then have had some cruel refinement, whether tipped with metal cylinders of bone-breaking power, miniature grappling hooks that would rip out great gobbets of flesh, or venom that would enter the victim's bloodstream to provoke further agonies just as the external wounds began to heal. Even so, Malabar had effectively taken seventeen lashes, compared to one for each of his teammates.

'Mbulu!' Sir Tristram got to the giant before Jakob, putting himself between the Zulu and the mangled Malabar. It was by no means clear that he had been prepared to leave it at one hit. 'What is this—?'

'My father's whip is broken. Now I must use my own.'

'That too will be broken soon enough, you black hound.' For a low fellow, Schwartz had a high-pitched voice. The mismatch in size between him and Mbulu drew a nervous laugh from a ranch hand in the crowd, soon stifled. He would be found face down with his throat cut when the crush abated.

Oscar had a pistol pointed at the whipmaster's stomach. Jakob spoke calmly. 'This could end for you here as in olden times, Mbulu, yet I will hear you speak first. Who poisoned your mind against our brother?'

The Zulu was nothing cowed. 'My weapon is the whip. His is the rock. It was a rock that killed my father.'

There was a sudden crack, louder than Nkulu's now broken whip. Tristan, scrambling for a view and to get near his own father, expected to see a gut-shot Mbulu fall and all hell to break loose in the square. Instead, it was Rumplebum who spoke, arm raised languidly to the skies into which he had just fired his Walther PPK.

'Just a minnit, gentlemen. Mbulu is the king's representative here. No harm will come to him on my watch.' It was a bold statement, since Rumplebum and his detail were outnumbered about five to one by Pirates alone. 'I was just talking to Mr Jakob O'Reilly about the unfortunate events of last night, on which forensic teams are still working. I can confirm the cause of death has not yet been clearly established.'

'How's that again? We all heard his head was smashed to a mush.'

The NCO did not respond directly to Vic's yell, addressing the Zulu instead. 'We were not planning to trouble you with this until your work was at an end. In the circumstances, I will tell you now that within the mu—the matter, the grey matter, a bullet was found.'

Mbulu seemed to have trouble taking in this information. Jakob O'Reilly filled the silence. 'I too was waiting before talking to our fellow Pirate. Matters darker than grey have now overtaken us. Is it not clear what happened?'

As the giant showed no sign of finding it so, Jakob elaborated. 'The Pirate keeper Nkulu was shot, his head then bashed in to deflect attention from the real killer and the real motive. I would find such an act hard to believe of my former teammate Victor, but have no trouble pointing to his serpent brother who has crawled here among us on his belly. We will have justice against the sot Ian Swallow.'

The accused showed the same readiness to stand up to the Arab as he had in his own home.

'Pirate justice, you mean! My neck's itchin' already from that lynchin' rope I can feel coming. I throw myself on the protection of the Army. Listen up yawl. Maybe it was the bullet as got planted.'

'You lie!' Jakob roared to be heard over the now buzzing crowd.

'Mr O'Reilly.' Rumplebum at least was keeping his cool. 'As I said to you a few minnits ago, our investigations are ongoing. There is indeed a question to be resolved about which came first – bullet or rock, rock or bullet. For now, I would rather end the dey without unpleasantness.'

'Without unpleasantness? Look at the state of my brother's back, soldier!' Oscar and Schwartz had been helping Malabar to his feet. Still without looking at the fleetmaster, the scourged Pirate hawked up a great gob of phlegm and landed it on Nkulu's whip at the foot of the pole.

'Jakob, Mbulu, hear me.' Sir Tristram spoke with all the authority he could muster, seeing the Zulu threatening to run amok, the Arab wound tight and ready to fight. 'We shall not know the truth of this matter todey. Whatever the instrument of death, we have no link of it to either of these two men, nothing to find anyone at this point innocent. If Mbulu represents King Henry, so do I, as head of the Seskie mission. I say this, to close matters and be on our way. We will resolve our own problems in the dressing room, while official investigations continue. Let Swallow, Ian, take the lash and join our squad.'

'What? With the Seventeener? You gotta be sh—'

'It is best, Ian, believe me,' Little Doe whispered in his ear at the same time he grabbed his left arm. White Eagle had his right, making any gunplay by the cavalryman impossible. 'It's the only way you'll leave this square alive.'

Ian allowed himself to be steered, not propelled, through the now rapt crowd to the pole. He threw down his filthy blue tunic to address Mbulu. 'In your heart you know the truth, boy. Have at it.'

Perhaps the 'boy' didn't help, or perhaps Mbulu was now in two minds. He brought the Seventeener down on Swallow with the same force he had on Malabar.

Ian was not shy of screaming. Helped to his feet by Vic and the ever obliging Little Doe, he made the same point of flobbing at the foot of the pole as the Arab had.

Mbulu would spend the night at the square, weeping over his father's broken and bespittled whip, which would be buried with Nkulu. He made some vows to the Cibolan moon and stars. Meanwhile, the Blood City squad had left the City of Blood: Tristram, Tristan, Knight, Septimus, Brittanus, Bowlegs, Chutney, François; Jakob, Malabar and Schwartz O'Reilly, Oscar; White Eagle, Little Doe, Yellow Cloud; Vic and Ian Swallow. They were seventeen.

4

Pink Viking

'You're expecting me to play right back?' Jakob's tone was as disbelieving as if he had just been asked to go on a pub crawl with Ian Swallow.

'I hadn't thought twice about it, to be honest. You wear the number 2 shirt.'

'I wore it, yes, in my early deys at City. You know full well I made my name for the Marauders and the Pirates in central midfield.'

'In my position, you mean?'

'Not necessarily, Tram. You know in later yeers you played right back yourself more than a few times.'

'I played centre forward when the team needed it, and

scored too, but that doesn't make me a striker.' Sir Tristram could not stop his own voice rising. The teammates were strolling in the extensive grounds of the Pink Palace. While both were cautious about being overheard anywhere indoors by soldier or automatic listening device, they each also found it obscurely oppressive to be inside. For all the space in the seventeen rooms of each wing in the palace (with a further seventeen at the centre where Pink Viking and his clique were quartered), it was too full of things that served no purpose: paintings on the walls, jars with flowers in them, tables at just the height at which you would bark a shin, cluttering areas where you could easily have marked out a five-a-side pitch.

The atmosphere on the team coach had hardly been relaxed during their long drive, distinct factions in the squad accentuated by the blood that had been spilled and the bad blood engendered before they left the city. Everyone but Tristan had, as a minimum, a sore back.

The Arabs had taken the bench seat across the rear, where they had persuaded Malabar to lie flat on his stomach. François' role in the squad was expected to be as magic-spongeman, and there was actually little more to be done with the Seventeener wounds than to keep them clean and dressed. The one-armed soldier was forever lurching between the back and front of the bus, where Ian Swallow, his other main patient, was considerably more vocal than the Arabs.

While Bowlegs, Chutney and Little Doe shared the driving, Sir Tristram and White Eagle sat at the front as navigators and to keep an eye on the cavalrymen. The captain had briefed Barrie, supported by Brittanus and Sir Septimus, to be handy around the toilet in the middle if ever the two parties should come together there. In fact those facilities were used only by Tristan and François, the latter merely to draw rather than pass water. The soldiers preferred to demand stops at any wayside cantina, where they could take refreshment as well as relieve themselves, as often as not in the open air.

The coach's suspension had taken a pounding when they pulled off the Pan-Cibolan Highway to cover the 100 varsts to Pink Viking's folly, the encampment he had built using ETechnolOGy, at what he and the Ogs judged to be the precise midpoint between Blood and Casablanca. This living apart, beyond the hugger-mugger of the big cities or any other natural settlement, was part of his mystique. He did not necessarily want to be king; he did want to be unique.

After wearing the red number 5 shirt conventionally enough at Blood City, over the pink tunic for which he was named, PV (as he had lately taken a shine to being called) had single-handedly broken the Cibolan league's transfer system. He refused to be bound to any one club, moving as a free agent to whichever one he fancied. All would be delighted to have him as, arguably, the world's best footballer. Just as in cricket he was an all-rounder, rivalled only by Barrie Knight, in football he refused to accept limitation or direction on his role. He had proved supremely effective at centre half – whether for the City or his current team, Ajax – and devastating at centre forward, where he usually turned out for the Pirates.

Many said PV was at Ajax mainly because of his long-standing special friendship with their skipper Red Cavalier, also named for the colour of his costume, which in truth had been more pink than red, or 'fuchsia, darling, fuchsia,' as he himself would describe the shade of his ruffs and frills. There was nothing luvvie duvvie about his tackling.

Red Cavalier (who did not yet aspire to be known as 'RC') was with Pink Viking when their host burst in on the Blood party in the central gathering space of the palace's Sarf Wing. Sir Tristram had not necessarily expected him to receive personally even a group including his one-time captain, so had taken no offence when Alaric, an up-and-coming Sun City Pirate centre-back, had done the meeting and greeting before leading them there.

'Red, come and say hi to this bunch of old has-beens – with the honourable exception of Jakob, of course – and never-wases. Trissie, you know I'm only kidding, and who's this lovely apple-cheeked new lady?' He moved with a magician's speed of hand to pinch the face of Tristan, who recoiled, instantly crimson. 'White Eagle my brother, Doey, Barrie, Sep, how are you all doing?'

Without necessarily remembering all of the seventeen, he made a point of greeting each one as if he did. Tristan could not take his eyes off the soldier whose arrival had stopped all the separate conversations, uniting everyone in wanting to be seen and addressed by him. He wore the horned Viking helmet over a pencil moustache, a standout white on his tanned face. When he had finished fooling with François, looking to shake the man's missing hand, he suddenly dropped to the marbled floor, as if to begin a set of press-ups. After twisting his head to both sides, he addressed Sir Tristram. 'And the summer Knight?'

'We shall be seeing Sir John in Casablanca when we complete the squad to cross the sea.'

'"*Sir* John", is it now? And has John Little yet signed on?' The banter over, he was now standing in front of Sir Tristram, looking down on him.

'Technically not perhaps, yet I am confident he will be as keen to serve our king as we all are.'

'You see, pretty one' —while Tristan knew it would only egg the Pirate on to tease him more, of course he could not stop from rekindling the blush that had not quite left his face since the first cheeky grab— 'I've not signed on myself yet. Pink Viking is a winner, and while he *could* still carry a team, he would see how time has treated the old City boys. *If* I go, it will not be to lose to the Yofas. Do you all feel the same, soldiers? I said: do you all feel the same?'

Barrie Knight and Jakob O'Reilly had bellowed 'yes' at the first time of asking. There were no negatives, but still a few muted responses to the second. 'You've got your work cut out here, Trissie, but golly, it's good to see you again.' Once more he moved with astonishing speed to wrap the stiff-backed Knight in a bear hug before holding him again at arm's length.

'I would like you and the lads to have a friendly against my house party tomorrow. We grow tired of playing with ourselves.' He gave Tristan a wink. 'You may join us at dinner tonight or prepare yourselves, as you please.'

'We'll be ready,' Sir Tristram bowed. Their host acknowledged this with only a flutter of his fingers, as if waving goodbye, before setting off arm-in-arm with Red Cavalier, who had not chosen to engage anyone in conversation. Ajax through and through, he was perhaps already in local derby mode against their arch-rivals.

Alaric remained at their service; Sir Tristram had no problem with him hearing his next words. 'You see the monk on Red Cavalier – one of the finest defenders ever to play the game, by the way. I bet he's furious not to be involved in the Seskie. All of you at least have a chance. The build-up starts here. From this momet on I shall be thinking about my starting eleven.

'I'll be taking counsel from Jakob, of course, and listening carefully to other senior pros' —he made sure to look in White Eagle's direction at this point— 'so never imagine what I don't see I won't know. Pink Viking keeps a sumptuous table and a fine cellar. Sample both, by all means, or get a good night's rest before tomorrow's game. The choice is yours, because I warn you it will be impossible to do both.'

Alaric had a stock of bedrolls for the men, explaining that while the wing had enough rooms for each of them to sleep alone, they were of different shapes and sizes, and not all furnished. 'In one or two you can see the stars,' he confided to Sir Tristram, 'but not yours, of course, the master guest.'

'Thank you, lad, we've camped in far worse places. We'll try not to trash this one.'

'It wouldn't be the first time, sir. On PV's last castdey he had a polo match running all the way through the palace, sarf to norf. There was horseshit everywhere – excuse my Morrocan – horse droppings, I mean.'

'No fear lad, shit is shit. It happens.'

Of the Sarf Wing's seventeen rooms, the Blood City squad eventually occupied only seven. The four Arab Pirates took one ('a dagger guarding the door at all times, I bet', Septimus referenced their legendary paranoia to his own roomie Brittanus); the Swallow twins took one bigger than their homestead; the three Indians were together, while Chutney and François were never likely to be separated. Only Bowlegs was put out to find he would not be sleeping at the foot of Sir Tristram's bed.

'Said our Tristan would be looking after him and I should squire for you,' he grumbled to Barrie Knight as he fussed about their quarters. 'Course I'm pleased to do that too, don't get me wrong sir, but how can a wee lad look after Sir T?'

'I expect Sir Tristram would say he has to earn his keep before he can earn his spurs. I suspect our captain just wants to spend some time with him, however much he dresses it up as a chore or a punishment.'

There was little enough work to be done in the master guest room, where Alaric had handed Sir Tristram and Tristan over to a spindly space-station auxiliary, pure unpainted white. He showed them the mechanism that would release the servant's bed, folded into the entrance door. 'We are mindful of our guests' safety, as well as their comfort,' Alaric explained. 'We know guards sleep, but any intruder forcing the door would have to shift their bed too.'

'Intruder?' Sir Tristram was looking out of the room's single window into the gathering night.

'It happens.'

It was the first time Sir Tristram and Tristan had been alone together since the morning of the whipping out, when the Knight had told Tristan he would not be going on tour.

The boy had been attentive all the way down in the bus, without drawing a word from him, other than thank-yous from reflex courtesy. The father had been biding his time. Still at the window, he spoke quietly enough. 'Stop messing with the clothes. I didn't really mean you to squire for me.'

'Why didn't you keep Bowlegs, then? I would have been happy to bunk with Barrie, and Bowlie would have been a *lot* happier.'

'And you think that would be appropriate? To have you room with the soldiers – even Uncle Barrie? Or alone? Are you being insolent to me on purpose, or was it born in you?' Now he raised his voice as he turned from the window back into the room. 'Tell me, girl.'

When Pink Viking had twitted him for a lass, Tristan had gone bright red. Now the blood drained from his face. 'You haven't called me that in yeers. I thought—'

'I never thought to call you it again, except it seems you need reminding what you are. It will soon be plain enough to all, as you know full well. You used it cunningly enough to get your way at Whipping Square – sure I could not allow you to take your top off there.'

'Do you think that horrible Pirate tonight somehow knew?'

'Pink Viking?' Sir Tristram laughed. 'I doubt it, though there are rumours he's omnivorous. He was probably having a bit of fun with you as a beardless newbie. You know that's what girls are in our world – something to taunt boys as being until they—until you reach the age of reverence. I doubt very much he realised you never will grow a beard, nor…you know.'

'Father, I did it not from defiance in the square, or to make you look bad. It was the only way I could think of to come with you.'

'You bested me, I grant you that. You are my first child and I love you. I thought you had understood, from as soon as you could understand anything, that you are different. You may be able to pass for a boy, but you will never be a Knight. You will soon enough have to take on your woman's name of Tristania, a lady's role.'

'And how lonely will that be? I understood – how hard I listened to you and how closely I listened. For every 100 Indian braves only one squaw is cast, for every 1,000 Robin Hoods only one Maid Marion, for every 10,000 Knights only one Guinevere. I remember exactly the numbers you told me, see. And I will assume my destiny as a woman, not a soldier. There is no shame in it. You taught me there is an honour in being different – you taught me that too. I just wanted to be your son on one last adventure. When my brothers grow, you will have support enough. Now it is I who must go with you into danger.'

'I don't want you in danger, dvaeba! I have trained myself for yeers to think of you as my son, to call you by a son's name even when we are alone together. You know I have, though you may not know at what cost. And I have been successful. We have been successful. Only Barrie knows your gender, and we have no friend truer than he. I had to tell someone at the time, in the initial shock at the honour done to my line, and what's told can never be untold.

'I swear it is not because you are a woman, or soon will be, that I never wanted you on this trip. My fear is no greater for you than it would be for Tramtrist or Tarquin, or Turgar.'

'Keep treating me as a son then, Dad, a son growing up faster than either of us might wish. You suddenly talk about a football match ending in a fight to the death, a fight in which my own dear father's life is at stake, then attempt to laugh it off. I listen too closely to you to miss things like that. Tell me where the danger comes from in football. Tell me so that I do not run into it blindly but may try to help you against it.'

'I have no option, do I? I mean, about continuing to treat you as a son. I would sometimes talk aloud to myself while addressing Bowlegs, stout fellow, yet knowing he could not grasp the thread, or, if he should by chance pick up something, would never betray me. You, my dear, are quite different. You are all ears. You grasp too much and too quickly for your own good. Let me think out a little more before I decide what it may be safe and proper to share with you. For now, let us say goodnight.'

Tristan felt a sense of relief, not that Sir Tristram's rage had abated – the rage had been understandable enough – but that his coldness had ended. Realising there was little hope of moving him further that night, he offered a simple 'Goodnight, Father.'

'Goodnight, my darling Tristania.'

'Goodnight, my darling Daddy.' She completed the infant formula she had never thought to hear or say again. They had usually been her last words before falling asleep, but she was no longer a baby. She so rarely allowed herself to be the girl she was, tonight she would take her father's address as permission to do so, flashes of the dey still playing in her mind. Before the deep rumble of Sir Tristram's snoring got into gear for the night, she ventured, 'Daddy, why did he call John Ivanhoe the summer Knight?'

'John's not the tallest,' he answered shortly.

Her next 'Daddy?' drew a sigh from the high four-poster. 'What does "omnivorous" mean?'

'Go to sleep, Tristan.'

The flay-backed Swallow did not fail to join the festivities in the central part of the palace, knowing he would not be considered for selection any more than Malabar, by virtue of their injuries and the charges hanging over them. Little Doe and others were with him; though voices were raised between them and their hosts in football banter, the night passed without bloodshed or gunplay. In their deliberations the next morning, Sir Tristram and Jakob O'Reilly were pleased not to have to factor any other disciplinary considerations into the process.

Once the captain and vice had compromised that Jakob would, with Pink Viking on the opposing side, play at number 5 – twin centre back with White Eagle – the rest of the team fell quickly into place.

'It's the only place Barrie can get a game at the Young Faithfuls now, so I'm happy to go with him at right back – Little Doe at left, of course. We may need to be more cautious when we get to the real thing, but let's go out and play here, 4-2-4 with Sep and me in midfield.'

'And Oscar on the right wing.'

Sir Tristram was quietly amused at Jakob's eagerness to secure that place. 'No worries on that. I've always wanted to see a natural left footer like Yellow Cloud actually play on the left, so we'll have him at number 11.'

'Brittanus down the middle picks himself. Who are you thinking of beside him? Not François, I assume.'

'No, we'll name him as substitute keeper,' Sir Tristram said of their one-armed teammate. It was about as close as he ever came to humour. Along with deferment of the potential rivalry for the spot of second keeper between Ian and Malabar, they had explicitly agreed to postpone further discussion of the reason the Seventeener came into play till they reached Casablanca, by which time the Army's investigations into the cause of the unlucky Nkulu's death might have shed more light on it.

'Listen, I know my brother Schwartz is small and relatively untried, but his position is left wing. We could put him there and bring Yellow Cloud inside, or try Schwartz feeding off Britt. Chutney and Bowlegs won't work any further forward than midfield, and I'd rather see them at the back if we have to use them at all.'

'You wouldn't know that Bowlegs also started off as a left winger, in the deys when Freddie One was still on the throne. Jake, I'm going to ask you an indulgence here. I'd like to start Tristan up front beside Brittanus.'

'Tristan?'

'Yes. I know he's never played top-class football, he'll be 30 yeers newer than anyone else in our team, and I promise I'll make harder-nosed footballing decisions when the time comes.' Although Jakob had still not raised any objection, Sir Tristram seemed keen to put them forward on his behalf before knocking them down. 'You may say I could give him a run-out as a sub, but you and I both know that's not the same as the honour of being in the starting line-up.'

'It is fine. I agree the real match is a different matter. Hopefully we'll have Pink Viking and John Ivanhoe both onside by then, so the lad may never get a sniff. Let's give him a game.'

The teamsheet Sir Tristram handed Alaric that afternoon thus read: 1) Swallow (V); 2) Knight, 5) O'Reilly (J), 6) W. Eagle, 3) L. Doe; 4) Tristram, 10) Septimus; 7) Oscar, 8) Brittanus, 9) Tristan, 11) Y. Cloud. Subs: François (GK), Bowlegs, Chutney, O'Reilly (S). The Mongol warrior seemed surprised at such formality. 'Thanks. Afraid I've got nothing to offer you in return.'

'Then how am I supposed to brief my boys? Can you at least give me an idea of your line-up?'

'Well, I expect to be at the back beside Red, A-Og in goal, PV up front and then whoever wants to make up the numbers – mainly Ogs and Sherwooders, I reckon.'

Hiding his irritation, Sir Tristram did not press the messenger. More than one of the Blood City squad were relieved he did not have details of their opponents' full starting eleven to run through soldier by soldier. For once, even Tristan was not listening to his father. He could barely sit still, thrilled not only to be starting but to be wearing the number 9 shirt of John Ivanhoe.

'They'll be solid at the back with Red and Alaric,' Sir Tristram droned, 'and A-Og in goal.' Tristan had, of course, seen the Sun City keeper play, the leading Og from the planet

Gog, which kept a generally benevolent eye on Cibola and its doings. The Ogs scattered throughout the population acted principally as peacekeepers, usually in support of the land's established power, as they were now of King Henry. Although bigger than most soldiers – and bulked up further by their space suits and helmets – they were far more than hired muscle. It was to their ETechnolOGy the Cibolans owed their only means of flying, whether by Tishoos for short hops or the fabled Far-Transporters for long jumps. Since the pilotry of these required at least one Og, their use was open only to the privileged few who had troubled to develop friendly relations with the Outworlders.

'Pink Viking will obviously be their main goal threat, as he is in whichever team he plays. You both know him well enough, but I would suggest White Eagle takes him on in the air and Jakob, you play more as a libero. I hope you'll be able to get forward on occasion. Count on me to cover for you.'

Barrie and Jakob might have been the only soldiers starting the match to take it as seriously as Sir Tristram, though neither could have been as keen to do well as Tristan. He was so keyed up in the early stages that whenever he did get a touch of the ball he played it too hurriedly, usually to the opposition. His strike partner, the old warhorse Brittanus, did his best to calm him down, without either of them getting much change from a defence capably marshalled by Red Cavalier.

All that changed, with the wonder of football, in a heart-beat.

Sir Septimus threaded a clever ball through the inside-left channel that Alaric left to the blue-skirted Zubian right-back,

Zambesi. Coming inside, he completely missed his left-footed kick, unlike Tristan, who ran in to squirt the ball into the bottom of the net at the surprised A-Og's near post. A front runner to replace the disgraced and dismembered Drake in the Pirate nets, his vast bulk alone made the Og an excellent shot-stopper; getting down quickly to either side he found more of a challenge.

While Brittanus offered only a manly Roman handshake, the Berserker Oscar was all over the lad. Jakob, too, ran the length of the field to embrace him. While he knew better than to expect similar effusiveness from his father, Sir Tristram's discreet thumbs-up meant the world.

As they crossed at the centre line, Pink Viking had the grace to congratulate him, albeit in such a way as also to goad his own teammates. 'I think we'll swap at half-time, lass, have you on our side, since my back four can't seem to cope with you.'

Smiling nervously in acceptance of the compliment, Tristan caught a look of sheer fury directed at him by Red Cavalier, who could not have failed to hear PV's booming voice, even as he was busy himself berating his fellow defenders.

They did not reach half-time. Vikings tended, with the huge exceptions of Pink Viking and the Young Faithfuls' Viking Attacker, to be more defensive players than midfielders or forwards, leaving the host's Select XI a little short on creativity. They had also, perhaps, been carousing a bit more heartily than most of the City boys. Brittanus gave the visitors a second goal with a firm downward header after a mazy dribble and cross from Oscar, whom Tristan had found in space wide right.

Maybe he was a little cheeky, or was it justified exuberance? When Yellow Cloud hit a low cross-shot that might have ended up somewhere near the corner flag had it not found Tristan first, his control was brilliant. He turned to slip the ball through Red Cavalier's legs. That he was allowed to follow it could only have been because the Pirate thought Alaric or A-Og would be covering behind him. Not so. Tristan was clear through on the keeper.

Cultured and elegant on the ball as he was, Red Cavalier was no stranger to the dark arts of defending. He spun and slid in hard at the lad's back, catching his foot and giving his upper body a nudge for good measure. It might have been a harmless trip had A-Og not been lumbering from his line. Tristan was already falling when his shoulder and neck collided with the Og's pecplate as Red Cavalier continued to steam into him from behind. While the two Pirates quickly regained their feet, Tristan did not. He did not move at all.

5

The Shooting Gallery

John Ivanhoe was a soldier driven to great heights by insecurities, rivalries and jealousies that went far beyond those of a classic little-man complex. It rankled with him far more than with François, whose hopes of such an honour were little more than a pot dream, that he had never been dubbed Sir, that he was not a full Knight at the Table of Trust. Camelot had been unmoved by his threat to take his footballing talent to the Pirate international team rather than the Knights, perhaps feeling they already had a better centre forward of the same name.

While John was making his name with Blood City as a lethal finisher with every part of his body, from dagger to heel

– and including head, despite his short stature – his brother Alan was scoring just as many goals for their capital rivals, Ajax. They were identical in cast apart from the strips they wore, and the fact that Alan had lost his dagger, with the hand holding it, in a boyhood skirmish. As if to make light of his disability, he would raise the cauterised stump to salute each of his goals.

When City were relegated, John had jumped ship to the Young Faithfuls in Casablanca. There he made a perfect foil to Viking Attacker through various trophy-laden seesuns. Alan had been the subject of a huge transfer fee from the Morrocan moneybags team the Continentals, which ironically meant staying in Blood, where they made their base on promotion to the first division. The Ivanhoes were rumoured not to have spoken in yeers, despite playing together as automatic first choices in every Knight international selection.

There was little high ground in the coastal city of Casablanca, where John made his home on the elite hill within the city's exclusive sports complex. Unlike Pink Viking with his extensive retinue, he received Sir Tristram and Jakob O'Reilly alone. They had brought his Young Faithfuls teammate Barrie Knight along to help in their soft-soaping exercise.

The meeting did not get off to a great start, for all Sir Tristram had greeted the goatee-bearded soldier in the famous all-red Yofa strip as 'Sir John'.

'I would have loved to see Red Cavalier megged by a kid, especially with his best boyfriend Pink Viking looking on,' Ivanhoe chortled as he released his former skipper's hand.

'That kid was my son, and the nutmegging could have cost his life.'

'I hear you nearly ended Red's deys there and then in your rage. I would not have shed a tear. But how is the kid? I hear he was showing great promise.'

'He learned the hard way that football is a soldier's game. I feared his neck was broke, and when that fear had passed it seemed his shoulder might be. Luckily the Ogs are as skilled at medicine as at mayhem. He will be all right. I have shaken with Red, allowing I might have done the same in his place.'

Sir Tristram had raced upfield after the collision, with murder on his mind. The brawl in the Palace team's box, involving most of the other players on the pitch, joined by their respective benches and fans, looked likely for a while to become a full-scale battle, rather to the amusement of Pink Viking, who stood watching from the centre square. Although it was contact with A-Og that had cold-cocked Tristan, no one attached much blame to the clumsy Pirate. He it was who called on others from his planet – G-Og and J-Og were among the players – to lay down their force-foam, lines across the field which the maddened Tristram and unrepentant Red Cavalier were quite unable to cross to get at each other once they had been lifted Oggishly and put on different sides.

What distressed Sir Tristram most in retrospect was that while he had been grabbing Red by the throat it was left to Barrie to attend to his stricken child. He was still musing on that as Jakob tactfully took up the conversational reins.

'It was an unfortunate accident, a good defender's foul gone bad. It looked very grave. If our friend here had not been speedily mouth-to-mouth the lad might have swallowed his tongue.'

71

'That's right, Barrie on the spot. I thought cricketing heroics were more your line, or did you go and score the winning goal as well?'

'Winners are more your speciality, John.' The imperturbable Knight bowed. 'The game was abandoned with us two-nil up, and I did not score either goal.'

'It hardly bodes well for the Seskie if you could not get to half-time in a kick-about without it ending in a riot.'

'We shall grow more disciplined, Sir John.' Sir Tristram rejoined them. 'We do not seek your help in that area.' He made the remark with a smile, knowing that Ivanhoe was proud of the number of red cards he had collected in a long career. 'Yet we know better than any how you grace and improve any team. We hope we can count on you to spearhead our attack in the Seskie.'

'Alongside Barrie, who was my willing water-carrier back in the dey?' He put a hand on the other Knight's shoulder, a conciliatory gesture.

'That is my hope. Dvida willing, I would like us to line up 1 to 11, as in those times.'

'How much do you want to win the match, Sir Tristram?'

'I never pulled on the City shirt and entered the field of play without wanting to win. I know the same is true of you, John.'

'You're right on that. I'm sure you also know I have a conflict of interest, or rather emotion, on this occasion. Half the Young Faithfuls originals may not be able to last half a game. If you mind that total-football eleven, many – Yashin, Más, definitely Frenchie – have mobility issues, Coluna is too old, Cavalry Man dead, Tuck may well be, and Tommy…well, Tommy – there's a big question. Do you suppose he will play?'

'We all hope to see him on the pitch again, John, but I have no say in that. Quite frankly I have enough problems with my own squad. I will prepare them as best I can to face a strong Young Faithfuls team – when did they ever field a weak one? That is all I can do.'

'There is talk of the legends taking at least some part in the match – a ceremonial one, perhaps. Many supporters want to see the strongest possible Yofa team turn out to win it, including some of the current stars. Without false modesty, including myself.'

'I don't doubt you are much courted, Sir John. I would not presume to suggest where your loyalties should lie. We shall not beg you to play for the City, though we all fervently hope you will do so.'

'At least, if Sir John should not, we have a first-class replacement centre forward in Pink Viking.' Jakob played their trump as agreed.

'So he is already signed up?' Ivanhoe's interest livened. 'I would expect nothing less, Jakob, than for you to press the interests of another Pirate. His success as a striker is mainly due to his size and bullying style. It is far more of a challenge to score headed goals from my height than his, though I have my share, as the Subbutay logs show.'

'If you are in doubt, John, may I suggest something?' Not being instantly overridden, Barrie continued. 'Why not show both sets of fans your best, starting the game with the City to make it clear you were the original number 9, then perhaps switching to the other side just before the end, to show yourself with the Young Faithfuls as still Cibola's best striker? You may be able to score for both teams.'

'I should certainly hope so, in a friendly or in any other game. To score a hat trick for each side might be amusing, I grant. As he shows such promise, maybe your son – what is his name again? – could replace me in the City colours for the second half, leave that lumbering Pink at the back for me to embarrass.'

Tristan would have been astonished and delighted to be mentioned (if not quite by name) in connection with two giants of the game as a result of his performance at the Pink Palace. He had no memory of the collision, which Sir Tristram assured him was all to the good. Far worse was the fact he could not remember his goal. The Ogs had put him into a healing sleep beyond sleep that took him all the way to Casablanca. He would never know his head had been cradled in his father's lap for the whole time on the road.

Had he been present at their farewells, the boy would have been amused to hear Pink Viking grant that he might feather in on a Fart to join the City squad in Zanzibar, amused in a way his elders never seemed to be by the common abbreviation for the Ogs' gas-powered Far-Transporters. Sir Tristram's handbump with Red Cavalier had been a necessary sacrifice to obtain even that degree of commitment from PV. They could only trust in his vanity and love of being at the centre of every showpiece event in Cibola to bring him through to the island.

While Sir Tristram, Jakob and Barrie were delicately playing out a line to hook PV's great rival by exactly the same

74

characteristics, Tristan was heading to the Casablanca Pleasure Beach with Little Doe and the Swallow brothers.

'White Eagle not a great one for all the fun of the fair then, Doey?' Ian asked.

'He tells me he is suffering from the gout.' He did not mention that the chief had passed to him the leadership of the expedition, originally offered by Sir Tristram to the older Indian.

'Suffering, more likely, from the bruising and battering he took from Pink Viking, in barely half an our's play. I bet he's hoping PV follows through on his Fart – why are you sniggering, Tristan? – to play beside him in the Seskie rather than against him, as he's quite capable of deciding.'

'Pink Viking would be a hard test for any defender in the world,' Little Doe stoutly maintained.

'Ain't none of us gettin any newer,' Vic said. 'Let's hope the Yofas put out their old stagers too.'

The shooting range was at the very end of the funfair – Ian had gone on the waltzers and bumping cars with Tristan on their way – for reasons that became clear as they approached. Some way behind the booth, in what was otherwise wasteland, were five cut-out life-sized figures of famous Cibolan goalkeepers.

'Come one, come all to Lascar's Seskie shooting gallery to play *Kill the Keeper*,' a foreign legionnaire wearing a blue kepi tried to sucker them in. 'You don't have to be a crack shot like our Blood City Historic Heroic Cowboy to win yourself a *cracking* prize. Come watch him, then have a go yourself. Come on in, squire, who do you support?'

'Blood City, in life and death!' Tristan yelled.

'All right – can't say I admire your taste but I think I can guess, with the Seskie coming up, which goalie you'll want to gun down. In case you're too new to recognise all the options, let me introduce them.

'So, we pass quickly nowadey over Drake for Blood City – we'll be removing him soon but haven't had the heart to chop his legs off yet. I'm sure your Indian friend will remember the Marauders' great Torreano, half-Pirate or not. The Continentals' Hitler – not such a big name. Mbulu the Zulu for Ajax and the Young Faithfuls' very own Red Cobra, the great Yashin. Which one's it to be? Everybody's waiting to know. Which one you want to plug?'

The historic hero indicated by Lascar was an exception to the supposed general anticipation. He slouched forward on a stool in his red shirt, elbows on the lowest shelf of the prize stand, hat almost lying flat on it. He had not turned at their approach.

'Right. I choose…Yashin.' The representation of the legendary Viking Pirate was him in his axe-wielding pomp, not the much-reduced figure reported in the Blood press as now good for little more than cricket.

'A true City fan all right. You hear him, Cowboy, that's the Yofas' Yashin, let's see if you can sit him down.' As Lascar leaned back against the counter where Tristan stood, Cowboy got to his feet, raised a rifle to his shoulder and, without the slightest pause, fired it at the distant keepers. There was a tinny clang, surprisingly close at hand, as the cut-out of Yashin flattened backwards on the ground. Cowboy resumed his seat and slouch, still not having turned to face the punters.

'Now, it may not be *quite* as easy as our Blood City speed merchant made it look, but soon as our staff out back put the keeper back up, if you can knock it down again just like he did, you win not only any one of our super-realistic action figures but a lottery ticket for a trip to the Seskie itself.'

Tristan did not hesitate to hand over a ten-spot. He had already set his heart on one of the figures of famous sportsmen and warriors. The use of firearms formed no part of a Knight's education, which made it all the more fun. He could hardly wait for Lascar to draw back the curtain again, passing him a rifle to aim carefully at the restored figure of Yashin.

'Close but no charuta, my boy. Fine effort, though. Any other of you gentlemen care to have a go?' Tristan thought his shot had been good, but all five figures remained upright.

'Pay my go, son,' Ian Swallow whispered to Tristan, stepping purposefully forward. Lascar must have thought he was a dead soldier. The rifle Ian suddenly had at his shoulder was pointing right at the legionnaire. It fired twice in instant succession. This time the sound was different from that of Cowboy's shot, more solid, and clearly from the distance where the whole figure of Mbulu the Zulu took off into the air.

'Thought I'd save you the trouble of working the lever to bring the keeper down. You might need to be after replacing that one too, never mind Drake.' Ian's tone was amiable, his voice restored to its usual volume. 'If you find Mbulu and I didn't blow him clean into the Straits of Zanzibar, he'll have holes where them big brown eyes used to be. Cowboy' —he turned his attention away from the goggling Lascar— 'I always knew you was more crapshooter than sharpshooter.'

Cowboy was looking at them now. He did not seem unduly impressed by Ian's marksmanship, or surprised to see his former teammates. He spoke for the first time. 'Just keepin' my head down, scratchin' a living, boss.'

'Right, Lascar, now you just give my pard the action figure of his choice – I bet I know which one, Tris – and, let's see, how about that other Historic Hero of Blood City, Little Doe? Give him the lottery ticket. I know the Injuns love gambling – never had much luck that way myself. I got a funny feeling you gonna hand him a winner, though.' He prodded the legionnaire in the chest with his rifle barrel, leaving a smoky mark on his uniform.

'Take your pick, and your ticket too, you crazy Westerner trash. I'd make sure you're not still around here come nightfall.'

'Oh, would you? Would—?'

'Hey, Ian, looks like you were dead right, we do indeed have a winning ticket.' Little Doe had used his hunting knife to scratch the gaudy card Lascar had thrust at him. 'All expenses paid to the Seskie, including a prime position in the winning squad. How's that sound to you, Cowboy?'

Ignoring Lascar's 'But it can't be…' Cowboy showed some of the athleticism with which as Blood City's number 11 he had hurdled many a full back's challenge, vaulting one-handed over the counter to land among his fellow Westerners and shake Vic's hand. 'Right now, that sounds a lot.'

'Looks like you lost your shill, Lascar. I don't doubt you can find plenny more who can't shoot.' Rifle still levelled waist-high at the huckster, Ian walked slowly backwards away from the range. Little Doe was laughing with Cowboy and Vic as he tore up the scratch card and threw the pieces back over his shoulder.

Swallow (V); O'Reilly (J), Little Doe; Tristram, Pink Viking, White Eagle; Oscar, Knight, Ivanhoe (J), Septimus, Cowboy: no sooner had Sir Tristram got his first eleven together, albeit in a slightly ramshackle way given the less than total commitment to the cause of Pink Viking and Ivanhoe, than it was disrupted by orders from the highest level.

Before setting sail for Zanzibar, the Blood City captain was summoned to the presence of Rab Rory, King Henry's smallest brother and unofficial representative in Casablanca. Specifically asked to come alone, so he did to the meeting itself, though Tristan and Bowlegs had accompanied him through the streets and as far as the entrance hall to the Highlander's imposing residence on the Malecon.

Sir Tristram knew none of the Morgans really well. He had never told anyone he liked Rab Rory least of the six, including the non-footballing Bonnie Prince Charlie. Undoubtedly talented as a left winger, Rory had a sly and malicious streak to him on the pitch, shared by none of his rough-and-ready brothers. Sir Tristram was surprised to find one of these, the inside left Albert, at Rory's side when he was called through after a wait long enough to have Bowlegs tutting in annoyance at the perceived slight to his master.

The interview was shorter than their wait had been. Both Morgans saw Sir Tristram out, without overextending their goodbyes. He strode past Tristan and Bowlegs, leaving them to walk behind him at a fair lick as they returned to their quarters. He dismissed Bowlegs there, saying he would dine alone that evening with Barrie Knight.

Tristan saw no reason to vacate the room when Barrie arrived, punctual as ever, with an affectionate greeting at the door. He busied himself in serving the two Knights, ensuring their tankards were regularly topped up.

'All ready for the off, then? Did Rab Rory wish us well against the Marauders' auld foe?'

'Let him not love us so much,' Sir Tristram answered morosely. 'To "give ye a better chance"' —he mimicked the Highland brogue, poorly— 'he, or King Henry himself, as I suppose I should believe when his brother tells me so, has seen fit to add another striker to our squad: their brother Albert.'

'There goes my place in the starting line-up, then,' Knight replied at last. His attempt at cheerfulness did not really come off.

'I pick the team, Barrie, not you. Sorry, I did not mean to speak so short. I appreciate your offer. You are certainly right that Albert will expect no less than a starting berth.'

'He was a fine player – more of a goalscorer than I ever was.'

'*Was* may be right. He has swelled his tunic since those deys, yet I grant he could be an effective battering ram beside the rapier thrusts of Ivanhoe. My annoyance is more that he has nothing to do with Blood City, nor the Young Faithfuls for that matter. It's sheer grandstanding, using the Seskie for political ends.'

'Is it not all about that anyway?'

Sir Tristram had no answer to Knight's question, which effectively closed their discussion. After Barrie had left, the captain sat on at table as Tristan cleared it around him. He was staring moodily at the action figure of his own self the boy had brought him home from the fair. It was in his official club portrait pose, legs braced as he prepared to swing a war-axe as long as his whole upper body from right to left diagonally down on an unseen enemy. Having initially refused it as a gift, saying that such dolls were only for little girls to play with, he had now retrieved it from the garbage corner of the room, where Tristan had hurled it.

Father and child had talked as never before since Tristan had come out of his induced sleep on the outskirts of Casablanca. He felt more of an adult now, in part because of the new respect shown him by the soldiers. At the same time, he felt it could not be long before new traumas were inflicted on his body – natural ones perhaps, but no more welcome for that.

Their late-night palavers had begun like Sir Tristram's monologues to the respectful but leaden audience of Bowlegs, until he realised Tristan could not only speak good sense but make him laugh on occasion. Tonight did not seem a time for humour. Tristan gently rubbed the close-cropped hair on the back of his father's neck.

'I sense there is something else on your mind – something you did not discuss with Uncle Barrie?'

'You are right, Tristania.' The use of the birth name by his father was still rare enough to make Tristan catch his breath. 'Before discussing something, you must have a starting position of your own. I am not there yet, let alone ready to seek counsel on a final decision. You say it was Ian Swallow who won you the do—the action figure. I thought they would have long disappeared from all shelves.'

Tristan did not tell him the one they were looking at had been a singleton, among serried ranks of Ivanhoes, Pink Vikings, Sinbads, Francos and Greenmans. He spoke enthusiastically, not for the first time, about the branded cavalryman's performance at the shooting gallery.

Sir Tristram cut him short. 'Do you think he is a murderer?'

Tristan considered carefully. He had seen the look in Swallow's eyes when he faced Lascar down and fired at the keepers. 'I think he could kill – no, I'm sure he could. But haven't you always told me, Papi, there is no shame in being a killer? That it is part of the soldier's life, whether Army, Pirate, Westerner or Knight?'

'A killer, yes. I asked if you thought him a murderer. Even to kill someone who is expecting no attack may be justified, except if that person is no threat to you and yours, no threat to anyone.'

'I hear you, Father, but what if Ian *thought* that poor Zulu was a threat to Vic's place in the team? You heard him say at the Whipping Square he was not desirous himself of coming to the Seskie, not mad enough for it to kill for the chance, as I almost felt I was myself. Did you hear news from Rab Rory, then? Was Ian found guilty?'

'If only it were that simple. I doubt the matter would have been mentioned at all, had I not brought it up myself as I was being hustled to the door. I still cannot say if the Highlander was speaking the truth or making it up as we went along.'

'What did he say?'

'Patience, boy. He said the Army's investigations were inconclusive on the cause of death, whether boulder or bullet. That I should execute either Malabar or Ian Swallow, according to my own choice. "Hang 'em both if you like" were his exact words.'

'But you don't know which one killed Nkulu. You don't know if it was either of them – it may have been someone else altogether. They may not be guilty.'

'They may not. Yet nobody looks more guilty than those two. Added to which, their presence together is causing a poisonous rift within my squad.'

'Let them sweat it out on the training ground, Dad, or have a square go at each other. Or just send Ian away from the squad. Surely you do not have to kill either of them?'

'Thank you for not saying "murder", the word in my own mind. Though the choice is mine as to which, I must choose at least one. Rab Rory made it clear that came from Henry himself, that I must sacrifice one of my squad – to leave a space in the seventeen for his dvidammed brother.'

6

The *Chupacabra*

The Cibolans were not a seafaring people. Many of them did not float. In the main port of Casablanca most soldiers had been no nearer to open water than that which flowed in the gutters of its streets. Since Zanzibar had been divorced from the mainland, for political reasons best (and perhaps only) known to Henry Morgan, business and pleasure travel there had alike been strictly limited. While football was known to flourish on the island as it did everywhere, being in the very blood of the Zunis, there had been no representative team for Zanzibar in many decards.

Tristan appeared to be the only one of the Blood City seventeen looking forward with anything like pleasure to the short trip across the Straits. Knights were justifiably leery of any deep water, since their armour was no great aid to buoyancy. Drowning was not, however, uppermost in their minds as they made their way quayside in two unmarked minibuses. They travelled without fanfare, knowing they could expect abuse rather than applause if recognised by the locals.

'Them porgee war-soldiers, not a bone in their bodies, not a tooth, yet they say they can swallow a soldier whole, or spit him back out as no more than a skeleton,' said Bowlegs, after making sure that Tristan was within earshot.

'Ar, but don't they keep to the deepest waters yonside of the Last Ground?'

'Depends how hungry they are. Why would you worry, Frankie? They'd hardly go for you first, couple of joints short of a feast as you are.'

'Nor you neither, Chutney. They'd need a can opener to get at your tough old nut.' François was evidently offended at not being a prime candidate for a terrible death at sea.

'The new 'uns they go for always,' Bowlegs clarified loudly, 'but don't let Tris hear you talking such foolishness – we're only *just* coming into their main hunting seesun.'

'How hazardous will the crossing be, Dad?' He caught up with Sir Tristram as they walked the last stretch to the *Chupacabra*, the galley that would ferry them across to the Seskie and their destiny. The sails were not yet unfurled from its single mast, with its lookout post or crow's nest jutting out like a basketball hoop high above them.

'The sea must always be respected, though it is not my main worry at this present momet. Of course it is your first voyage. Let me give you two tips. For your tender heart, do not visit the engine room. For your tender stomach, do not eat too much before we weigh anchor.'

'Of your other cares, have you yet made a choice?'

'The sea may bring answers of its own, setting at naught any choice of mine or anyone else. If we all make land safely, we shall jury-rig a scaffold on the very beach in Zanzibar and let a jury decide.'

'A jury?'

'A group of soldiers peering into the darkness and deciding between them whose face they see. I have in mind White Eagle and Barrie to sit with me.'

'Not Jakob?'

'As vice he would sit in any other case, but here it is his own kin involved. He could not vote except in favour of his brother, nor would I expect him to. Now stand back, as we board in good order.'

Mbulu, easily recognisable on the slightest acquaintance, had been standing at the masthead as they approached. He was talking to a Pirate in the all-white of Ajax, right down to his doo-rag and pigtail. Just soon enough that he could not be accused of turning his back on Sir Tristram, the giant Zulu wheeled away, disappearing below decks.

Even the actual Pirates within the Pirate nation did not often have much to do with sea-going vessels, though Tristan heard his father greet this one as a boat son – Bates – before continuing less formally. 'Now then, Slasher, so the fleetmaster left you to welcome us aboard?'

'That's about right. There's some of your party he'd

sooner usher to the gates of hell or the bottom of the straits than onto the *Chupacabra*. He'll be in the engine room till night, I guess, before I take over.'

'I didn't know you'd still be using these poor devils.' Sir Tristram indicated with his chin a heap of soldiers at one end of the vessel, apparently dead to the world.

'Devils is right in some cases – that's why you'll see the foot irons. The sails serve at least to give them a break if the wind is set fair, but the art of using them properly is a lost one, and beneath the notice of the Ogs to help us with. It's still the lash and the slash in the Cibolan Navy – just as well for me, who don't know how to manage anything much apart from my cutlass. Unless you're looking for a centre forward for the Seskie?'

'I might be if John Ivanhoe and Pink Viking don't come through. Somehow I can't see you turning out for the City rather than Ajax, Slasher.'

'I'll pipe a tune for whoever pays me, stand on that.'

Offered by his father the choice between cot and hammock in their tiny cabin, Tristan chose the novelty of the latter, which soon proved a mistake. Once they began to move, albeit slowly at first, the pitching of the vessel amplified that of the hammock. He had taken Sir Tristram's advice and pushed himself back from table while still hungry. After his fifth bout of vomiting, he wondered if he would not have been better with more solids to throw up, rather than the bile which seemed to draw his very heart up into his throat with it.

Waking in the night, he left the now suffocatingly hot, cramped quarters, with some idea of mounting to the deck before his attention was caught by a cry of pain coming from a lower level. No coward, rather than return to wake his father, or Bowlegs in the cubbyhole next door, he went down a narrow and steep flight of stairs to see if any one of the seventeen needed help.

There was no door at the foot of the stairway, one of three opening into a large space where scores of soldiers, naked from the waist up and wearing precious little below it, were plying banks of oars threading out to the waters on either side of the *Chupacabra*. Directly opposite him, on a high chair like a judge at a royal tennis match, sat the boat son, calling out instructions from time to time to two men-at-arms, whose arms for now were short whips.

'Sir Tristram's lad, isn't it? Remind me of your name. Come to take a turn at the oars, or just a turn? Walk with me a little.'

The movement of the boat seemed less here than above. The rhythmic plash of the oars in the water could almost be felt as soothing. This was the engine room, however – no tranquil place. As they walked up and down the ranks of rowers, Slasher explained that he and his crew were there essentially for maintenance. 'If we need to set a faster pace, there's none like Mbulu. I've seen him wield two long whips at once, covering twenty backs with each.'

The flat of Slasher's cutlass was reserved for individual slackers, its blade for sleepers, as Tristan wished never to have seen. Finding that one soldier slumped at his oars did not respond to a hefty thump between the shoulder blades, Bates pulled him upright by his hair to take his head off with one stroke. At the side, one of the men-at-arms rang a handbell.

'Slave down, you load of skivers,' Slasher yelled as he swung the head above his own, drizzling the bent backs around him with blood. 'Ye'll have time enough to sleep above decks when we make landfall.'

Having thus encouraged the others, Slasher dropped the head at his feet and flicked it left-footed under the nearest bench. 'Never lose them scoring skills, matey, under the diving keeper. Not much blood there – that one may already have died at his post. No reason for the rest to know that. Steady, you still struggling to find your sea legs?'

'Something like that. I'll leave you to your work. What time is it, please?'

'The darkest – you know, just before the dorn. Our Mbulu is such a nightjar he's probably prowling the deck still. He'll come down here and catch some kip during deylight ours.'

While Tristan had no great wish to meet Mbulu on a dark night, the prospect of waiting for dorn below decks – he had no hope of any further sleep – was no more appealing. Sir Tristram had stirred in his absence to use the bucket for bodily functions more routine but even less aromatic than his own sick. Rather than wait for Bowlegs to attend to it in the morning, Tristan decided to tip it over the side.

Entirely by luck he sent the foul slops overboard in the right direction, so that they were carried swiftly away by the wind rather than coming back at him. Dorn in Cibola cut as cleanly as Slasher's cutlass, so that from darkness when he approached the taffrail, as he turned from it he could clearly distinguish two figures.

Mbulu was sitting cross-legged on the deck, straight-backed and still rising to an impressive height. He appeared to be speaking quietly, urgently, to a person standing by the masthead. Only on moving closer did Tristan realise the person was not standing. His feet were well above the deck, in thin air. Also, he could hardly be called a person anymore.

Tristan's screams brought most of the seventeen and various crew running, Bowlegs – for once bald-pated, without his balaclava – at Sir Tristram's shoulder. Chutney put his hands on his knees and bowed his head to puke – not from seasickness.

His father tried to prise Tristan away from the flayed corpse of the cavalryman. It had been flogged so hard that the shreds of the faded blue tunic and trousers were embedded in the raw, tenderised flesh. That this had been done without waking the whole ship could only be explained by the red gash of cloth across the face, serving as a gag but so drenched with blood it might have provided the mercy of choking him to death.

The Zulu was unmoved and unmoving, continuing his patient litany.

'Barrie, Septimus, lend Bowlegs a hand there and cut Ian down. Did you think to leave my boy to do that all alone, trying as he was?' Sir Tristram was hugging his child's face to his breast, though of course Tristan had already seen everything. He struggled to pull himself free.

'It's not Ian, Dad.'

'I'm sorry, Tris, I know it looks nothing like him, it's not something you should ever have to see, we'll—'

'It's not Ian. Look at the feet.'

Jakob O'Reilly was the first to grasp his meaning. 'He's right. You mind, back at their hovel, the criss-cross of knife marks on the sot's feet scored by his brother. Apart from a few calluses, the soles of this one are clear.'

'But the uniform—' White Eagle began.

'It must be Vic, Uncle,' Little Doe gently explained.

'But why would he? And where's Ian, then?'

Chutney had recovered enough to contribute. 'Me, Ian and François was drinking and dicing on deck until late. Frankie must still be sleeping it off down below. Ian said he couldn't stand being cooped down there, said he was the best sailor of us all, reckoned he'd shimmy on up to the crow's nest and catch him some zees where the air was cleaner. That's what he said, and by Dvid he got up there too – like to have broke his neck.'

'And wish I had, an' all.' As the soldiers looked upwards, it was into the barrel of a 17th Cavalry standard issue Winchester, with some enhancements to it made by Ian.

The quality of the weapon was of no concern to anyone. The quality of the shooting took Mbulu first. In truth, he already seemed to have moved away from any soldier community. The bullet entered the top of his head and he slumped sideways, silenced.

Malabar fell next, hit in the chest. The Knights had no weaponry to respond and save themselves from being shot too, if that was Ian's intention. They would never know, as the third shot came from the deck.

Jakob was already halfway up the rigging, which he had

begun to scale with a terrible roar before his brother was hit. The third O'Reilly present, Schwartz, was kneeling to hold his rifle at a steady elevation against a biscuit barrel which also provided him with a measure of cover. He fired only once, a different timbre from the Westerner bullets but with the same deadly intent.

Slasher was not on deck, presumably still keeping his oarsmen to the mark, since the forward motion of the *Chupacabra*, as well as its pitching from side to side, continued. Its incline meant that when Ian Swallow came out of the crow's nest, he hit the waters of the Bay of Casablanca rather than the deck.

As if fearing the sharpshooter might fire up from the depths, just as he had fired down from the heights, nobody approached the taffrail. There was enough to hold the attention on the bloodstained deck, with the three dead or dying goalkeepers. Mbulu's passing had been as swift as Vic Swallow's had been, to all appearances, slow and agonising. Schwartz, having carefully laid aside his gun, was nursing Malabar's head. He called for medical aid in vain, the *Chupacabra*'s strength not including a ship's doctor. Although Brittanus bullied François onto the scene from his drunken slumbers, the Arab was far beyond any help from his limited resources. A red stain was spreading on the fanatic's chest, a red froth bubbling from his mouth. It was impossible to tell if he was cursing or praying.

'Hardly a well-disciplined squad you're running here, Sir Tristram.' Albert's laughter drew everyone's eyes to him. Morgan's brother, who had embarked just before they set sail and spoken to no one since, was standing with bare feet planted on the deck, a cudgel in his hand, wearing only a blue kilt. 'Room for a new teammate now, no doubt, but don't expect me to go in the nets.'

'Albert, now is hardly the time for levity.'

'Aye, Tristram, the time for action was before now. An open wound must not be allowed to fester. Since we are afoot so early, I ask you to attend me over breakfast. Levity the dead over the side first, by all means.'

Tristan, still held tight by his father, felt every muscle in the Knight's body tense. His only response to Albert was a nod.

Jakob was kneeling at his brother's side, paying little apparent heed to the Highlander's intervention. Equally he spared the dying Malabar only a glance. 'Did you get him?' he asked Schwartz.

'It was a hard shot, but not beyond me.'

'This is no time for braggartry, you fool. Did you kill him?'

'Did you not see him fall as you were monkeying in the shrouds?'

'Do not provoke me, brother. I don't know. I don't know if I saw him fall or dive.'

7

Morgan's Fist

Although Sir Tristram no longer needed to consider building a scaffold on arrival in Zanzibar, there was plenty of wood to do so on and around the small crescent beach where they made landfall. The loss of its captain had enforced the change in the navigational plan of the *Chupacabra*. Piedra, with its tributary port of Pedrilla, was on the sarf coast, with the whole island between it and Casablanca. Slasher Bates may have been a competent enough number two, yet expressed no confidence in his ability to steer the vessel well enough around the island to avoid coastal shallows and miseries. 'My respectful recommendation, sirs, is that we land at Morumbi Cove. With luck the wind can drive us most of the way.'

'With luck? *Most* of the way? Are you capable of getting us there or not?' Slasher's 'respectful' had been for Albert, who cowed even the tough bosun. By virtue of his kinship to Morgan he was head soldier on the boat, and made sure everyone knew it.

Sir Tristram and Jakob O'Reilly had been at the meeting mainly, they realised, so they could see to implementation of whatever would be decided – and blamed if the decision went wrong. 'Morumbi Cove is the trafficking point for smugglers,' Jakob said. 'I do not doubt our friend Slasher knows it well.'

'It is an unfortunate way to arrive, sneaking in the back door.' Sir Tristram was always conscious of his own dignity, and the status of Blood City. 'How will we reach the city?'

'For all aboard including kit and caboodle, transhipment would be the easiest option. A smaller group could perhaps arrive more quickly by land, through the jungle between sea and civilisation. No stroll in the park, mind.'

Sir Tristram's sparing contribution to the debate was in part because the manner of Albert's address to him in the immediate wake of the bloodbath still rankled. If the Pirate had been trying to put him in his place above decks, he was only marginally more friendly when they met for chops and chai below.

'Bad business, that. I need hardly say, if you had taken action to punish one or the other, it might have been avoided.'

Sir Tristram had considered this carefully in the short interval between his abrupt summons and their meeting in Albert's cabin: short, but long enough to encompass the death of Malabar, expressing one last war cry or malediction followed by a gout of arterial blood.

'I fear the fleetmaster had run mad. Why he should have decided on the Westerner's guilt, who can tell? Say I had chosen to sacrifice Malabar, he would probably still have gone after Swallow.'

'You would have chosen to sacrifice Malabar? An O'Reilly? With Jakob as your vice, and heading to the land of Tommy? Have you run mad yourself?'

'There is such a thing as justice in the Knight's Code. It ranks higher than expediency.'

'Bosh, enough of your Knight's Code and long words. The word of my brother ranks highest of all, and I am to give it to you.' Suiting action to word, he handed Sir Tristram a letter folded into oilskins.

The Knight moved closer to the open fire to read Morgan's message, not for the heat – there was enough of that in the closed quarters to make him wonder when Albert had last bathed – but for any additional light. He had reached an age where the smallness of Tristan's script made it as unreadable to a prying parent as if it were written in one of the tongues from over the seas.

Henry's untutored fist was, fortunately, much larger. Hardly in joined-up writing, it presented little challenge. Nor did the length of the missive: 'Albert shall be my Regent in Zanzibar. Give him every support to make it so.'

The seal of the king of Cibola dated from the time of the Fredericks. Morgan had not bothered to have it changed from their totem of a wolf, glaring red-eyed from the centre, with a quadrant around it for stylised representations of each of the four peoples. Sir Tristram hardly needed to see it to know the message was authentic. He refolded the single sheet and put it into the flames.

'What?' Albert had been lounging back in his chair, which he turned over in springing to his feet. 'You dare so disrespect your king's orders?' He bent over the fire without quite completing the idiocy of sticking his hand in for the already consumed note.

'On the contrary, Albert, I follow them to the very letter. I have read and understood the king's desire. Surely it is better kept here' —he stabbed an index finger into his own forehead— 'than on a scrap of paper that may fall into the wrong hands.'

Sir Tristram would have given much to know if Albert had seen the actual message. The Pirate's response did not enlighten him.

'*I* was supposed to destroy it.' The hulking Highlander was clenching and unclenching his fists, like a boy sulking at his parents' insistence on lighting the pyre on Faggot Night.

'I wonder why the king did not tell me face to face, or when I attended you and Rab Rory in Casablanca. I understood mine as a diplomatic mission primarily, with force to be applied only should the Grand Vizor not return voluntarily to the mainland. If you are to be named Regent, he must see that as a disgrace to himself, making violence more likely.'

It seemed Albert would not deign to answer, but his vanity won out. 'Your "diplomatic mission",' he sneered, 'does that mean a con job? You will be telling O'Reilly there's a greater role at Henry's side awaiting him on the mainland, will you? Good luck. I know nothing about diplomacy. Still, you can count on me to be gracious, say the right things about following in the footsteps of such a distinguished Grand Vizor of such long standing. Such long standing that for all we know he's gone totally bush.'

Albert laughed. If he was expecting complicity from Sir Tristram, it was not forthcoming.

'He *is* a distinguished soldier – among the greatest of his generation. And a proud one too. What if he should decline to leave this "bush"?'

'Then butt-kissing diplomacy will have to become butt-kicking.' There was no hint of anger in the sentence. Sir Tristram realised he could not afford to underestimate Morgan's brother, however uncouth, as Albert put an arm round his shoulders to continue. He almost gagged at the Pirate's breath.

'Look Tristram, I probably shouldn't tell you all this, but hell I'm a simple fellow. You know me and Viking Defender are tight, like brothers ourselves?'

'Yes.' That tightness was rumoured to owe much to shared gaol time in Morroco many yeers since, before their families had opted to buy them out of a double-murder charge. 'But having been so long the second, would he not aspire to be the first if Tommy were to leave?'

'There's no "if" about it. O'Reilly will leave on a boat or stay in a box. And Viking Defender will stand with me. Your department is the butt-kissing. If it comes to it, we're your soldiers for butt-kicking.'

Sir Tristram was pleased not to have to spend any more time in the putative Regent's company during the remainder of their passage. He gave orders that everyone was to remain below decks after nightfall, bitterly regretting he had not done so the previous dey. His squad was now only fifteen plus Albert, and not one goalie on board. That issue could wait till landfall. Meanwhile he had Tristan to look after.

Since giving the word to identify the dead Swallow, the boy had scarcely spoken another. He attended the unceremonious funerals of Malabar and Vic, pitched overboard with only a cannonball each for company. The Westerners and Pirates attended to their own. White Eagle joined Sir Tristram and his cohort of Knights – Barrie, Septimus, Brittanus, Bowlegs, Chutney, François and Tristan – at both committals, without favour. The figures were thrown off different sides of the *Chupacabra*, largely in silence, though Little Doe did express the sentimental hope that the cavalryman might be reunited with his twin below the waves.

There was no funeral for Mbulu, whose body had disappeared as completely as Ian Swallow. Apart from the Blood City squad and the *Chupacabra* crew, the galley slaves who were not on shift had been woken from their exhaustion and sent milling around the deck by the gunfire. Slasher showed no inclination to make enquiries of them or his own soldiers. 'Let the dead bury the dead. I saw the bullet split his head like a womelon. I know he ain't coming back, but it may serve us if the devils at the oars half-believe he might. Superstitious beggars, the lot of 'em.'

When they were settling for the night in their tiny cabin – the *Chupacabra* was not designed for luxury of any kind – Sir Tristram asked if the boy wanted to talk over the events of the dey. Tristan shook his head. When he woke screaming in the night it was another matter.

'Dad, Dad, did you see him? It was like he was doing a magic trick, floating in the air, till I saw the rope. Then I saw you could hardly call him a soldier anymore. I mean, at least it was fast for Mbulu, and probably Ian too, unless he drowned or the porgees got him, but Malabar, the way he fought before going under, he still wanted to fight the whole world. All of them, all three might have been guilty, but it was Vic, that's who I was seeing in my dreams. He was lashed to pieces. Did you see him, Dad, did you *see* him?'

'I saw him, child. You found him. That was the greatest horror. I would not have let you face that alone for the world. To be trying to drag him down off the masthead alone – many full Knights would have baulked at that. You did all you could and more. Do not let the memory overcome you when the event did not.'

Tristan quieted in his father's arms. Just when he appeared to have fallen back to sleep, he presented his calculations in a calm voice. 'That's four gone – five, with the poor old Zulu in Blood – and we're not in Zanzibar yet. How many more will there be?'

It was too late to remind Tristan that he had warned their expedition was not to be lightly undertaken. It gave Sir Tristram no comfort to have been proved right so quickly, so brutally. He could only continue to rock the boy until he did sleep. His father could not. The butcher's bill so far had shocked him to a deeper realisation of what he was leading his squad into, most of them all unawares.

Above the belt of beach on Morumbi Cove as they approached was what appeared a carelessly patterned, seamless shirt of green and brown woodland. There was no welcoming committee, no one at all visible on shore. Bates had told Sir Tristram most of the soldiers living in the forest and its surrounds were Indians. 'They'll be more frightened of us than anyone need be of them.'

'No doubt. And what about the smugglers? Pirates, I assume?'

'There you go, give a dog a bad name,' the Pirate answered. 'This island has been cut off from commerce with Casablanca and beyond so long that everyone with an ounce of gumption is a smuggler. The Army are always looking to supplement their naffy rations with stuff from what they call Morumbi market. It wouldn't be in their interests to come barging in and turn the stalls over, but they keep an eye on it all the same. Sure, there's a few hard cases around here, but not by dey. Even at night there's more risk of having your purse snatched than your throat cut.'

'I would have thought the same on the *Chupacabra*. I'll be mounting a guard anyway.'

Sir Tristram sensed relief to be off the boat and onto dry land again in most of his squad, though Albert was no more cheerful. He turned on Slasher. 'I thought you said there was a way on foot to Piedra? That brush looks pretty thick to me. Not that I'll be walking far in this heat.'

'There is a way through, but I wouldn't expect you to take it, sir. They may already be sending transport. The Grand Vizor has a Mobo – a motor boat,' he clarified. 'If not, we can wait for a local craft or at least a pilot to help me on the *Chupacabra*.'

'If you've any hope of becoming its captain and expect me to put in the word, I'd better not be stranded here too long. Have a couple of your crew set me up in the shade for now.'

It did Sir Tristram good to see his son splashing about in the shallow waters of the beachline, the only one of the party to do so. Bowlegs was keeping an eye on him, probably having convinced himself of aquatic dangers from his own tall tales of porgees.

It occurred to the Blood City captain that Tristan might be lonely. He pulled himself up sharply when he caught himself thinking it might have been well to bring another squire along, perhaps Barrie's blue son, Christian. While his friend knew the secret of Tristania, the boy would not. It might cause more complications than it would resolve. Besides, they were not on a seaside outing but a deadly serious mission. It was not easy to harden his heart, tell himself the kid needed to toughen up, having just spent a sleepless night watching over him.

When Sir Tristram woke, he judged from the angle of the sun that there could be no more than a couple of ours till nightfall. Most of the party had, like him, stretched themselves out in the area where the beach faded into the forest, out of the worst heat, in knots tied by friendships, house or clan loyalties. Some were now stirring. Rather than see them pass an evening in idleness, bickering or worse, he decided it was time to remind them of what they were, what they were here for.

Jakob had moved apart from the main group, almost to one end of the cove's horseshoe. He continued looking silently out to sea as his captain climbed to join him on a rocky shelf. Sir Tristram was uncomfortably conscious that his closeness with the vice-captain when they began to reassemble the team of City's pomp, not to mention their sense of optimism and adventure in doing so, had been greatly eroded since they left Blood. The potential differences in their personal agendas, and the third one imposed above them both by Henry in the shape of Albert, were the most likely causes, though Sir Tristram asked himself if he had not perhaps been too much among his Knights at the expense of others in the squad.

'Again, I'm sorry for your loss, Jakob.'

'Malabar was an unquiet spirit. Perhaps now he can rest. Which does not mean' —he suddenly switched from his reflective tone to something altogether sharper, looking at Sir Tristram for the first time— 'we can ourselves rest until he is avenged.'

'Avenged on who, Jakob? The Swallows are already at the bottom of the sea. Did not Schwartz already take your revenge? Are you saying Malabar was entirely innocent?'

'I say that of no soldier, but Malabar was *an* innocent. I was the one who brought him on this mission, against advice from many in the clan O'Reilly.'

'And now he's gone.' It was the Knight's turn to speak more harshly. 'Our mission continues. Come on, Jake, help me organise a training session, defence against attack.'

A designedly multi-house detail of Sir Septimus, Chutney, Little Doe and Oscar using their various sharp weapons – dagger, halberd, hunting knife and scimitar – had soon rigged respectable goalposts from saplings growing in the shade of much bigger trees. Bowlegs enlisted the aloof Yellow Cloud to help him plait and stretch creepers between them for crossbars. The whole squad except Albert, who had only said 'might join you later for a bit of a kick-around', were called together by Jakob, picking up the various balls they had been playing with, unloaded in a bag from the *Chupacabra*.

Sir Tristram's gaze panned the semicircle of soldiers. 'We are here, lads. Here in Zanzibar, where many of us never set foot till this dey. We will hold silence for those who did not make landfall with us.'

Knowing the concentration span of various in the squad was as limited as kittens', and not wanting to plunge others (Tristan foremost) into too deep an introspection, he kept their gesture of respect brief. Then he turned to football.

'The death of Victor Swallow, that horrible and unnecessary death, made me face up to a serious mistake I made. I had a fixed idea, one I know I communicated to some of you, that our team to take the field against the Young Faithfuls would be the Old Truebloods, the first painted City 1 to 11. I am spared the temptation to persist in my error by the loss of Vic. We can also not yet be certain that our number 5, Pink Viking, or John Ivanhoe at 9, will be pulling on those shirts for the Seskie. I pledge this to you all: I shall pick our starting eleven purely on present merits, not past glories. My own number 4 shall be first up for contention.

'At the same time, I repeat my earlier comment that everyone within our squad has a role to play, one I will not undervalue. François, you will, for instance, continue to exercise your keeping skills in the nets for attack during tonight's game.'

'What about defence keeper, Tram? In training we can defend an open goal if you like, but what are your thoughts for the Seskie? We can hardly play rush goalies against the Young Faithfuls.'

'I know, Jakob. Drake would have been an ideal guest star. I did not speak in jest about my own shirt. If we have no better candidate, I will take the gloves myself.'

'We shall need you on the pitch. For now, shall I bung Bowlegs in, or Chutney?'

'Dad? Er, sir—I mean, skip.' Tristan broke off from his keepie-uppies within discreet earshot, fearful they might not be planning to involve him in the session. 'I'm sorry to interrupt. If you want to train all the defenders, I'll be glad to go in goal behind them.'

'From striker to keeper? Will you promise not to get yourself knocked out this time, boy? No heroics, then. And no showing off.'

They put Jakob beside White Eagle again in the heart of the defence, Chutney in Jakob's berth at right back and Little Doe in his normal position at left. Sir Tristram and Bowlegs would play as defensive midfielders in front of the back four.

The attack, also lacking a star in John Ivanhoe, was nominally captained by Barrie Knight, who would work with Sir Septimus as attacking midfielders in front of François. They had a full forward line of five to feed, with Oscar wide right and Cowboy wide left. Yellow Cloud was asked to work the inside right channel. Schwartz, similar to John Ivanhoe in height if nothing else, would be inside left, with Brittanus at centre forward.

It was no wonder that a forward line containing four wingers did not immediately achieve a great balance. Septimus, a subtle passer of the ball when he could escape the harrying attentions of Sir Tristram, would need a little time to rekindle his understanding with the wingers, while his attempts to find Brittanus were baulked as often by Schwartz and Yellow Cloud as by defenders. Barrie's offensive strengths in a midfield role were surging runs, relying on brute force as much as finesse, for which there was little room in the crowded box.

Tristan proved agile and dependable on the rare occasions attack were able to throw off the smothering blanket of defence. Perhaps because they did not need to think of doing anything creative, the back four came together quickly as a unit, Jakob playing slightly deeper than the rest to provide cover where needed, often to the game but less talented Chutney. Tristan conceded only from deflections, the first a deliberate side-footer by the canny Brittanus on a pull-back by Cowboy, the second when a thunderbolt from Yellow Cloud looped up off Little Doe's heel.

They were all playing barefoot in sand still warm from the dey's sun, which at its height had made the beach too hot to go bootless. The sand was deep enough to highlight the soldiers' overall lack of stamina. Some of that could be improved by training, some of it was gone forever with the yeers since they had all been top players. All except Schwartz, at any rate. Sir Tristram soon concluded that he lacked the necessary quality, or rather confirmed the contemporary judgements of more than one manager. Because he was an O'Reilly, he had been on the books of several clubs, drawing a salary – if never a compliment – on the occasions he was pitched for a few minnits into games already won or lost.

Schwartz was the obvious soldier to sub off when Albert ambled over to join them, had Sir Tristram not been keen to avoid offending the Arabs' sensibilities. He would switch the sniper with Cowboy, to Schwartz's preferred position, fully expecting him to confirm his uselessness so comprehensively that even Jakob would be unable to make a case for him. Brittanus, whom the captain trusted to be fit and capable whenever required, made way for Albert.

A modest crowd had gathered to watch Blood City's first training session in Zanzibar. The galley slaves remained on the *Chupacabra*, with those of Slasher's marines not required to watch them beside him on the notional touchline. They were joined by soldiers emerging from the jungle – Indians mainly to start with, coming with their hands on their heads to signal their lack of any hostile intent, then a few Army and Sherwooders. Slasher had a quiet word with his sergeant-at-arms before turning back to the makeshift pitch to watch the new recruit to the squad.

Tristan realised only with the arrival of Albert how easy Brittanus had gone on him. The hulking Highlander saved his full strength for battles, in the air and on the ground, with Jakob and White Eagle indiscriminately, never moving far from the centre of the goals or the mini-box. In a full eleven-a-side his lack of mobility might have been an issue, particularly playing offsides. In the close quarters of this session, he served as a focal point for the other attackers, far more vocal than the legionary in constantly demanding the ball.

While Albert disdained to use his extra strength and weight on the new keeper, he was up to every other trick in the book. He was not always quick enough to get in the boy's face (and nostrils), but at set pieces there was no escape. The first time he found himself unable to jump for a cross because Albert was standing on his foot, Tristan appealed to his father, as referee, for a free kick. He got no joy. When he found himself bound to the brute by a sweaty paw gripping the side of his shorts along with a painful pinch of thigh, Jakob O'Reilly, blood streaming from a broken nose inflicted by a blind-side Highlander elbow, was equally unsympathetic. 'Welcome to the big leagues. Keep on the move and take your hits like a soldier.'

Albert, especially adept at bringing the ball down from his chest and firing in powerful shots with either foot (as well as entirely selfish in front of goal), quickly claimed a hat trick. Schwartz, meanwhile, was more than fulfilling Sir Tristram's expectations on the left wing, in the pocket of Chutney. While Cowboy, at inside left, was also largely anonymous, a cramped pitch like this did not play to his strengths of bursting past players at speed and delivering good crosses. The question of how much of his pace he had left at the Casablanca Carnie was one for another dey.

So, too, was the right wing starting berth, occupied by Yellow Cloud since a swap made with Oscar by the captain at half-time. Jakob could be expected to see reason about Schwartz – he wanted to win the Seskie, after all. He could equally be expected to press for Oscar's inclusion, with some justification. The Berserker relied more on trickery than pace, which helped in the inside right position he was now occupying.

Yellow Cloud brought something different to the table, more apparent now he was out wide. Almost as greedy as Albert, he preferred to cut inside and shoot with his left foot rather than hit the byline and cross. If his shots were not always on target – though he did score another to add to the goal he was claiming from the first half – they could easily lead to own goals or chances for alert teammates. It would be a difficult choice between him and Oscar.

There was no set duration for their match, Sir Tristram's goal as much to tire his boys as drill them. The pace had slowed considerably when a murmur from the Indians in the crowd and a shifting of their attention had the less-focused players also looking out to sea. Tristan heard first a low buzzing. Having just fielded an unusually tame effort from Yellow Cloud, he booted the ball upfield for attack to come again. As the noise increased, he saw a low-slung boat, all red, come surging into view round the edge of the horseshoe.

Albert was not slow to pounce on the boy's lapse in concentration. Found by the simplest of through-balls from Barrie Knight, he pivoted to smash his fourth goal under the pliable crossbar. 'Last goal wins,' he grunted in satisfaction before abandoning the mini-box at last to walk towards the sea, a further layer of sweat added to the many already permeating his pale blue jerkin.

The Mobo came sweeping up, closer to the shore than the *Chupacabra*, spraying white water on either side. The bare-chested helmsman, sweatbands on his thick wrists, must have cut off the motor at the approach, since it nosed onto the beach towards the footballers and spectators in complete silence.

'Wow, how cool is that!' Tristan said to no one in particular.

The shaven-headed Pirate remained at his wheel as two Tommies disembarked, holding sub-machine guns at an almost apologetic half-slope. They stood with the water lapping their boots as a much bigger soldier hitched his skirts over the prow. He had a heavy war shield on his braceleted left arm, a sword poised to strike upwards in the other hand. His head and back were bent forward as he began to advance, a Tommy a step or two behind on either side.

'Viko, it warms my heart to see you!' Albert was apparently capable of enthusiasm after all. He almost ran to greet his old friend. Viking Defender allowed himself to be hugged, the shield coming round as if to protect Albert's back while he lowered his sword parallel with the ground. He seemed to be talking to the Highlander while inspecting those behind him. Sir Tristram had beckoned forward Jakob on his right and Barrie on his left to form a symmetrical welcoming committee.

Albert was almost skipping, excited as a girl being picked up for junior prom. 'I told you my brother would not keep us waiting – and to have come in his own person! You can see space is limited on the launch, and we must be gone before nightfall, but of course there is room for you aboard.'

'And welcome too, Sir Tristram,' the Viking growled through his beard, which was teased into a single plait running from chin to his spreading waist. 'A little warmer here than in Blood, no doubt.'

'Indeed. I am glad to see you looking so well after these many yeers. The island climate obviously agrees with you.'

'Is the English influence so strong here' —Albert waved an arm vaguely at the Viking's uniformed escort— 'that all you can find to talk about is the weather? Whatever the skies send, I have not changed this tunic' —he proudly thumped his chest— 'since the dey I was cast.'

'I am sure that is true,' Sir Tristram answered coolly, while still looking at the Viking rather than the Highlander. 'We were just observing the courtesies.'

'Longer and deeper conversation must wait until we are on the water or back in Piedra. The lights on the *Torvid* – the vessel's name was painted in black on its side, merging from a distance into the red all around it – 'need an Og to look at them. Will you come on board now?'

'I regret I must stay with my team, Deputy Vizor.'

'You would not present yourself to the Grand Vizor at the earliest opportunity?' Albert's good humour vanished as quickly as it had appeared.

Sir Tristram continued to address the Viking. 'Tommy is a captain himself – few more experienced. He will understand the responsibilities that entails. Jakob is more than capable of doing the honours in my stead, if he consents.'

'If he consents?' Albert exploded. '*I* do not consent. For all your talk of courtesies, if you as captain will not go, I shall certainly not take the vice. Let us waste no more time here. I am ready to go, brother – alone, except I shall need someone to buttle for me. Your lad will do for that, Tristram. Come, boy.'

8

At the Toryanka

'Cuff this for a game of marballs,' Chutney grumbled to Bowlegs and Cowboy as they toiled with their Indian guide to clear a fallen tree from the narrow jungle path. 'Why couldn't we just wait for another boat to come for us? And why do we have to pull the path-clearing? What's got into your old man?'

Bowlegs had been more than surprised to have their waking duties reversed by his lord that morning with a rough shake. 'Gather the squad – we leave for Piedra in seventeen.' He knew better than to question a command. While he had pondered on it since, he would not show his ignorance to Chutney. 'You heard what he said. It's a punishment for our laziness in training, a yomp to get us in better shape for the Seskie.'

Cowboy too was resentful at being involved in the heavy lifting occasionally necessary to make a way for the main body following them. His role was to provide firepower against attack from rogues in the forest, whether on two legs or more. 'I reckon the skipper just had second thoughts about letting Tris go off ahead to Piedra. I never saw him so protective of his other wains. He'll be making a quean of him if he's not careful.'

If he had not heard the excitement, the wonder in Tristan's voice when he saw the *Torvid* racing towards them, Sir Tristram would have fought any notion of him going with Albert, the more so as he knew the Highlander was only making a spiteful assertion of his authority. The Knight saw nothing but innocent enthusiasm in his son at the prospect of a ride in the speedboat; he thought it might help banish the grisly memories from the *Chupacabra*. Still, he had been grateful when Tristan's godfather, Barrie Knight, took a step forward. 'With permission, as an original Blood City and current Young Faithfuls player it would be a signal honour for me to present our team's initial compliments in Piedra.'

Albert glanced at Viking Defender, who shrugged his heavy shoulders. 'Come on, then. You Knights and your bluddy compliments.'

They were soon gone, Tristan waving at his father and friends on the shore as the *Torvid* gathered speed. It was now full dark, at least until a powerful beam from the vessel came on to light its way, with red taillights winking them goodbye.

'Don't look much need of an Og repair crew on them.' Sir Tristram heard Jakob softly behind him. 'A word, Tram?'

They returned to the rock where they had talked earlier, not speaking until they were settled on it side by side. Jakob had fished two primo cigars from Busted Jaw out of his robes yet was mildly surprised when the captain accepted one.

'After that show I'd say PV and Ivanhoe can't get here fast enough.'

'I know. And how both of them would love to hear you say it, Jake. Is that really what you want to talk about?'

'The team will need to be addressed, for sure. But no, I guess not.'

'Do you mind if I speak first? I owe you an apology for not doing so before now.'

'Is it something to do with the arrival of Albert? Dvaeba, it's great to have a reminder of how much I hate the Morgans.' Carefully gripping the bridge of his nose, Jakob expelled a dollop of blood and snot over the shelf of their rock.

'I should have talked to you before that. I have a mission to fulfil on behalf of King Henry himself, who, whatever you may think, is a beast of a totally different stripe from that lummox Albert and the rest of his clan.'

'He is not king without cause, I grant you. Whether he is still the right king for Cibola is another matter.'

'He is my king, right or wrong. As a Knight, I am bound by the Table vow to cleave to him, unless and until a decision of the Table relieves me. However little I am cast for secrecy and plotting.

'I know Tommy forever. Viking Defender too. They are both of an earlier tradition, if not generation. The difference is that while you, Ulf and the rest are clearly sons of your fathers, Pink Viking and his cohorts, back to the very Hulk, are soldiers of another mould altogether than Videf and his peers like Yashin.

'But I do not need to lecture you on the history of the Pirate nation. While Hulk is in Morroco and Tommy here – Casablanca I regard as fundamentally ungovernable, no matter what the viper Rab Rory may attempt – there are limitations on King Henry's power. The other important distinction between his clan, the Arabs and the Vikings is that lack of a second generation.

'Henry is a realist – knows he must plough with the oxen he has. I am partly here – I say "partly" because I am deadly serious about winning the Seskie with Blood City – to open channels of communication between the two great men, Henry Morgan and Tommy O'Reilly. I believe they need to talk. I hope to persuade Tommy back to the mainland with us.'

'And if he will not be persuaded?'

'I hope to persuade him with your support, just as I know I can rely on it in melding a team to beat the Young Faithfuls. I am sorry not to have told you of this before – glad to have done so now. Please, have your own say.'

For a while it seemed Jakob had nothing to add. At last he turned to look at the Knight. 'I will support you in trying to get Tommy O'Reilly to Casablanca. I must in all conscience also warn him of dangers he may face there, or even here under his own Vizordome. I did not like the speed with which Albert insisted I should not go on that boat. Glad in one way, for I am no sailor, much less a lover of his company, I do not like the collusion between him and Viking Defender. Forgive me my frankness. I would not have let Tristan join them on board, a thousand times not were he my own boy.'

'Come, Jakob, I know Viking Defender and Albert are murderers many times over, and not by proxy, yet I cannot believe they would threaten the life of Tristan. What would it profit them?'

'Nothing, unless they can by holding him with that threat bend his father to their will. My uncles Tommy and Zito would sacrifice second generation as promptly as their own if need arose. I do not believe you Knights are the same. I noticed Barrie was not keen to let him go to sea alone.'

'Thanks for the smoke, Jakob.' Sir Tristram tossed the butt into the breaking waves below.

They left François with the team's supplies and kit, to follow with Bates around the coast to Pedrilla. Sir Tristram's campaign experience made him cautious in unknown territory, hence the advance group of three with the Indian guide he had saved during the night from being pressed into Slasher's crew after he was found lurking around their camp. Schwartz, with his rifle, was at the front of the main party with the captain, followed by Jakob, White Eagle, Little Doe, Sir Septimus and Brittanus. Yellow Cloud and Oscar were deputed to follow on behind to cut off any attack on their rear.

'I bet you only one of them makes it through the forest,' Septimus offered Brittanus. 'They're liable to kill each other for the number 7 shirt.'

'That would be one less problem I'd have,' Sir Tristram overheard him.

At best it was usually only possible to walk two abreast along the forest floor. Although the route was clearly one of some traffic, the tropical vegetation grew so quickly that the maintenance and clearing work Chutney, Bowlegs and Cowboy were grudgingly putting in was more than welcome. The soldiers were not bothered by any large animals, but were soon slapping away insects ranging in size from the microscopic to that of gorged bumble bees. When these let up, the heat became a torment, despite the shade of the jungle canopy.

After a stiff enough march to satisfy Sir Tristram's second purpose of a good workout for the squad, his group came through gradually thinning trees to the end of the forest. The advance guard had been taking a break from its labours, Bowlegs the first to get to his feet to greet his master. 'Welcome to the pan-Zanzibar highway, Sir Tristram.' He gestured at shrubland, featureless apart from a narrow path to which the Indian had brought them.

They walked under the unrelenting sun until the earth became tarmac. The paved road began, or perhaps ended, with a Brittain's tank blocking its whole width, cannon pointing straight at them. The soldier watching their approach from its turret through a pair of binoculars had left any order to fire too late, as they were now below the gun's elevation.

'Halt! Who goes there? Name yourselves with the password of the dey.'

'The Blood City football team, heading to Piedra for the Sesquicentenario, which should be password enough,' the captain replied. 'I'd be obliged if you would organise us some motorised transport.'

'You'll have to see the lieutenant about that. Head on to the customs posts.'

A hunnert yerds or more beyond the tank were what looked like tollbooths on either side of the road. There were no windows facing towards the jungle, but as they left the tank horizontal slits appeared in the wooden walls, through which they could see the glint of gun metal. These would not have a problem with elevation.

A tall Cossack wearing a red-trimmed shako above a heavy woollen uniform stepped from one of the blockhouses and repeated the formula of the soldier in the tank. Mindful of the guns, Sir Tristram kept his cool and repeated what he had said there.

'Of course, I recognise you Sir Tristram, we just have to say the words. And Jakob O'Reilly, as I live and breathe. Is John Ivanhoe here? Or Pink Viking?'

'They are finding their own way.'

'Lieutenant Muntian at your service, sirs. I was on the Amalgamated Unions' books. I'm surprised to see any of you coming this way. Delighted though, since it will likely be my only chance. I was hoping to be at the match but I'm already on jankers out here' —he mimed tossing an invisible drink down his throat— 'and they wouldn't have it. Can I offer you chai?'

'Thank you. If you were not expecting us, what kind of army *are* you expecting to face that you need a tank against?'

'It's more a ground-clearer for us to deploy our own troops, if I'm honest. The tank hasn't moved in yeers. Engine needs an Og overhaul, turret still swings through a full circle, but we expect to use it on the forest, if at all. We can load shells or fireballs, kill the bad guys or smoke them out to a fair fight in the open.'

Sir Tristram shook his head at the barbarities of modern warfare.

The canvas-topped, open-sided lorry to take them to Piedra took long enough for Muntian to summon that Sir Tristram – consumed by impatience to find Tristan – was on the point of marching his squad off again. While they relaxed outside, fraternising with the Russkies, he and Jakob took chai in one of the blockhouses. Muntian's assertion that his outpost was more a customs station than a fort was somewhat belied by the twin machine-gun emplacements that dominated the space inside the booths. The gunners would sit back-to-back in bucket chairs on a single rotating base, so that if one were to be disabled the other could swing around to his post. 'We've got mirrors rigged outside so that we can see the road on both sides without revealing our own strength. You wouldn't have seen the guns if we hadn't opened the slats. Actually, I was only showing off a bit there – didn't really expect to have to use them.

'There's not much motorised transport at all on Zanzibar – sorry again for the delay – but we can put up a roadblock if we want. There's a weighbridge built into the road, but most of the stuff that comes through here is smaller scale.' Muntian did not go so far as to admit the informal taxing of anyone emerging from the jungle. Often the victims were Indian fishermen or hunters, satisfying the troopers with something to fry for their dinners.

'I can understand lorries having to use the road, but why doesn't other traffic just bypass you?' asked Sir Tristram, more from politeness and to stop the lonely officer's flow than any real interest. 'The terrain away from the road doesn't look too problematic.'

'It doesn't, does it? All heavily mined though, the whole area.' He winked at Jakob. 'And if anyone wants to crawl though the crap in the roadside dykes – our cludgies discharge into them – I'm not sure I want a taste of whatever they're smuggling.'

For a while after they passed the welcome-to-Piedra board – more welcoming than that of Busted Jaw, at any rate – there was still little evidence of a major population centre; more tepees than walled dwellings, few soldiers to be seen. Sir Tristram and Jakob were in front with the Army driver while the rest of the squad sat facing each other in the body of the lorry behind. They seemed in good enough spirits, no doubt enjoying the breeze generated by the vehicle's speed coming through its sides after their earlier sweaty tramp. Bowlegs and Chutney worked them up at one point to some tuneless serenading of their vice, who did not turn to acknowledge it: 'J O'R, O'R, he's going to Pee-ey-dra, J O'R, O'R.'

The truck pulled to the side of the road by a gap in a stone wall – surely a remnant of some pre-Zuni race – where a sign announced 'Piedra Old Town'. 'You'll be quicker anyway walking from here, which is where I hand you over to the city garrison,' the driver advised them.

Sir Tristram was surprised and pleased to see in the representative of that garrison a familiar Blood City face, albeit now that of an Ajax player. 'Sergeant Reaney, who did you upset to pull this duty?'

The smart Redcap gave a crisp salute before shaking the Knight's hand. 'No one, Sir Tristram, I'm across from the mainland as ADC to the CIC.'

'Take me with you.'

'Sorry – Army TLAs. I'm a glorified dogsbody, really. The commander-in-chief, General Myhigh Syhigh, is over as part of the Seskie beano. The Army will be putting out teams against both Blood City and the Young Faithfuls as curtain-raisers for the main event. Everyone's looking forward to the football. Word is our security job, crowd control, might get a bit hairy though.'

Trying to keep any note of concern out of his voice, Sir Tristram asked Reaney if he had seen Tristan. 'He should have arrived last night, late no doubt, with Viking Defender and…' He was suddenly leery of mentioning Albert in case his presence on the island was not widely known. 'And Barrie – Barrie Knight.'

'Negative, sir. Which does not mean he's not here. There was a bit of a kerfuffle at the Toryanka last night, for sure. They may well have been brought already to your lodgings, Hosteria Videtor, pretty central and close to it.'

As they walked the narrow streets towards the centre of Piedra, the Blood City squad drew some friendly attention from the pavements and the buildings rising on either side, seeming to lean towards each other like gossips at their higher levels. Most of the buildings had seen better deys; the unhoused of Zanzibar too.

'Of course, Tommy doesn't live at the Toryanka for all it's his official building. Nobody knows for sure where he lays his head. Most of the bigwigs nowadey are out at the Zuteca – that's one phenomenal complex, sir, latest ETechnolOGy in one of their famous bubbles, you know, temperature-controlled and everything.'

'I can see that would be welcome here. I would like to call and pay my respects to the Grand Vizor at once.'

'I don't know if that's on todey's running order, sir. My understanding is that Viking Defender will receive you. I gather MySy hasn't seen Tommy himself yet.'

Sir Tristram wondered if Albert had made some unhelpful comment about arriving with a newbie and a teammate rather than the Blood City captain, leading Tommy to keep him waiting to restore a proper sense of his own importance. He could only trust that Tristan was being well looked after. He swore silently that he would find him by nightfall.

They stopped at what appeared to be a gigantic bar, open to the street but with armed soldiers at each of its supporting pillars. Ceiling fans provided the only temperature control. White-jacketed bar staff stood behind a double rank of pink drinks. 'Most locals can't aspire to a cocktail here, the guards are more to keep beggars and rowdies out. You won't have the whole place to yourselves, but any other guests will have been carefully vetted.'

'Jakob, I'm pressing straight on to see what I hoped would be your clansman but turns out, more likely, Viking Defender. You want to come or settle in the boys?'

The vice-captain understood at once Sir Tristram's worry

that a good proportion of their teammates, already with eyes glued to the long bar, might not make it past that to their rooms till all the morning's conditioning work had been undone. Nevertheless, he opted to go with the Knight, who put White Eagle in charge of the rest.

Crowded in by the Old Piedra buildings, they did not see the Toryanka until they emerged suddenly into a square, of which it occupied the centre as the only building. It was perhaps five stories high with a cupola. Stone steps rose to the main entrance. Its massive wooden doors, covered by gun turrets on either side, were wide open, though it was impossible to see what waited inside.

'Pretty impressive, no?' said Reaney. 'Especially in the middle of a beaten-down burg like this. Apparently it extends as far below the square as above it. In the offices from the first floor up, you get strangled by red tape. In the basements, you get strangled. That's what they say.'

'Let's hope we are received on the ground floor, then.'

There was a strong Army presence on that floor, a wide-open area large enough for a full eleven-a-side. Jakob confirmed the second comparison to come into Sir Tristram's mind, muttering 'A killing field.' The floor was overlooked by walkways extending all around the higher storeys.

They were not received on the ground floor, which Reaney explained was as far as the Army mandate ran. A full-blood Pirate by the name of Sambo, wearing the Young Faithfuls' colours as a sometime reserve keeper of theirs, led them to a broad internal flight of stone stairs. 'The assender's blown, sirs, till the Ogs can get to it.'

Beyond the second set of stairs Sir Tristram was glad to be led along a corridor rather than further upwards. Their host was leaning back against a table in a room otherwise devoid of furniture, through the only open door on either side of the hallway. As he rose to greet them, the marks left by the big man's buttocks and hands showed up clearly against the layer of dust on the empty table. 'Will I have Sambo fetch you food? Or drink? I had thought you would arrive at your leisure, fed, watered and rested, but perhaps not.'

'We were keen to get here. On mature reflection, I should have come with you last night. I trust you explained my concerns about my soldiers to Tommy if Sir Barrie and Tristan did not meet him. I have not seen them yet.'

'Tommy is occupied with Albert. I doubt you have had a chance to mingle here yet. I would ask you mention to no one the arrival of Morgan's brother. Impress the same on your squad. Under pain of death.'

Before Sir Tristram could ask if he was serious – though he gave no sign of being anything but – Jakob spoke for the first time. 'Why? I mean, the way you met Albert on the beach looked like you were somehow expecting him. Why should it be such a big secret now?'

'You do not know Zanzibar. We do things differently here. The whole island is flooding into Piedra to be near the Seskie, most without any hope of getting inside the Zuteca. We must entertain them. Allow us to keep a few surprises. Rumours of an all-star parade are everywhere. Only the stars remain to be unveiled.'

'At the Seskie? Three deys from now, right?'

'That is so. Tomorrow you will face the VD Army XI. Tomorrow past it will be the Young Faithfuls' turn against the TO'R Army Select. On the third the Seskie itself, Blood City v Young Faithfuls.'

'And should we expect Albert to turn out for us tomorrow? He was talking of it, or would that spoil your surprise? I need as captain to know my options.'

'I'm not sure his head will be in the right place tomorrow. I would advise you to count on seeing him again only at the very kick-off of the Seskie.'

'And your tribesman, Pink Viking? Has he arrived yet?'

'Not that I'm aware of. He marches to his own drum, as you surely know.'

'I surely do. And where did you leave my son and Barrie Knight if they were not received with Albert?'

Viking Defender was evidently pleased, a grin of yellow teeth in his yellow beard, to have drawn at last a question from Sir Tristram that betrayed his anxiety. He did not rush to answer.

'I left them here. On the ground floor. I have not seen them since last night. Are they not capable of shifting for themselves? I will see you again tomorrow.'

The Knight barely managed a curt nod of farewell to the Deputy Vizor, clattering down the stairs far more quickly than they had climbed them. As they regained the square he turned angrily to Jakob. 'The oaf! To be received in a broom cupboard, then threatened as if we were tattling bairns. "Under pain of death", dvaeba. I know your clansman Tommy would never have treated us so, however aggrieved that we did not come to him at once.'

'I am aggrieved myself, Tram. Reaney, give us some air, please.' The Redcap obediently moved further ahead of them. 'I too wish we had come last night. I do not believe that Viking is a true friend to my uncle – far less a defender.'

Having been so preoccupied with the whereabouts of Tristan, the captain only now saw the justice of Jakob's remark. How much sooner should he have reached the same conclusion! He knew of Albert's mission in Morgan's writ. He had heard the Highlander brag how close he was to Viking Defender. Could the two of them have already made a move to unseat Tommy? For the first time it occurred to Sir Tristram that the Arab chieftain may have been unable, rather than unwilling, to receive them.

Before he could do more than acknowledge Jakob's concerns – which he had no intention of exacerbating by his additional privileged knowledge – Sir Tristram was cheered at last by the presence of Barrie Knight at the Videtor bar, talking to Sir Septimus with Bowlegs in attendance. His delight turned to dismay when he saw how gingerly his friend descended from the stool and, as his eyes adjusted from the street sunlight to the indoor shade, how Barrie's own eyes had both been blacked.

'What happened to you? And where is my son, in the name of Dvida?'

'He came here safe to the Hosteria with me.'

'Unharmed? Don't tell me the two of you were found out in some street brawl.'

'Never in life, sir.' Barrie confirmed that Viking Defender had left them on the ground floor of the Toryanka before disappearing with Albert.

'Your lad was asleep on my shoulder before long. The late hour and the few soldiers around – Army, mainly – made the noise from somewhere upstairs carry, though not distinctly. Raised voices, loud bangs and thumps—'

'Gunfire?' Jakob asked.

'I think not. Everyone else ignored the sounds altogether. Perhaps they are customary in that place.'

'Hardly the sound of red tape,' Sir Tristram said to Jakob.

'Eventually, not far from sleep myself, I realised not only had we paid our due courtesy, we would be disrespecting ourselves and the Blood City mission by dancing attendance any longer. I made to leave and find our own lodgings as we might. It was, perhaps, a mistake to draw my sword when a bold Desert Rat said we were going nowhere. Tristan fought valiantly too, but we were overpowered and taken downstairs by main force.'

'Downstairs?'

'Yes, a dungeon, tar-black. I told the lad it was a mistake, must be – at worst we would be there till morning. Then they came for me. For both of us, though I prevailed on them to leave him there, saying he was no more than a squire. He told me this morning he even managed to get a little more sleep.'

'I see you have taken some heavy blows, Barrie, probably more than are visible. If any of them were meant for my son, I thank you. I would hear your full story, but first—forgive me—I must see him. Why is he not here?'

'He cannot be far.' For the first time, Barrie looked uneasy. 'I told him I must sleep – he should not go far if he left our quarters. I did sleep. On waking I met Bowlegs and the squad. We were about to go for him—'

'About to go for him? And instead we've been jawing here? Bowlegs, gather the whole squad at once. Reaney, how many soldiers do you command?'

'I command none, sir, but I will put together a detail ASAP. The streets in this part of Piedra are heavily patrolled and relatively safe, at least until nightfall.'

'Which will soon be upon us. If I do not have my child back by then—'

'Dad, Dad. What a surprise. When did you arrive? And Jakob – hi.' The subject of their conversation breezed into the bar, evidently with no idea that he might have been missed. Going to hug his father, he was soon enlightened.

'You dviddam little fool, where have you been?' Sir Tristram slapped him hard across the jaw – Barrie stirred but thought better of it – and shook him by the shoulders till he registered the bewildered look and tears starting in Tristan's eyes. Then he hugged him, very tightly – to save him the embarrassment of being seen to blub in public, he would later tell the boy. In fact, the hug was almost entirely for his own comfort.

Bowlegs had efficiently assembled the squad, many of them probably chafing to be out exploring this new city before their captain's curfew kicked in. He took the opportunity to give them their briefing for the following deys.

'You'll all be guaranteed some game time against the Army tomorrow, playing in borrowed boots and bibs unless François arrives in time with our belongings. Counting him we're fifteen, with Pink Viking and John Ivanhoe making up the numbers to the full seventeen. Please don't anyone let on I spoke of either of them as making up the numbers.'

Although his comment did not rank as a witticism, when he saw he was not getting so much as a courtesy smile he understood nobody was listening. 'All right, on your way. Don't make us have to come looking for you – under pain of death. Which reminds me. Our guest Albert, who is also our possible guest centre forward, is about the king's business. Make sure it remains just that, not our business or that of anyone you might happen to run across in Piedra's concert halls and theatres.'

Tristan's natural exuberance was not fully restored by the enthusiastic welcome back from his friends in the squad. Sir Tristram was glad he made no request to go out with them. The boy did ask for an urgent word in private, which Sir Tristram told him curtly would have to wait. He was still annoyed at the emotions he had shown in front of Viking Defender and his own teammates when the tyke had been happily running around the streets on his own.

'So who worked you over?' Jakob and Sir Tristram sat facing Barrie and Tristan in a small room the hotel had made available to the Blood City captain for meetings with his soldiers.

'Impossible to say, Jake. In the cell it was like fighting panthers in a coalhole. They had covered my head by the time we reached the other place, hands bound behind my back so I could not guess by touch. I caught a sleeve, a shirt, but could not swear they were Army or Pirate.'

'Could have been Cowboys or Indians. Not all braves go bare-chested. What did they say?'

'They asked who I was first. I told them I was here to

play football in the Seskie, which they pretended to doubt. They kept asking me "what else, what else", and every time I said "nothing", they hit me. Punches to the face, clubs to the body and legs.'

'The cowards. Tommy shall hear of this.' Sir Tristram was glad he had not confided more of their secret mission to his best friend. While it might have brought him short-term relief, it would likely have led to a worse ending. Knight's injuries were another dollop on his growing burden of guilt.

'And how long did this go on?' asked the ever-practical Jakob. Tristan was looking on with mounting horror at the torture Barrie had suffered while he slept.

'All night. It was a Pirate who eventually brought me out – Sambo, a Young Faithfuls colleague.'

'And what did *he* have to say?'

'He was apologetic but would not tell who had been behind it. He spoke of an "admin error", whatever that means.'

'Reaney said he knew nothing of your whereabouts,' Sir Tristram mused. 'If not Pirates, if not Army, then who?'

'And why? What can have been suspected? How could they not have known we arrived with Albert and Viking Defender? At the time I was more anxious to see no harm came to Tristan. He stood up well.'

'I ask your pardon, Sir Barrie. It was a noble gesture to come in my stead, to take a father's role and a father's blows. They will be returned with interest in due course, I vow. Tristan will of course bunk with me now – you go and rest those bones. Will you be fit to play against the Army tomorrow?'

'A few bangs and bruises, a couple of sprung ribs maybe, will not prevent me from taking the field if selected. Believe me, I shall be listening carefully for any familiar-sounding voice in the Army squad.'

Tired though he was, Sir Tristram ended up breaking his own curfew. Tristan was insistent once they reached their room, no bigger than the 'broom cupboard' in which the captain had been received at the Toryanka, that his father come out to see something very important he could not otherwise explain. Rather than threaten to paddle an explanation out of him, as he might have done had he not felt guilty for his earlier slap, at last Sir Tristram agreed to take to the night streets of Piedra Old Town.

The lad said nothing more once they had left the hostel, beyond muttering to himself from time to time, 'First left… third right…second left.' Sir Tristram found his hand gripping the pommel of his sword as they moved into ever darkening, ever narrowing streets. At the door of a dive its swinging lamp identified as the Spartan Officer, he looked at Tristan in disbelief when told it was their destination. There was no sound from within. The saloon door gave readily to the touch.

'You will answer me later how you ever came to find this place, never mind expecting us to enter it at this our.'

'Welcome, sirs, though I was on the point of closing for the night and leaving him to it.' The Cowboy barman gestured at what appeared to be his only other customer, sitting with his back to the wall. He had a beer to his left, whiskey to his right, rifle on his lap. It was Ian Swallow.

9

The Spartan Officer

'Course I didn't go in the Spartan Officer on my own, Dad. I would never have found it at all if Ian hadn't led me there, making me memorise the turnings. He said he wanted to be somewhere out of the way where the rest of the team wouldn't come across him by chance. He said he'd happily wait there for you all dey and night.'

'I bet he did.'

'At first I thought I was seeing a ghost – might have fainted in the street if he hadn't grabbed my arm – then that it might be a tripling of him and Vic. But it was definitely Ian. He offered to show me his feet.'

Although it was already the small ours, Tristan's excitement was keeping him awake. His father did not want to tell him to shut up, for all his own tiredness, struggling to organise his thoughts around this latest development.

By his own account, Ian had been winged by Schwartz's bullet 'enough to knock me out of the crow's nest, but I knew I was gonna have to jump – couldn't see me getting a friendly reception on deck. I was lucky the shot fell nice with the pitch of the boat and that it passed right through me. Otherwise I could easy have hit the deck, and if I'd lost conscious in the water it would of been curtains too.'

Never separated from his rifle, he had used it first to keep himself afloat then to bully an Indian fishing crew unfortunate enough to help him from the water ('them not knowing if I'd fire, me not knowing if *it* would fire after its dunking') into returning to Zanzibar rather than Pollockgate market in Casablanca where they were heading.

'Why would you want to come to Zanzibar?' Sir Tristram, sitting over a pewter mug in the Spartan Officer, was genuinely baffled. 'Why not go back to Casablanca, where you could easily have vanished and made your way home?'

'Home. That's about it. You were at our "home" – mine and Vic's. It was never sweet – now there's nothin' to take me back. Besides, I knew you were kind of short of keepers now,' he glossed the deaths of three custodians on the *Chupacabra*.

'And you dare face Jakob? You killed his brother.'

'And he killed mine. Sure, it was Mbulu did the deed, and he had to go first for that, but he was mad from the death of his pa. And why did he turn on me, as he thought Vic was? Cos that crazy Ayrab had been in his ear ever since the whipping post.'

'You're saying it was Malabar that killed Nkulu, then?'

'My own pa told me never to badmouth a dead soldier. Course I could say it was him now he can't answer back. If I did, I 'spect you'd still have your doubts about me. Am I right? All I ask, Sir Tristram, is can you use me? Your word as captain should be enough to keep Jakob and his murderous little sh…idekick brother, who already had one potshot at me, you can keep them onside. At least until after the Seskie. I'll take my own chances then. You can even have your original starting eleven back if you name me as "Swallow, V". I wouldn't mind one bit having that Seskie winner's medal struck in ole Vic's name.'

Having had his say, Ian leaned back against the wall and took another pull on his beer. Tristan looked anxiously at his father, who also drank before replying, elbows on the rough wooden table.

'I can use you, Ian. And not only for football, it may be. Can you find the chief of that Indian fishing crew again?'

'Thunder Cloud? As it happens, I can. I told him to come here at dorn and I'd either have money to pay for his rotten fish or work off the loss myself. Maybe you can help with the first option, captain?'

'Good. I'll come to meet him with you.'

Having agreed that, Sir Tristram realised he had to speak to his vice first. After much less sleep than his body was pleading for, he took Jakob for a pre-dorn walk through the mainly still-sleeping streets.

'I knew it. I knew it was a dive, not a fall. I am glad he lives so I can have the pleasure of killing him myself. Take me to him, Tram. I promise a fair warning. I would not catch him unawares, as the murdering dog did my brother.'

'No, Jake, it can't be that way. If you meet Ian Swallow, I will not ask you to shake his hand, nor agree a lasting peace. It must, however, be on condition of a truce until the Seskie is over. I remind you, he too lost a brother in the most gruesome way – a far crueller death than Malabar's, most would say.'

'Death is death, I would say. What of Schwartz?'

'Schwartz had his shot – from cover, if I remember well. If I take you with me, are you saying you cannot keep your little brother under control?'

Jakob flushed. 'I am not saying that. What does the cavalryman bring us?'

'A safe pair of hands in the nets. Safeish, anyway. Tristan was willing enough, but he is not a keeper, never mind one to put against the wiles of Suarez and the power of Viking Attacker. I had thought we might ask A-Og to guest, but A-Og is not Blood City. The Swallow twins are part of club history.'

'I do not like it.'

'I know, Jake, I understand that. If you say no, turn back now and we shall head to the Zuteca without him. I shall still deal with him, though – that is my right. Let me ask you this. Have we received the welcome we expected? We have not so much as glimpsed the Grand Vizor. Swallow is a resourceful fellow who can help us in ways other than football. He is a crack gun, and there is more. Are you with me, Jakob?'

Ian Swallow's arrival at the Videtor was a five-minnit

wonder with the rest of the team. Jakob, to whom many eyes turned when Sir Tristram brought him out from the hostel's cramped kitchen, had his hand on a surely forewarned Schwartz's shoulder, like a careful owner walking an unpredictable dog. 'As a mark of respect to our departed first-choice keeper,' the captain concluded after an abridged version of Ian's adventures since they had last seen him, 'his brother will wear Vic's number 1 jersey and be registered in his name. Apart from the fact he may be wanted by the authorities, it would give our rivals comfort to know we are playing a reserve rather than first choice.'

'Thanks for that vote of confidence, cap'n. I'd never have allowed him as a better goalie than me in life, as I will now to all of you. I'll be doin' my very best in Vic's name not to let nobody down.'

'By the curls of Dvida, is Zanzibar indeed an island of miracles?' came a cry from the street. François had arrived with Slasher Bates.

Sir Tristram laughed at the welcome breaking of the mood. He had feared Ian Swallow, maudlin-drunk, was about to cry. 'Bowlegs will explain all, Franc. It is miracle enough that you have made it in time for our opening match.'

Slasher, delighted with a guest spot in the squad for the Army game that afternoon, was happy to organise transfer of its kit direct from the repiloted *Chupacabra* to the Zuteca. Reaney reached the hostel precisely at the agreed time, leading them on foot to the main road they had left at the gates of Old Piedra, at another point in what he referred to as the gyratory, which ringed the walled city. A 55-seater coach awaited them there, the name *Tommy Fender* painted on its side.

At the entrance to the Zuteca was a massive statue that explained the name of the drinking den where Ian Swallow was found. Three times higher and broader than the tallest soldier and cast in silver and gold, this Spartan Officer stood with right arm outstretched, a spear planted on its plinth with its business end rising above the warrior's head.

'Local Zuni craftsmanship, with a bit of help in the heavy lifting from ETechnolOGy,' Reaney told Sir Tristram as his teammates marvelled and clambered about the statue's silver boots, trying in vain to snap or at least bend the shaft of the spear. 'The Spartan, known worlds over as a supreme fighter, is apparently supposed to represent the whole Zuni nation – all four Houses of Cibola in a single figure. The Army hierarchy and structure, in that it's an officer. The Knights – well, you can see the armour, the greaves, the breastplate moulded to look like a hero's wall of muscle. The Westerners – look at the headgear, not just a utilitarian metal helmet but the gorgeous plume above it.'

Jakob looked at the Redcap suspiciously. 'And the Pirates?'

'That would probably be in just that mixture, that juxta-position of qualities, sir, not limited to any one race – above all a warrior, one you would not waste your breath asking for mercy.'

While the statue provided only a symbolic deterrent to intruders, the Zuteca reportedly had an absolute shelter against the heaviest ordnance as well as massed attack by ground troops, in a dome that could cover the whole complex, rising from the ground when required and disappearing like a burst bubble by a reversal of the same ETech mechanism. Internal barriers could be activated for more localised crowd or riot control.

To the Blood City veterans of the Cibolan league's origins, the footballing facilities of the Zuteca were more impressive than the Spartan Officer. There were synthetic and grass training areas as well as courts and tracks for other sports. The changing rooms for the Zuteca itself, the showpiece pitch where the Seskie would be contested, were underground, the two teams emerging from a tunnel onto the halfway line.

Sir Tristram was shocked to see the welts and bruises all over Barrie Knight's body, cause of much ribald comment from his other teammates about the night of supposed deboshery he had enjoyed in Piedra before the arrival of the main party. 'Is that why Tristan got changed at the hostel, ashamed of his own battle scars? Let's have a look, lad.' Chutney moved towards him ready for a rag, with a few others showing interest behind him.

'All right, enough banter, this is where the serious business starts.' Sir Tristram headed Chutney off, thrusting him backwards with a solid palm to the chest. 'Make the most of this luxury.' He indicated the marbled floor, the individual shower cubicles, the steam baths. 'I suspect with Tommy in the Young Faithfuls team we'll be in the away dressing room for the Seskie.'

'Any idea about the make-up of this Army team, Tram?' Jakob began their selection huddle. 'Not that we have too many permutations we can make.'

'I tried to pump Reaney – he's normally gabby enough but kept a tight lip. Couldn't resist bragging he'd be playing left midfield, though.'

'What? He was a full-back pure and simple last time I looked.'

'We don't know if they've got all the Army stars out here for what are really only friendlies. We do know they're not over-blessed with attacking talent – Little Boris, Chick Brody and this new Sigi, that's about it. Looks to me if they've got Reano in midfield it's going to be an ultra-defensive line-up. As Viking Defender's XI it may be made in his image.'

'We might struggle to break them down without John and PV. I almost wish we could count on that blowhard Albert.'

'I agree, Jake. That's why I let Slasher join the squad. He could be a useful foil to Brittanus and if Oscar and Cowboy can get them some good service—'

'I wanted to talk about the wingmen. I was hoping you could find a place for Schwartz. Don't look like that, Tram, I'm not asking for the Seskie, just for todey.'

'Have you promised him?'

'What if I have? The fact he can't play for carob don't mean he has any less love for the game than the rest of us. And frankly, with Ian Swallow in goal, I'd rather have him on the field where I can keep an eye on him.'

'Are you saying he might put a bullet in our keeper from the dugout?'

'It wouldn't be the first shooting of a goalie in Cibola. Remember when Spindle of Casablanca Kids got hit against AU. They never did catch the fan.'

'A fan, yes, but a teammate? Go on then, I suppose in the grand scheme of things it's only an extended training session.'

The seventeen Sir Tristram handed to Viking Defender as referee before kick-off read: 1) Swallow (V); 2) Knight, 5) W. Eagle, 6) L. Doe, 3) O'Reilly (J); 8) Tristan, 4) Tristram, 10) Septimus; 7) Y. Cloud, 9) Brittanus, 11) O'Reilly (S). Subs: François (GK), Bowlegs, Chutney, Oscar, Cowboy, Bates.

'Read it to me, that's the chap, I don't have my specs about me.'

Sir Tristram obliged, doubting very much whether Videf had ever seen a pair of eyeglasses, a curiosity of ETecholOGy that had enjoyed a brief fad on the mainland some yeers earlier. He was surprised at the old man's vanity, with illiteracy the norm throughout Cibola.

'Glad to see you're looking after your own – you with your boy in the team, Jakob with his brother.'

The captain did feel a little uncomfortable at Tristan's inclusion, to which Jakob had made no objection once Schwartz's place was confirmed. 'He's a willing runner, Videf – newer legs, you know. May we see the Army selection, please?'

'I haven't been to their room yet.'

'No problem. Tristan can make himself useful in that too. Boy, go with the Deputy Vizor and bring us back news of what we will be facing.'

'Talk about parking the bullock-cart,' Chutney laughed when Tristan returned a few minnits later with the Army team by heart: 1) Flagger; 2) H.V. Rumplebum, 3) Bollis, 4) Sylo (cap), 5) Rofe, 6) Thugface, 7) Cruz, 8) Held, 9) Beef, 10) Reaney, 11) Crumplebum.

'Reaney at number 10. Wonder how much he had to pay for that shirt?' Jakob mused. Sir Tristram saw at once he had been far too conservative in his own selection. The only two attackers they faced were Beef, once a fine header of the ball but now broken by injuries as well as age, and Held, a second division player with the Probables of Morroco.

For the Seskie the Zuteca would be packed and a degree of segregation by race might be enforced for security reasons. Todey admission was free, but with little advance publicity only the traditional Indian side, the one in full sun from which the players emerged, was approaching half-full, including a good number of off-duty Army.

The thin crowd had little to cheer until half-time. None of the Army's top stars were on display, either up front or in midfield. Even in goal the solid veteran Flagger stood in for the acrobatic Limdenberger. It was a team of journeymen, if not outright cloggers in the case of Thugface, Cruz and the cousins HVR and Crumplebum. Thugface and Jakob exchanged a few words before the off. Thereafter the Army central midfielder let his studs and elbows do most of his talking.

The Army's attacking moves were limited to high balls pumped in the general direction of Beef, the superannuated sapper. Sir Tristram had put Jakob at left-back, to mask the intent of using him in midfield in the Seskie, and Barrie at right-back, to spare him too much running. Tristan worked hard at Barrie's normal foraging role in the middle of the park, usually nimble enough to avoid the scything attentions of the opposition.

The Blood City captain had to face the fact that, with

Jakob in a limited defensive role and absent Pink Viking and John Ivanhoe, his team lacked inspiration. His own game had always been more about drive and energy than subtlety. Although Viking Defender disallowed one perfectly good goal from the ever threatening Brittanus for some imaginary infringement, and was quick to blow offside on other occasions when the City threatened – there was no mistaking which dog he had in the fight – they could not grumble too much that the match remained goalless as half-time approached.

Thugface's creature Vera Cruz, the smallest soldier in a big Army team, made up in malice what he lacked in brawn. Rather than wait for Schwartz to fall over his own feet or pass conveniently to the opposition (both skills he had shown to have in his locker), he raked his studs down the back of the Arab's leg, bringing him to the ground. The two were being separated by Thugface and Jakob, between whom Sir Tristram was sure he caught a look of complicity, when Viking Defender whistled for the interval.

The teams moved to the goalmouths they had been defending for their half-time talks. While Jakob appeared to be furious, it was in an uncharacteristically verbose way. 'Sir Tristram, the ref is obviously not going to protect any of us, and especially not my brother, from the looks of that last challenge. You did well, Schwartz, just beginning to get the measure of Cruz and HVR, but I won't have you try to play through that injury. Please take him off, Tram. Looks to me as if it'll keep him out of the Seskie too. Bad luck, brother.'

Sir Tristram quickly named Cowboy to replace Schwartz, then Chutney to come on for Barrie Knight. 'You shouldn't have much defending to do, Chut, so get forward any chance you can.' Before he could further strengthen his attack, the biggest cheer of the dey rose from the largely muted crowd. An Og Bubble-Fart had plopped gently into the centre square.

10

Pledge of Fire

From the miniature two-seater version of the Far-Transporter range emerged Pink Viking and A-Og. The former milked the crowd's standing ovation, waiting regally in the centre square as if to receive homage from the players as well.

'Carry on with the team talk, Jake, I'll see if I can get him on as centre forward.' Sir Tristram grudgingly made his way to hear PV bragging on himself to Viking Defender and the Army captain Sylo (a nephew of Myhigh Syhigh). 'Yep, I'm the first non-Og ever to pilot one of these thingies.' He pointed to the now deeply unimpressive membrane into which the flying machine had collapsed as if to protect some crop under the grass. 'Isn't that so, A-Og?'

The giant spaceman nodded from inside his orfish-bowl helmet.

'Nothing to keep the fans happy yet, then. It seems my services as a centre half are hardly needed – eight or nine on the pitch already. I'll be with you for the Seskie, of course, Trissie' —he must have noticed the way the Blood City captain winced whenever he addressed him thus— 'but Videf, my honoured kinsman, asked if I'd lend his boys a hand todey. And speaking of boys, I'll take your Tristan to partner me up front. If I can't set him up a couple of goals, he can feast on my scraps.'

The second scenario was more likely than voluntary assists, Sir Tristram thought sourly as he returned to his own group. Pink Viking was no more noted than Albert for his unselfishness in front of goal. Having apprised his teammates that they would be facing rather than feeding the monstrous centre forward, a very different proposition from Beef, he completed his changes for the second half.

'We all know PV's power and talent. Let's remember also he's a teammate and treat him well – treat him to a couple of goals if he doesn't grab them for himself. No need to handle this sprog with similar indulgence' —he put a hand on Tristan's shoulder— 'I shall view it as a personal affront if he gets an easy ride.

'White Eagle, I know you're the best equipped to cope with PV in the air but I don't want you destroying his confidence before the big one, so I'm going to stand you down this half.' In truth, it was not the Viking's confidence he was looking to cosset.

'So I'll move into the middle beside Little Doe, then?'

'No Jakob, and for similar reasons' (in this case without the unvoiced ones). 'I want you low profile still at left back before exploding in the Seskie. I'll slot in between Chutney and Doey and we'll go 4-2-4. Looks like they've been given instructions to kick you out of the Seskie Sep, a bit like Schwartz' —he somehow managed to keep a straight face— 'so Bowlegs will come on for you, and Oscar, I want your wizard dribbling from right midfield. Yellow Cloud, keep firing in those crosses from wide right – good first half despite Bollis' hacking; we'll bring in Slasher beside Britt so we've got more chance of getting someone on the end of them.'

'Am I getting a run-out, Sir Tristram?' François deadpanned.

'I think you missed your chance first half, Franc, when Ian hardly had to make a save. I suspect he'll be busier when we change ends.'

So it proved. Blood City were soon three down. Ian had no chance with a majestic header and thumping cross-shot from Pink Viking, to whom every player in the Army team was now striving to get the ball at every opportunity. The City keeper made an excellent parry on another header, only for Tristan to reach the ball before his father or Chutney and tap it into the empty net. 'Good goal, son,' Sir Tristram congratulated him, just as he had Pink Viking on his brace.

Obviously considering the game won, Pink Viking took his notoriously low boredom threshold from the pitch at 3-0 to rapturous acclaim. It was disheartening for the remaining players that he took so many of the crowd with him back to the city.

146

PV's departure saw the Army unit throw yet another centre back (Blood United's Crank) into their already hugely congested penalty area. Despite the fact they often had two or more soldiers on the line, Viking Defender had no compunction in continuing to award offsides against Blood City. He did allow them two goals, one from Bates and the other in sheer delight at the talent of Oscar beating five defenders before dinking the ball over Flagger.

'Looks like only Pirates can score for us,' a frustrated Brittanus remarked to Yellow Cloud. Even Pirates, it soon became clear, would not be allowed an equaliser. The match ended Army 3 v 2 Blood City.

The Seskie circus, opened with the arrival from the sky of Pink Viking, continued that evening with a parade of the Young Faithfuls squad, fresh from the sea. Reaney, scrupulously avoiding any mention of the afternoon's result, was embarrassed to tell Sir Tristram and Jakob there would only be one float in the parade, and that reserved for their opponents. 'But Blood City could always take part on foot.'

'Good of you, or whoever you speak for, to give us the option. So we can either march ahead, as if providing the Yofas with a guard of honour, or trail behind like gawping fans. I don't know what you think, Jakob, but I don't fancy either option.'

'Agreed.'

'All most regrettable – the second tractor is in the Og workshop and…' As if sensing it was better to move on, Reaney brightened in offering the Blood City squad prime spots on the very steps of the Toryanka should they wish at least to view the parade.

'Processions are no more than flimflammery, but it may keep our soldiers amused. I must ask formally before you go for an audience with Tommy O'Reilly. Viking Defender won't do. I would see Tommy himself.'

'I will take your message, Sir Tristram, though obviously I cannot guarantee a response. Is there any particular subject of your meeting?'

'I want to talk about the officials for the Seskie. I'm not joking,' he said before Reaney's smile could get a fair start. 'I understand today's game was only a friendly, and that we were playing against Viking Defender's own selection. Still, the question of an impartial referee is of major importance. A couple of brave linos wouldn't hurt either – people who understand the offside rule.'

'No one understands the offside rule,' said Jakob.

'Have you had no attempt at contact with or from your uncle, Jakob?' Sir Tristram asked when Reaney had gone.

'None. I have been reluctant to seek a meeting, since I lost one of my brothers on the crossing, the shame of which is with me still. Perhaps he is also punishing me for that – until now I always had the impression of being a favourite with him.'

'You believe he is still master of Zanzibar, then?'

'I believe so, though it is no longer an absolute belief. As we have discussed, I fear the brute Highlander and do not trust the Deputy Vizor. I hope to seek counsel tonight from my uncle, Zito. If he is not received by his brother, then we will indeed have reason to suspect the worst. Such a breach of O'Reilly clan loyalty would be unthinkable.'

'I hear you. Although there is no clear picture in my own

mind, I believe tonight we must test the loyalty of the Blood City squad – loyalty for our darker purpose, not the Seskie, though Dvid knows that will be trial enough.'

'I need no proof of Schwartz's loyalty, nor Oscar's, unless I were to ask him to go against his fellow Tuaregs. Can you not count on the Knights in the same way?'

'Our way is not the same as yours. Bowlegs apart, they owe me no personal fealty. They have a right to decide for themselves under the Knight's Code. It does not sit well with me to lead them into danger ignorant of the true situation.'

'You will tell them the whole truth?'

'Whoever knows the whole truth, let him tell it. I shall say I am charged, as are you, with bringing Tommy O'Reilly back to the mainland. This may not be easy, to put it mildly. I shall tell them we have arranged with Bosun Bates to have the *Chupacabra* at anchor for as speedy a departure as we need, which is the truth.'

'With another truth behind it.'

'We are not in a reeve's court, Jakob, on our oath. I need also to speak to our Westerners, who may not wish to be drawn into a battle for primacy between Pirate chieftains.'

'We can speak to them together if you like. With three crack riflemen – I cannot deny that the sot Swallow is one such, to go with Cowboy and Yellow Cloud – they would be good to have on our side rather than against us. Are you planning on battle?'

'Planning for it, yes – hoping to avoid it, also yes. If all goes well, we shall see Tommy free and he will come freely with us. I do not believe—forgive me even mentioning the possibility, my friend—he can have been killed. After such a play there would be no reason to delay announcing it and seizing power. If we are right about the conspiracy between Albert and Viking Defender, I can only think they will produce Tommy as an apparently willing party to their accession. The Seskie, with the whole population either present in the stadium or watching on community Far-Seers, would be the logical time for such an act. We must be prepared to move quickly and in concert.'

'As well as winning the match.'

'Aye, as well as winning the blessed match. Do not think I forget that mission for one segund.'

In the hope of seeing Tommy plain that very evening, whether in private or among the dignitaries and the Young Faithfuls on their float, the captain and his vice agreed they would talk to their teammates only after the procession. The Blood City squad found nothing strange in their opponents being so feted in contrast to their own unheralded arrival; the Young Faithfuls were always the glamour club of the whole of Cibola. Sir Tristram made a mental note to focus before the Seskie on eliminating any trace of an inferiority complex in his players.

The punctilious Reaney came to escort them to the Plaza de Armas with a couple of Desert Rats, shouldering their way through the dense crowds. There were people of every race, though Westerners and Army predominated. Reaney explained the capital had seen a massive influx of soldiers, many from the mainland with or without legitimate travel documents.

There they all were, above the crowd, on the float being towed by a tractor driven by George Buck, a Young

Faithfuls player himself as well as a farmer: the living legends of Cibola's first ever football team, including Yashin, Zito, Suarez, the captain Coluna, Ferdinand and crippled Frenchie; stars of subsequent and current generations like Atilla, Viking Attacker, Hun, Lancelot, Scarface and John Ivanhoe; even a few players the Young Faithfuls were now supposedly courting from other clubs, the likes of Limdenberger, Greenman and – Sir Tristram was furious to see, as a low growl suggested his lads were too – Blood City's own Sinbad. Talking to his brother Yashin was Viking Defender, with the Army's commander-in-chief. Myhigh Syhigh hailed from Morroco, an imposing putteed and gaitered WWl officer with his knapsack on his back. There was no sign of Albert or Tommy O'Reilly.

As the Videtor was already busting full, Sir Tristram had not expected their rivals to be lodged there. Reaney offered him up to five tickets – 'I'm sorry, I don't dispose of more' – to attend a reception at the Vitoritz Hotel, on the seaward side of the Toryanka square.

'Let the Young Faithfuls enjoy their party,' the Knight ungraciously declined. Apart from the need to speak to different groups within his squad, reinforced by the continued invisibility of Tommy O'Reilly, he could not have chosen which ones to go without creating jealousies; nor was he sure he could find five he was confident of behaving themselves.

White Eagle would have been one eminently suitable ambassador to the Vitoritz, but the oldest member of their squad looked tired when he assembled with the other Westerners. Had he been leaning on Little Doe for support when they came into the conference room? Well, there was a reason most of them were already retired, Sir Tristram had time to think, before addressing them with Jakob at his side.

'Friends and teammates. I shall not keep you long. I have gathered you under the convenient banner of the Westerners while recognising you may not speak with one voice – perhaps it will even be with five. I have seen you all work together on the field of play, prepared to put your bodies on the line for each other. Tonight I ask – not demand, ask – if you would join another team under my leadership – mine and Jakob's.'

He had made no attempt to gather them round a table. White Eagle had laboriously lowered himself to the floor, Little Doe similarly cross-legged beside him. Yellow Cloud stood alone in a corner. Cowboy sat on a table, his spurred boots scuffing the floor. Ian Swallow had his feet fully up on the table, resting his back against the wall.

It was Ian who spoke first when Sir Tristram had outlined the plan to take Tommy O'Reilly back to the mainland, with an occasional supportive nod or clarification from Jakob. 'Can't say I much care who rules in Blood, let alone Zanzibar. You're my captain, chose me when you didn't have to. I choose to follow you now.' In conclusion he raised his knee to put a boot in Cowboy's back and propel him to the floor.

'Quit that, Swally.' He made sure his hat was still square on his head. 'I'm just a hired hand, always have been. Reckon I may be more use to you now with my gun than with this left peg. I'm in.'

The other two Indians were clearly waiting for White Eagle, who took his time. 'If you have to depend on my once-strong right arm, Sir Tristram, then I feel sorry for you. Time was I would have spoken for my whole tribe, without fear of contradiction. As far as I can see this is not a tribal matter. Each Zuni must speak for himself. You have my personal loyalty. I thank you for giving us a choice. I choose to stand with you as always in the colours of Blood.' He batted aside Little Doe's aid in rising to his feet.

'I stand with my uncle, and so with you, Sir Tristram.' The usually more talkative Little Doe suited action to his words.

Yellow Cloud was the last of the Westerners to open his mouth, sounding almost bored. 'Our esteemed Chief White Eagle understates his power. While I may raise my rifle, he has only to raise that still strong right arm to command multitudes. I have been among our people in Piedra in the short time since we arrived. Though life is still hard for many of them, they seem to agree O'Reilly' —a brief nod at Jakob— 'has been a just Vizor. If what we are doing is to help him, I am with you.'

The implications of that 'if' were not lost on Sir Tristram. Was he really acting in Tommy's interests? Or was he taking him from his own place of safety to an uncertain future on the continent? Morgan's instruction to assassinate the Vizor if he would not bend to the king's will did not betoken undue concern for his well-being. While the captain was still trying to cough up some weasel words – they did not come easily to his lips – Jakob stepped in.

'Yellow Cloud. Do you think I, revering Tommy in the same way you do White Eagle, would be here if I thought we were acting in other than his best interests?'

The chief, having just made his longest speech since Busted Jaw, reverted to type, merely nodding his feathered headdress in sign of his commitment.

Sir Tristram had sugared his order for the whole squad to return to the Hosteria Videtor after the procession with the promise that they would be allowed out again later, with no curfew or any training the next morning before they gathered to watch the Young Faithfuls take on Tommy O'Reilly's Army side. Once Bowlegs had brought in the rest of the Knights – Jakob had discreetly left with the Westerners – he outlined the secret mission to them.

He knew Barrie and Sir Septimus, and probably Brittanus, appreciated the gravity of what they were being asked, which made the promptness of their pledge to be with him till the death the more gratifying. Bowlegs' support for any wish or request of his master was automatic, unblinking. Chutney and François, half an eye already on their evening ahead, may not have distinguished too much between a street brawl in Piedra and a scrum to rescue Tommy. He knew they were not shy.

Having already taken Tristan, during their evenings together, more into his confidence than he would ever have thought possible, he had seen no reason to exclude him from the meeting. It was another matter when the boy showed every sign of wanting to take the pledge along with the others.

Seeing their captain hesitate, Barrie spoke. 'Sir Tristram, I understand you may not wish to show favouritism to Tristan. I have no such scruples, invoking a godfather's privilege. Let him not put his hand to the fire on this enterprise. Let him participate, by all means, in football and logistics, but not in battle.'

'And why not? I know Franc lost his arm before he was my age, and Chutney was already a veteran of many battles.'

'Do not always trust in campfire tales, boy,' said Brittanus.

'I will not, then. Were we at a campfire in the Toryanka, Barrie, when you told me of your own first campaigns? And Sir Tristram, my sire, were you not newer than I when you first – how did you put it? – christened your war-axe? I *will* put my hand to the fire.'

'Will you indeed, lad? Then maybe I will too,' came the voice of John Ivanhoe from the doorway. 'I escaped with Zito and Suarez the boredom of the Vitoritz reception – not for simple soldiers like us – to see if you were having any more fun. I did not expect to stumble upon a council of war.' His tone hardened. 'I am nowadey maybe half Blood City and half Young Faithfuls, but I remain a Knight. I would know the goal of this cabal.'

'Gladly, Sir John.' The by now well-rehearsed Sir Tristram went over his proposal again as the new arrival listened intently.

'I too had wondered at Tommy's absence when everyone of note in this backwater was either at the port or the Plaza de Armas to make a great fuss of us. Present company excepted, which is fair enough as we have a football match to play. Their clan-leader's whereabouts is one of the things my Arab friends came here to discuss with Jakob. Like Barrie, I am a teammate as well as an admirer of the Grand Vizor. I am with you.'

At a nod from Sir Tristram, Bowlegs lit a candle. The captain put his hand over the flame, John put his on top of it, and so on, Tristan's hand among them, his face defiant. His father looked him in the eye without making any objection or comment.

'I pledge myself to what we have agreed here, Knights made one and indivisible by fire.' It was a matter of pride and honour to speak slowly before removing his hand to the top of the heap, as the rest did after repeating the solemn words: John, Barrie, Septimus, Brittanus, Chutney, Tristan, François (perforce with his left hand) and Bowlegs, before coming back to Sir Tristram. 'So are we pledged together, not always to victory, but to that or extinction,' upon which he extinguished the candle under the palm of his hand.

With more haste than they had made their pledge, the cohort of Knights dispersed. Planning to join the Arabs in the bar with Ivanhoe and Knight, Sir Tristram saw Tristan hanging back. 'Will you not be off with the others to the fleshpots of Piedra, having been so keen to join our mission?'

'I would rather stay here with you, Father.' Tristan studied the floor. 'I have no interest in fleshpots.'

'*Now* he's submissive, Barrie. Come then, you can fetch and carry our drinks from the bar so we will not be over-looked or overheard by the waiters. I think he's a little bit starstruck at being in your presence, John.' He deliberately embarrassed the boy, with a stroke to Ivanhoe's ego that was never unwelcome.

Jakob and the two other Arab leaders, his uncle Zito and Suarez of the Tuaregs, were seated around a corner table at which stood Reaney, immaculately uniformed as ever. He snapped a crisp salute at the Knights.

'I hear you were not best pleased at the standard of officiating in today's match, Sir Tristram.' Often Suarez's words had the undertone of a sneer or jeer. 'It seems we shall be luckier tomorrow.'

'Reaney has just invited me to take the whistle in tomorrow's friendly in representation of Tommy,' Jakob said, inviting them with a gesture to sit.

'A deserved honour for you.' Sir Tristram remained standing. He decided there was no need to be coy, since Jakob would surely have taken his older kinsman and clansman fully into his confidence. 'Does the word come from Tommy himself, Reano? And is there an answer to my request for an audience?'

'Not directly. Though he has asked for a meeting with the two captains tomorrow night.'

'The two captains? He will receive Coluna with Tristram, but not his nearest clansmen?' Any spite in Suarez's comment at the expense of the two O'Reillys was dashed by Reaney's reply.

'No. Zito and Jakob will see Tommy after Martin and Sir Tristram.'

'So the two vices are to follow the two captains,' Zito remarked without surprise, hands folded on his belly.

'What a surprise when John Ivanhoe walked in, Dad. Were you expecting him to join us?' Tristan had been respectfully silent in the larger group but now, as they returned to their room, became talkative. Sir Tristram, who had played a full match among all the dey's other comings and goings, was tired.

'He will make all the difference.'

'Are you being sarcastic, Dad?'

'Not at all. How are you at your numbers?'

'Not my best theme.'

'I shall quiz you, then. How many do the Arabs contribute to our squad?'

'That's easy. Jakob, Oscar and Schwartz – three.'

'Correct. And the Westerners?'

'There's Ian, Cowboy, White Eagle, Little Doe and Yellow Cloud – he spooks me sometimes, do you know what I mean? So that makes, er, five.'

'Correct again. And how many were we Knights before our number 9 arrived?'

This time Tristan used his fingers. 'You, me, Bowlie, Barrie, Sep, Chut, Britt, Franc. That makes eight. And John makes nine as well as wearing the number 9 shirt – I get it.'

'Do you? Add the numbers together and what do you get?'

'Three add five add nine. Seventeen!'

'Correct. Seventeen.'

Tristan did not quite dare wake his father a few minnits later to check. It had occurred to him to wonder if he had been allowed to take the pledge only to complete that auspicious number.

11

The Capula Sancta

Sir Tristram had known Martin Coluna since he was first Martin. They had played with and against one another many times in schulboy football, not often competing directly for a place, as Tristram tended to be more right-sided while Martin favoured the left, though he had later played everywhere in the Young Faithfuls' famously fluid five – numbers 2 through 6 in front of the peerless Yashin. He had recanted his knighthood, after only a brief spell as Sir Martin, in order to represent the Pirates at international level. There had been no precedent, no ceremony, for such an action, which reverberated into the next generation. Although Coluna ignored equally his two sons, Stefan and François were alike in no other way. To call the aggressively white-painted Ajax stalwart anything other than Sir Stefan was to risk the flat or blade of his broadsword, depending on your own status. François had flirted with the Pirate nation, lost his arm in the Little Rock Candy Mountains, and still aspired to be both Sir and son.

Some said Coluna had been tossed the juicy bone of the Yofa captaincy only to stop bigger dogs fighting over it. Less commonly than it was called the team of all the talents, their original side had sometimes been known as Captains Eleven. Like much in Cibolan football, this was an exaggeration. Frenchie, as selfish as all the greatest goalscorers, would have had no interest in the title, and nobody would have given it to the effete conquistador Armando Ortega, usually the stumbling block for quizzers or alehouse historians seeking to name the whole team.

Coluna, now sitting beside Sir Tristram on the ground floor of the Toryanka, was shorter than the Blood City captain, considerably shorter therefore than the likes in that Yofa starting line-up of Cavalry Man, the Tommy O'Reilly they now waited to see and Zito. Nevertheless, his squat, powerful form, always visored and armoured on the field of play, had made its presence felt enough to legitimise his legacy as skipper, in whatever circumstances he had been appointed. If it came to that, Zito was said by some to have been elected vice-captain not as the best of the rest but as the only candidate acceptable to the competing claimants Tommy, Suarez, Ferdinand (those two more jealous of each other than of any O'Reilly) and Yashin.

The Arab vices had not yet arrived as Sir Tristram and Coluna sat silently, uncompanionably but uncomplaining, having soon exhausted their meagre supply of small talk. Sir Tristram felt a tingle of anticipation at the prospect of seeing Tommy O'Reilly again after so many yeers, not unmixed with trepidation, albeit surely much less than many in his present seat would have felt. While he did not consider himself in any way diminished by the passing seesuns, he thought Coluna much shrunken off the field. He wondered if he would find Tommy similarly so.

If they were attended by Sambo, he planned to ask the Pirate some questions about the night Tristan and Barrie had spent at the Toryanka. In the event, it was Viking Defender himself who appeared. The Deputy Vizor greeted them with a bare minimum of civility, just as they declined to show him the slightest deference.

'So the assender's working again.' Sir Tristram stated the obvious as they found themselves rising in its cage, attended by a skinny white spaceman.

'After a fashion,' Viking Defender granted as the two unprepared captains clattered onto his shield at a lurch when the astronaut threw a lever. 'A-Og did something with it.'

The albino opened the gate without accompanying them into what turned out to be the dome of the Toryanka, a reduced space compared to the atrium below. A railing ran round it at shoulder height, which would have prevented anyone suicidal yet energetic getting a fair run at any of the small windows. Around the room cushions and blankets were scattered. No chairs or tables. No soldiers either. Viking Defender hollered 'Tommy!' with as little formality as an emboldened drunkard returning home after midnight.

161

There was no answer, unless in the shape of a spiral wooden staircase, suddenly ejected from the ceiling to land in the very centre of the room.

'Do we come up or you come down, Tommy?'

'Send the captains up, Vida. You keep watch below.'

'You heard the Grand Vizor. He does you the honour of receiving you in the Capula Sancta.'

Politely Sir Tristram let an unthanking Coluna lead the way, his sheathed sword clanking awkwardly against the staircase's central pole as they mounted.

They emerged into a much smaller room, shaped like an orange half, flat side down, waiting for a thirsty footballer at half-time. It had four small windows, above which the letters 'N', 'W', 'S' and 'V' were illuminated, each by its own candle.

'Hope you can see your way, my old beauties. The only electrics up here come from lightning, though by dey the light streams in through the four cardinals. You are not missing any view but the sky. If you have not already seen it, we can look later at Piedra by night.'

The burnoused figure was between 'N' and 'W', wearing the Young Faithfuls' red as always, all red like Coluna and Sir Tristram's shirt, so that the only white among them was the latter's Blood City bottoms. The craggy, beardless face was undoubtedly that of Tommy O'Reilly, in confirming which Sir Tristram could finally admit how much of him had never expected to see the old Pirate again.

'Thank you for visiting my lair, Martin, Tristram.' He extended his hands, not to shake but to indicate they should be seated, cushions again the only option. Tommy looked to be sunk in at least a score of them. 'I see less reason to leave it nowadey.'

'Indeed? I had thought perhaps to see you at the Zuteca, spectating if not playing.'

'I saw you, Sir Tristram. At the risk of chafing a sore, I also watched a rather more entertaining game than yester's.'

The Blood City captain could not deny it. Tommy's Army Select, skippered by Myhigh Syhigh himself, had come to play. Reaney was relegated to his normal full-back position, the flamboyant Limdenberger was in goal, Pierre Garçon, the elegant Ackerman and Persson energised the midfield, while older stars Brody and Little Boris flanked up front the newer generation's supernova Sigi.

They had scored five goals yet still been held to a draw by what was virtually the current Young Faithfuls team. Their legends of the past had paraded round the pitch pre-match to an almost full house, particularly raucous behind the Pirate goal. At the kick-off Frenchie had put the ball into play with a header from his wheelchair, and they had all returned for the penalty shoot-out with which it was agreed to give the fans a result. Yashin came out then to replace Chory in the Young Faithfuls goal.

With the confidence of the latest big thing Sigi took the Army's first spot-kick. He tried a little chip down the centre, a panyanka. Yashin, who had no intention of diving until he saw the ball leave the forward's boot, caught it comfortably at waist height. He hurled it back with some venom, smack into the face of the opponents' number ten. 'Try to make a fool of me, you pup – you've just cost your team the match.'

He was right, without ever needing to go to ground. Unnerved, the foreign legionnaire Persson chose to blast the ball with his cultured left foot after Augusto had scored for the Yofas. Yashin fisted the powerful effort away two-handed from where he stood. Although Ackerman and Brody beat him comfortably, after Viking Attacker and Lancelot had scored, the Faithfuls' fourth penalty was a potential winner. Put forward by Suarez and Ferdinand, each unwilling to cede the glory shot to the other, Coluna took the ball from Atilla.

'First goal you'd ever scored, wasn't it, Martin?' Tommy asked.

'Second.'

'Let's hope tomorrow's game is equally full of them,' Tommy continued, when it became clear Coluna was not going to remind them of when he had ever scored before. 'There has been talk of little else in Piedra, in the whole of Zanzibar.'

'The same in Blood, Tommy, I tell you. All Cibola will be involved in the Seskie in one way or another.'

'We shall give them something to talk about for yeers to come.' The Grand Vizor's pledge admitted of no doubt. 'Viking Defender will referee the Seskie. I know' —he raised a hand as Sir Tristram struggled to lean forward from his nest of cushions— 'you were looking for someone more… someone else, but you must not judge him on Blood City v Army. He was reffing his own team then, and in a friendly. He will be conscious of the importance of tomorrow's game as a showpiece, and I would have him on the pitch with us.'

Although O'Reilly spoke as one accustomed to command, Sir Tristram could not quite give up yet. He tried a conversational rather than hectoring tone. 'I was only thinking that as Myhigh Syhigh is in Piedra he might be ideal, a soldier of great distinction and undoubted impartiality.'

'True enough. We should be grateful that the Army here does not play at politics, nor take sides among those who do. Syhigh may be busy enough tomorrow with crowd control. In any case, the choice is made. Because I respect you, I shall say more than I need. Viking Defender will not favour either of your teams. He is a Marauder, remember. If anyone should be complaining at the risk of bias, it is Martin.'

'I am sure he will be as fair as your brother Jakob was todey.' Coluna nodded at Tommy. 'I would not mind playing as we used to, with no arbiter but Dvid to our match.'

'When we used to settle arguments on the pitch with machetes or knives,' Tommy rumbled with laughter. 'Believe me, there will be at least one nod to the old deys.' The smile showed his teeth, a startling white in his jaundiced face. 'The occasion merits a certain amount of formality. As long as the ETechnolOGy works, the match will be seen all over Cibola, from the sylvan abode of the humblest Indian – rehearsing the speech they wrote for me here, lads,' he barked in continued good humour, 'to the sumptuous quarters of King Henry Morgan himself. Viking Defender will be fully involved at my side throughout.'

He paused as if to allow further challenge. Sir Tristram saw no point. If Tommy really was the victim of a plot between Viking Defender and Albert, he would surely not still have this easy authority, nor be trusted by them to receive the two captains alone.

'There may be organisation required beyond the match also. I am not generally a fan of penalties to decide, though without them we should not have enjoyed Martin's *second* goal, of which those present will surely tell their grandchildren. Only if the pens are not conclusive will we go with the sword, the fight to the death.'

Sir Tristram and Coluna both nodded.

'I know you two are old friends. It is not necessarily the two captains who have to fight, as long as it is someone named in your squad. Understood?'

'Understood.' Each fancied his chances against the other.

'You will exchange team sheets half an our before the match. Every minnit of delay will see one player cut – a player chosen by the other captain – so you may care to be prompt. I shall not be so crass as to ask you your likely team, Sir Tristram. I hope Martin will not mind me saying I shall wear the number 5 shirt for the Young Faithfuls.'

'And I the number 4 of Blood City. It will be a pleasure to do battle with you once more, Tommy. One question, about guest players. Albert said he was of a mind to turn out for us – do I then include him in my squad?'

'And in whose roster should John Ivanhoe appear?' Coluna offered a few of his carefully rationed words.

'He is mine,' Sir Tristram said flatly.

'He is a Young Faithfuls player—'

'Now then, captains, let us not squabble. Ivanhoe can stay in the City squad. I shall have Albert with me at the start, as befits a brother of the king. Number him among us, Martin, much though he would, as a Marauder, hate the thought. Kick-off is at three.'

The rival captains rose effortfully from the cushions. Instead of following Coluna in bowing to the reclining Pirate, Sir Tristram extended his hands in front of him, palm to palm. 'Grand Vizor, I know your clansmen and our vices are waiting for their own meeting with you. Will you spare me five minnits first? Alone?'

'To talk football?'

'No, sir. To talk of matters which need not detain Martin. On which you can, of course, form your own judgement and apprise him afterwards if you see fit.'

'You will have Vida think we are plotting together. Will he join us?'

'You must decide, Tommy. My respectful recommendation – suggestion, rather – would be no.'

'Be careful in even suggesting "no" to me. Give us the room, Martin.' The respect of a Young Faithfuls defender to his captain was gone.

In the silence between them while Coluna negotiated the spiral staircase Tommy had conjured into place with a flick of his fingers, Sir Tristram resumed his seat, more from innate courtesy than any illusion that his standing posture might intimidate the lounging Arab. 'I naturally meant no offence to Viking Defender. I thought you might prefer to hear me alone, as my message is from King Henry.'

'And why would he send a message by you and not his own brother?'

'I know he did so. Since I arrived, I have not seen Albert to tell if he has delivered it. I would not fail to deliver mine, whether or no.'

'The unbending Sir Tristram. I can see why he would choose you.'

'Tommy, I would ask you on Henry Morgan's behalf to return to the mainland with me.'

'Would you? So he can chop off my head at Mini-Gilli?'

'I have no indication that is his intention.'

'And if I say no?'

'Then I have my orders for that too.'

'To chop off my head yourself, with that great war-axe, no doubt. We shall see. You have given me Henry's message. I shall answer it at the Seskie. I wonder not at your personal courage – that is well attested – but that you would bring here your child, your dearest-born by all accounts – that does surprise me.'

'The world is full of dangers, yet I know a child, mine or any other, has nothing to fear from the clan O'Reilly.'

'Not from us, no. You know the truth in that. We shall meet tomorrow.'

Only walking back into the Videtor, Bowlegs again at his shoulder since the steps of the Grand Vizor's palace, did Sir Tristram realise he had still not seen the much-touted views from the Toryanka's upper floors. He suspected now he never would. If he had any further business in that building, it was more likely to be below ground.

In the Videtor bar, suddenly crowded with soldiers of all races, from the Blood City contingent they found only Barrie Knight and Tristan in close conversation at a corner table. 'Why the red face, my son? I hope Uncle Barrie has not allowed you at the Cabeza de Piedra special brew?'

'I would not fail in my duty to you or your kin.'

'I know it, Barrie. And the rest – all in the streets? Perhaps we should have had a last supper together to keep them sober and in their beds before dorn.'

'They know we meet for breakfast, my lord,' Bowlegs spoke. 'I took the liberty of saying the place on the bus would be forfeit of anyone not appearing at the appointed our.'

Sir Tristram did not individually scrutinise his soldiers duly assembled in their private room for any signs of a deboshed night. For good or ill, he had already made his pick. He stood at the head of their narrow table, Jakob to his right and White Eagle to his left.

'My teammates, my mates. We are here in readiness for the most important match in the history of Blood City. No league title is at stake, no Four Cities Cup, but a unique trophy. I am determined to take the Seskie, as I am the other prize we plan to lift todey – one that may cost us dearer. You all have a part in both missions, the second to be detailed individually between now and kick-off. I know you will uphold the proud traditions of Blood City in both.

'Our tour began in disorder followed by division and death. All three may be with us again this dey. While we are together now, let us raise the shot glasses in front of us: to absent friends.'

They all tossed off their drink, Ian Swallow grimacing in theatrical disgust at finding it non-alcoholic.

'It will be important to keep the faith. Our opponents may be fitter, newer, more skilful than us, but as a team, if we have faith we can compete. That is all I ask of you. Only compete. I ask you each to stand as I call your name and squad number.

'1. Ian Swallow, in honour of his brother Victor.

'2. Jakob O'Reilly, bearing the memory of his brother Malabar.

'3. Little Doe, pride of the Cherocree nation.

'4. Your captain, Sir Alfred Tristram of the line Galahad.

'5. Our linchpin, his own greatest hero, to join us later, Pink Viking.' The applause directed at the other players as they rose was replaced by thumps on the table, setting the crockery ajangle.

'6. Spiritual leader of the Indians from the city of Blood to the forests of Zanzibar and physical mainstay of our defence, White Eagle.

'7. Wizard of the wing, the Baffling Berserker, Oscar.

'8. King of all sports, master of both, by name and nature Sir Barrie Knight.

'9. In absentia, a blazing firebrand to light up our attack, Sir John Ivanhoe.

'10. The locksmith legionary, able to unpick any defence, Sir Septimus.

'11. Cowboy.' Sir Tristram allowed their blushing outside-left to scramble to his feet, both hands fidgeting with his hat, before adding simply, 'A soldier of few words.

'That will be our team to take the field at kick-off. Some may feel they have a better claim to a starting berth.'

In ensuring he did not look at Yellow Cloud, the captain's eye fell on Schwartz. He nearly burst out laughing at the small man's offended face and fiercely nodding head. 'In terms of footballing skill, they may be right. But the first eleven is the first eleven. Number 12 is Chief Yellow Cloud, 13 Schwartz O'Reilly, 14 Sir Brittanus, 15 Sir Chutney, 16 Horace Bowlegs.'

Only two were still seated. 'Sir François, stand up to take your bow.' That was it, then: seventeen. Tristan knew better than to have expected any special favour from his father. Still, he had hoped to make the squad on his own merits, at least ahead of a one-armed soldier with a gammy leg. Fighting to restrain the tears, he wished Barrie had not put an arm round his shoulder, which meant he had to fight even harder.

Sir Tristram was still praising François. 'We have all found much to amuse – I mean, admire – in Frankie's footballing skills, whether between the posts or at left back. I will not stoop to the old joke of saying he should be left back in the pavilion – his presence among us is most definitely required. His role will be that of my Deputy Manager, Medical Officer and Logistics Coordinator.'

'There you go, Frankie – bibs, balls and the magic sponge.' Chutney punched him in the ribs on the armed side so his friend had nothing to wind up for a good swing at him.

'Which means, to complete the playing squad, I am pleased to name number 17, Tristan son of Tristram, and no father prouder.'

Now Barrie was shaking Tristan with the arm round his shoulder, pinching his cheek with the other hand. 'Did you really think your dad would leave you out? Shame on you. Get up and take your place – well earned.'

The applause, louder than ever for the squad's newest member, merged into one of the old fans' chants for his father as Bowlegs allowed the bored kitchen staff back into the room to serve breakfast.

'Number Four,

He knows the score,

He's our skipper ever more,

Tristram with his chopper.'

Watching his Sesquicentenario squad tuck in, Sir Tristram wished he could have found even the crude eloquence of their tribute to him, suffering a similar access of melancholy as when they were first gathered in Whipping Square. He was ready to die for the seventeen, individually or as a collective. Harder to bear was the thought of any being sacrificed to his mission. Any more, he corrected himself dismally, pushing his plate away and standing to meet whatever the dey would bring.

12

The Trophy

The Spartan Officer saw with equal indifference the teams arriving at his feet for their historic match. The Young Faithfuls came in a carnival atmosphere on the same float that had carried them round Plaza de Armas. The Blood City bus inched its way through the growing crowds, largely heedless of those within it. John Ivanhoe rode on the float. Pink Viking had his own vehicle, with A-Og driving and two other Ogs minding the superstar. The mob would happily have pushed the pink Eldorado, its top down to allow PV to schmooze and favour them with his touch. The strong Army presence's good humour would be tested if the crowd grew fractious, when it became clear there were many more seeking admission than would fit in the reduced Zuteca stands.

'I'll be your OLO, Sir Tristram.' Sergeant Reaney greeted the Blood City captain as he led his team off the bus. 'Sorry – Official Liaison Officer. I'm afraid you've been drawn to the away dressing room.'

It was indeed a stark contrast to the luxury of the home team's they had used against the Army, more Spartan than the stadium's tutelary god. 'One bench, one bath, one bog – this is what we left civilisation for,' Ian joked to Cowboy, not at all put out. Perhaps it reminded him of home.

Leaving the squad in the cramped quarters, Sir Tristram called Reaney outside to the pitch with Jakob. 'Whatever have they done?' He was diverted from the initial purpose of their sortie.

They had emerged from the tunnel at the halfway line on the sunny Indian side. Facing them was not the sombra stand, which would normally account for 30% or more of the ground's capacity, but a gigantic screen, running the whole length of the pitch and reaching as high as row ZZ of the terraces.

'It's the Ogs' Farseer Supersensurroundomaticron,' Reaney explained (for once an acronym might have served). 'Bigger the audience, bigger the screen they tell me, and since this has to go out all over Cibola—'

'Yes, sylvan abodes and all that, but what about the people expecting to take their normal places to see the match live? There'll be a riot.'

'We do expect to have to break some heads. The bigwigs think if we can get to kick-off and you can give them a good game the fans may stay off the pitch. Everybody wants to put on a good show for the rest of the country.'

'The country will get a show, all right,' Jakob said grimly.

Sir Tristram looked at his vice. He had been abed when Jakob returned from his and Zito's meeting with Tommy at the Toryanka. Over breakfast there had been no opportunity to talk in private. Now was the time to make one.

'Reano, I know we're the second-class citizens here, expected and understood. I would like to give my team individual Pep talks though, and the only space for that seems to be the cludgie. Will you see if you can scout me up at least a private office for the time left till kick-off?'

'I'll see what I can do, Sir Tristram.'

'How about seeing what you can do right now, soldier?'

Without hesitation Reaney snapped out a salute and left them.

'I sometimes wonder if he is tasked with helping us or spying on us,' Sir Tristram ventured.

'Trust no one. That is the best policy.'

'Except it doesn't work. It can't work between team-mates, Jakob. I'll tell you mine if you'll tell me yours, how about that?'

'Will you really? Will you tell me of your message from King Henry?'

He should have realised that Tommy O'Reilly might be frank with his closest kinsmen. He tried to keep his tone light.

'I see you have me at a disadvantage, Jake. If Tommy already told you of our conversation, I have nothing to offer to hear of yours with him. You know I had shared with you my intention to take him back to the mainland. I thought we were at one on that?'

'Take him? Last night he blew away my misgivings that he might not be the power in Zanzibar he once was. He will make a declaration this dey – an answer to Henry, he assured my uncle and me. We still want him in Casablanca to raise the O'Reilly standard there, but he made it clear he will not be bidden. We were petitioners only, like so many he has received over the yeers.

'Like yourself, Sir Tristram.' Jakob put his hand on the Knight's arm to stop their walk and face him. 'He does not show his anger before striking, my Uncle Tommy, yet I could sense it. He asked how with a handful of soldiers you dared to enter his fiefdom. How you presumed to enter alone the Capula Sancta, to say what you would have him do.'

'I was there at Tommy's own invitation.' Sir Tristram was finding it hard to hide his own mounting anger. 'Alone, when speaking in the king's name? A handful? Is that how you see the Blood City squad, Jakob, our squad – hardly more significant than a handful of plastic?'

'Very well.' The Arab had neither answered nor lowered his gaze. 'O'Reilly blood is thicker than Blood City. Let the marballs roll where they may. We need to talk football now.'

Returning to the pitch in good time to submit the Blood City teamsheet, they had the curious sensation of walking towards a funfair mirror, one that magnified their frames and features many times over. The huge screen gave a strange feeling to the ground, already almost full on the other three sides. Indians, as usual, were the main constituents of the long stand facing the screen, able to amuse themselves by viewing their reflections when it was at rest, showing the pitch with them in the background. Technicians appeared to be experimenting before the match began, showing at times shots of the clear sky – it looked as if the Zutecadome would not be needed – and at others zooming in on individuals anywhere in the ground.

Army detachments occupied each of the stadium's four corners, protecting the elaborate video installation as well as separating and enclosing the fans behind each goal. Those to the right of the players as they came onto the pitch were mainly Pirates, already rowdy. At the other end Cowboys were perhaps the largest element, though Pirates, Knights, Indians and Army were also represented. Reaney had explained that, as well as those in uniform, Army irregulars would be embedded in the main blocks of spectators. Sir Tristram thought briefly of Lieutenant Muntian, hoping he would at least be able to watch the match from his customs post.

Coluna and Zito brought out the Young Faithfuls' listing just as Sir Tristram was wondering which player he would elect to cut from it first. The Arabs embraced while the two captains exchanged the sheets and a cursory handshake.

'Not many surprises, lads,' he told his players, packed in their cubbyhole once he had allowed Tristan to read out their opponents' team. 'Cavalry Man was decapitated yeers ago, and I doubt anyone went looking for Friar Tuck – I'd be surprised if he's still above ground stumping the poorest barrios of Blood. Apart from those two, the whole original team is named – even Frenchie, who surely won't play.'

'Not unless they let him career around in his wheelchair. I know he was in talks with the Ogs to see if they could motorise it for him. He'd do anything for the chance to score a few more goals.' John Ivanhoe was closing in on the great legionnaire's all-time scoring record for the Young Faithfuls.

'They'll still have Viking Attacker up front. I've been assured his uncle will referee fairly todey, for all that the Yofas also have Hun and Atilla in their squad, not to mention Viking Defender's own brother Yashin.'

'And Blood City have Pink Viking,' that very soldier announced. His tendency to speak of himself in the third person was one more tiny thing that grated on Sir Tristram. 'He carries a mighty weight among the Vikings of the Pirate race, and far beyond. The crowd will not be all for the opposition as long as I am with you. We must simply score irresistible, undeniable goals. That's all.'

'Amen to that' Barrie Knight endorsed the sentiment. However little their ostentatious self-belief and self-trumpeting were to his personal taste, Sir Tristram knew the arrival of John Ivanhoe and Pink Viking had bucked up the team, because in their presence he himself felt much greater confidence in the match's outcome.

The roar as the two columns, led by Martin Coluna and Sir Tristram, trotted out was underwhelming, since there was no accompanying announcement of names, which had surely been the whole idea of handing over the sheets to Reaney a few minnits earlier.

The Young Faithfuls made as if by right to the Pirate goal for their warm-up. Sir Tristram was nothing loth to take the other end, spotting there some of his own crusader banners, red cross on white.

Viking Defender beckoned the two captains towards him in the centre square. He looked far less comfortable holding the big old microphone than he would have the billy club it somewhat resembled. His shout into it having stunned the crowd into a total silence, he realised he could speak in his normal harsh mutter and still be heard. 'Before the Grand Vizor talks, I will ask the captains of the Young Faithfuls and Blood City to announce their teams.'

Viking Defender randomly handed the skippers their opponents' sheets. Coluna read in a monotone the Blood City squad his father had made Tristan write out in his best copperplate, rather rushing the early names, so it was not until they heard Pink Viking that the crowd began to cheer at each one. The whoops from the Indian side for White Eagle exceeded in volume those for his centre-back partner, an inconvenient fact PV chose to ignore.

Sir Tristram gave due weight, pausing for the crowd's acclaim, to each of the Young Faithfuls' legends: Yashin; Zito; Coluna; Atilla; O'Reilly, T; Hun; Ferdinand; Más; Suarez; Frenchie, the iconic number ten; even Ortega drew a respectable shout. The Indian Chory, face obliterated when new so that he could never be mistaken for his illustrious father Tory, was the second goalkeeper. Augusto, Scarface, Viking Attacker and Little Boris made for an attack-minded bench, while the last-named Albert Morgan was an out-and-out striker.

Albert's name provoked reflex cheers, which then led to a degree of confusion and debate on the terraces. Was the

Blood City captain talking about *that* Albert Morgan? The chatter stilled when the big screen alerted the crowd to Tommy O'Reilly's progress to the centre square with his brother Zito, both fully robed in their Young Faithfuls red. In the same colours but unfilmed, Sambo approached from the touchline, balancing on his head with both hands a big silver platter covered with a cloche, also of silver.

Tristan, entranced by the spectacle of the multi-raced fans behind the goal they were kicking into as much as legendary Young Faithfuls at the other end of the pitch, assumed the Pirate was bringing the trophy for which they would be competing, to be unveiled to all for the first time by the Grand Vizor. As the three soldiers converged at the centre spot, Sambo lowered his burden to waist height, while Zito took the microphone from Viking Defender. He held it as Tommy began to speak.

'Soldiers of Zanzibar, you have done well to fight your way through the crush to claim your places this afternoon. Sometimes it seems life is all about fighting. You will see live what others will see only on the screen we installed for the benefit of all Cibola, from the favelas of the poorest Indians to the vast, sumptuous, sybaritic quarters of Henry Morgan.

'What you see here will appear in the pages of history. You will see a Torneo Sesquincentenario – a Seskie – fit not only to mark history, but to make history. We shall commemorate the beginnings of the Cibolan World Football League with a clash between two of its founder members: Blood City from the capital; and the Young Faithfuls from our country's greatest port, its beating heart, Casablanca.'

Tristan sensed the crowd were listening to the Grand Vizor in rather the same way his favourite mastiff, Rufus, would listen to him: appearing highly attentive yet only recognising, and giving tongue at, one word in ten – 'Seskie'... 'Blood City'...'Young Faithfuls'...'Casablanca'.

'Some of you will remember those founding yeers, as many of the players here to entertain you do. We had no luxurious carpet-smooth pitches. We had no goalposts. Tall soldiers were trained to stand still and play that part. And the balls. What were the balls we used back then?

'What were the balls we used, Sir Tristram?' Zito thrust the microphone into the Knight's face. Tristan thought his father looked uneasy, but he answered firmly enough.

'We used heads.'

'We used heads. We used soldiers' heads,' Tommy repeated as the mic swung back to him. 'They weren't as smooth as the footballs newbies grow up with nowadey, by no means. But they served. They had to serve. I'm sure Henry Morgan' —for the second time he failed to refer to the Highlander as 'king'— 'remembers those times. He and I have a long history together. This match is to honour history, to remember. I will remind Henry of his old friend, Tommy O'Reilly, with the help of his brother, whose name you heard announced in the Young Faithfuls' squad.'

If many of the crowd looked to the dugouts on the touchline to see Albert emerge from the dressing rooms, their eyes were soon brought back to the centre square, not least by the giant screen's focus on it, and particularly the heavy trophy pot. This was blocked by Tommy's broad back as he bent to remove the cloche, tossing it carelessly to the grass. As he turned towards the screen it was filled by him alone, holding aloft by the hair the head of Albert.

The picture on the screen followed Tommy in a slow circle as he showed his trophy to each sector of the crowd in turn: ragged cheers and some boos from the end where the Blood City players were frozen, almost complete silence from the long Indian stand, then a louder mixture of approving and dissenting noises, accompanied by some commotion, behind the Pirate goal.

Tristan had moved unconsciously closer to the group including his father. He had no need of the screen to recognise Albert, despite the fact that the Pirate's tongue was somehow affixed to his chin, a grotesque goatee, and his lips were crudely stitched together. If the boy did not know this was the traditional death mask of a traitor, his father did, and King Henry certainly would.

'Albert thought to play a bigger part on this island, as his brother's creature. While I could not allow this, neither could I entirely refuse to give him his head and allow him to participate in the Seskie.'

Turning once again to the screen, with his famous left foot Tommy drop-kicked that head high into the sky towards it.

13

The Seskie

It was not the smell, which set at naught the pungent, unwashed living stink of Albert. It was not even the splitting of the face and the spillage from it when it landed near the touchline under the screen.

Someone had cauterised the jagged edges of the slashed throat and treated them to provide a smooth, bright-red kicking surface already curved for Tommy's boot. That was what, for some reason, made Tristan fall to his knees and spew his whole breakfast onto the pristine turf.

For perhaps the only time in his career, during the first fifteen minnits of the match Sir Tristram could hardly focus on the game in hand. The stench of Albert's head was still in his nostrils, the implications of Tommy's act running through his mind. It amounted to an open declaration of revolt against the king. Instead of betraying Tommy in cahoots with Albert, Viking Defender must have lured his sometime friend into the clutches of his long-time master. Were Vikings and Arabs, then, in unlikely alliance, one strong enough to make any kingdom tremble? Neither Viking Defender nor Zito had appeared surprised at the unsavoury dish presented by Tommy to the world. Did that mean Jakob had also known?

'Get a grip, Tram!' that very soldier yelled as he came clattering through Ortega halfway inside the City half. Sir Tristram had neglected to apply the reducer in the opening exchanges that would surely have discouraged the conquistador from tricks like the nutmegging he had just administered to the Blood captain.

The crunching tackle from Jakob came only after Ortega had slipped the ball wide left for Más, who was able to exploit the space vacated by Blood's number 2. Pink Viking, drawn out to meet his threat, was bypassed by a floated cross. Viking Attacker got in front of White Eagle to plant a header into the net, despite a brave attempt to save by Ian Swallow, fingertipping the ball onto the post before it squirmed over the line. The big striker had come on for Frenchie in the first minnit, neither the prolific legionnaire nor his son Franco who wheeled him off getting the applause they would have expected from the dumbfounded spectators.

Sir Tristram and Jakob stood watching as Ian retrieved the ball, lumping it back over their heads for the restart. 'I had to come for him, Tram, he's been making a monkey of you.'

184

The knowledge that Jakob was right, and the shock of going a goal down, brought Sir Tristram's mind back fully to the match. 'You're right, Jake. My bad. It won't happen again.'

There was no further danger of being embarrassed by Ortega. This was worse news for Blood City, since in place of the ageing fop the Young Faithfuls brought on Augusto, an O'Reilly, son of the fabulous Eusebio, a current Pirate international and a much more aggressive midfielder. Sir Tristram needed all his concentration and skill to stop himself and Sir Septimus being totally overwhelmed by the powerful Atilla, crafty Suarez and the dynamic newcomer. He summoned Barrie Knight back into midfield at least to balance the numbers. It was not enough.

As if challenged by his brother's contribution to the opening goal, Ferdinand began to take on Little Doe. While not as fast as Más, he was quicker than the Indian. Gaining a yerd, he chipped in a ball to the near post. This time White Eagle was with Viking Attacker, so close it was not entirely clear whose head the cross flicked off, towards the centre of the goal. It landed perfectly for Luis Suarez to sweep in left-footed on the half-volley: 2-0.

As Suarez celebrated the goal with his Tuareg brothers, Viking Attacker was struggling to separate himself from White Eagle. Whether intentionally or not, one of the horns on the Viking's helmet had gored the Indian, penetrating his neck and emerging at his cheek. His attempts to disentangle it had only made matters worse.

'Sorry, Alfred, did they score?...Getting too old...'

'Don't worry, dear friend, you take a breather. We'll

recover and so will you.' Sir Tristram spoke with more confidence than he felt on either count. 'Doey, take him off for treatment. See if there are any Og physicians that can help.'

Viking Attacker was still trying to reclaim his helmet. With unexpected tact the referee pulled him away. 'No matter, Vika, take my own for the rest of the match.' Viking Defender passed it across, leaving his yellow hair covered only by a grey skull cap.

I see you're not giving a foul then, Videf,' Jakob O'Reilly addressed him quietly.

'For an accidental clash of heads? Your tackle on Ortega was worse. If I hadn't played advantage and the Yofas scored they'd have been shouting red for you.'

Sir Tristram diverted Jakob from the confrontation as Yellow Cloud helped Little Doe get the senior Indian into shelter. The whole terrace above the dugouts stood as one soldier in perfect silence as the gravely wounded chief passed, unable even to raise a hand to acknowledge his fellow Indians. Tristan might have puked again if he had anything left to bring up, at the sight of the Viking helmet attached so unnaturally to White Eagle's face, the horn coming out just below his right eye.

Sir Tristram waited till the Indians had disappeared down the tunnel before addressing his bench. 'It's a tragedy, yes, just like our performance so far. We're two down already – one more and they'll be out of sight. Britt, Bowlie, you're both coming on, help us sort it out.'

Either from professional courtesy between Vikings or intelligent forward play by Viking Attacker in targeting the weaker of the centre-back pairing, the scorer of the first and assister of the second goals had matched himself mainly against White Eagle. With a two-goal lead, the Young Faithfuls were in no hurry to resume after the sickening injury to Blood City's number 6, so Sir Tristram laid out his team's new shape.

'Right, Jakob, you take over White Eagle's spot to keep us solid at the back, sweeping up behind PV as necessary.' Said Pink Viking was at this point in deep conversation with Viking Defender and Yashin.

'Barrie, you'll drop to Jakob's position at right back. Bowlegs, you're in for Little Doe on the left. You're both going to need all your experience against the Tuaregs. I'd try to get a bit more defensive work from the wingers, only we need them to press forward.'

'Speaking of Tuaregs, it would be good if someone could stop Suarez creeping up the middle. He left me without a prayer there.'

'I'm on it, Ian. Britt, up front beside John – make a bluddy nuisance of yourself. I'll threaten Oscar and Cowboy with substitution by the mighty Schwartz if they don't get you some service going. If Yellow Cloud was here I'd probably hook one of them for him right now.'

The injury to White Eagle had caused a shift in the sympathies of the crowd, or at least of the Indians who formed such a large part of it. Viking Attacker was roundly booed by them every time he came near the ball. This did not faze him as much as it did the Yofa fans gathered behind the goal his team was defending. The Army detachment separating them from the Indian side was reinforced by a troop of Tommies in anticipation of trouble.

The intensity of the Young Faithfuls had slackened notably, perhaps from complacency at their 2-0 lead. As the Blood City forwards were brought more into the game by some tigerish tackles from Sir Tristram, playing with controlled fury, the monument that was Yashin proved hardly more mobile than the Spartan Officer. Sir Septimus, having been given a rollocking by his captain and perhaps inspired by his example, beat the Viking keeper with a header, as did Brittanus; both efforts pinged off the woodwork to safety. John Ivanhoe was luckier, or more precise, his low shot finding the corner of the net after he spun on a cross from Oscar: 2-1.

With Little Doe and Yellow Cloud attending the stricken White Eagle in the depths of the Zuteca, where they hoped to find more professional help than any François could provide, there were no longer any Indians on the pitch to channel their fans' support to Blood City. Though Yashin did not suffer the indignity of a subbing immediately after Ivanhoe's soft goal, it was not long before the Young Faithfuls replaced him in the nets with the only Indian on their books. Chory was a renegade, physically as well as mentally scarred by the fame of his father, running with Pirates as much as Westerners. He was a competent keeper (still kept out of the international team by Tory), but he was only a keeper. He could not stir the crowd by attacking moves. Even his defensive capabilities were not showcased, as it was Blood City's turn to run low on energy and invention.

When they returned to their bench at half-time, still a goal down, Sir François was waiting.

'He's gone, Sir Tristram.'

Despite medical counsel to the contrary from a grey-tunicked Confederate Colonel, when White Eagle recovered consciousness in the bowels of the stadium, maddened by the pain he had wrenched the horn from his face. It was his last act of strength. The blood his tribesmen had tried to staunch, already with limited success, came flooding from the hole in his throat. He died within segunds.

Sir Tristram found Little Doe hunched over his elder's body. Yellow Cloud was circling them in slow, intricate patterns made with hands and feet, eyes closed, murmuring steadily though pinched lips. Even as Sir Tristram paid his sincere last respects to their fallen comrade, he was wondering if either of the two surviving Indians would be willing or able to take any further part in the match.

Before he could begin to find a tactful way to raise the matter, Jakob O'Reilly was at his shoulder. 'I'm sorry, Tram, Viking Defender has called you to the ref's room. I offered to go as vice, but he wasn't having any of it.'

'That's okay Jake, I'll go. You can do me and the team a bigger service. See where our friends' heads are at, if they're with us at all. It's like a battle zone in here, and outside it looks to me as if your Uncle Tommy made a declaration of war.'

The referee's quarters at the Zuteca were larger than the away team's dressing room, though the Army CIC and Viking Defender were hardly using the space, standing almost toe-to-toe in the centre of the main room. The only other soldier present was Coluna.

'To cancel the match at this point...' Syhigh was almost

189

shouting, a sheen of sweat on the florid face emerging from his buttoned-up, thick khaki uniform. He may not have heard Sir Tristram's thump on the door, followed immediately by his entrance.

'This had better be important, Videf, to have called me away—'

'It *is* important,' the Viking snarled back. 'The match is done. The Grand Vizor will be arrested for Grand Treason. I am explaining to General Syhigh that we must not allow such an insult to HM to stand, especially since he has designated Pink Viking as the maximum authority here, with full power of life and death over Tommy and all others.'

'And I am explaining to the Deputy Vizor that unless and until I have written orders to the contrary, however much we may deplore his rash and unconscionable act Tommy O'Reilly retains that maximum authority in Zanzibar. Furthermore, to cancel the Seskie at half-time poses a very serious risk to public order.'

'Public order?' Sir Tristram had never seen Viking Defender so animated. 'That is your job to maintain. If you cannot, there are Ogs seeded throughout the ground, friends of Pink Viking, with their own nuculars to restore order.'

'To restore public order at the cost of destroying the public? I don't think so.'

'How can we let the match continue when from the start it was made an open mockery of the king's authority? I take some blame – I should never have blown the whistle for kick-off. I was too shocked by what Tommy had done to grasp its full implications. Martin, you would not object to calling an end to the match?'

'Not at all. As long as the 2-1 stands, and we are awarded the Seskie.'

'That's not going to happen,' Sir Tristram said at once. 'We have come too far and lost too many friends to abandon the match now. Besides, that would only be a further insult to King Henry, whose whole idea the Seskie was. Whatever divisions may have come between him and O'Reilly, they are both football men. We are all footballers. We have a duty to the beautiful game too.'

'Tommy O'Reilly is still the Grand Vizor. The Army must support the office, not the soldier as such. Where is this Viking authority?'

Sir Tristram thought Viking Defender would strike the CIC. He advanced close enough to him, well within dagger range; the general did not flinch. 'The authority is in my word,' the Viking hissed, 'and in that of Pink Viking. The authority should be in yourself, soldier, after what you have just seen with your own eyes.'

'Authority lies with the king, above all' Sir Tristram intervened. 'I have Henry's writ, to prove his intentions were other, with no mention of Pink Viking.'

'"Henry's writ"? What knightly nonsense is this? Will you hear him or me, CIC?'

'The two are not mutually exclusive, my dear fellow. I shall always listen to Sir Tristram. If he has written orders direct from the king, of course he is right – they will bind me. Where are they?'

'Not here, obviously. I can send for them.'

'If we are to play, the second half kick-off time has already passed,' Coluna reminded them. 'What news on White Eagle, Tristram?'

'None good. But Blood City will be ready to take the field.'

'And continue with the act of defiance we saw before the start? I have tried to respect you as captains. Do I have to bring in Pink Viking to add his voice to mine?'

'No. I agree with Sir Tristram – the match should continue. Here's a thought. Martin, could you substitute Tommy? If it was his act alone – unlikely though that seems, Videf' —the CIC returned his pale-eyed gaze to the Deputy Vizor— 'we shall at least have removed him from the king's sight at the earliest opportunity.'

'Our decisions on team changes are taken collegially. As it happens, I do believe Tommy intended to take a breather for the second half, only returning in case of need, or perhaps to take a pen.'

'Splendid. Before we go arresting anyone, let's at least get the GV out of the spotlight. I shall look to you for documentation of your claim after the match, Sir Tristram.'

'For Dvid's sake, try to make a better game of it too,' Viking Defender conceded peevishly. 'The fans will be fighting among themselves from sheer boredom if not.'

Sir Tristram knew Syhigh would look in vain for any documentation. The letter of Morgan he had consigned to the flames on the *Chupacabra* would have only confirmed a motive for Tommy to kill Albert. His own orders from the king were written only in his heart. The Grand Vizor as a prisoner of the Vikings did not square with them. He was sure Pink Viking's authority was spurious because he knew of that granted to Albert, as Syhigh did not. He did not know if the Vikings' grab for power was opportunistic or long-planned. In strict loyalty to his teammate, he reminded himself he had only Viking Defender's word for it that Pink Viking was even aware of his sudden elevation. Viking Defender's word...

'Jakob, we need to discuss the line-up – how best to rejig. Lads, give us the room please, we're not out of it yet. Wait for us in the dugout area – we will have a better second half.'

The rest of the squad, lacking its three Indians, trudged out in a silence that did not bode well for their chances of getting back on terms. Even Jakob's energy seemed low. 'Things could get worse yet, Tram. Their heads are down. The news of White Eagle hit us all hard.'

'I know, Jake. Me too, if I let it. There will be time to grieve him properly hereafter, but only if we get our act together. Did you know Tommy was going to pull that crazy stunt before kick-off? No matter, I need to tell you anyway: there may be a double betrayal, not only of Albert – for whom none of us may weep – but of the Grand Vizor himself. It is more urgent than ever for us to get him out of here as soon after the match as possible.'

'He has plenty of support without us.'

'Maybe in Casablanca, but here on the Last Ground – are you sure? Soldiers will always follow the power, and it seems to me the Vikings have a big chunk of power right here and now, between Videf with his machinations and PV with his tame Ogs and rabble-rousing nature. I shall act as I must at the end.

Whether I succeed or not, as in the match, will depend heavily on your support.'

'I know. And we won't succeed in the match unless we focus on it. Here we are gassing about everything but the game. Let's rob Tommy of the Seskie first, then think about saving him from his enemies.'

Sir Tristram's subterfuge on Morgan's supposed written orders had been not only to gain time for Tommy but to provide a plausible reason for sending some of his squad out of the ground. The CIC might have wondered why it would take three soldiers to retrieve a piece of paper, except that such administrative overkill was typical under his own command.

'Barrie, Bowlegs, thanks for helping to steady the ship after we went two down. Tristan, you will have to wait to make your official Blood City debut. We may have to leave the Zuteca and Zanzibar in some haste. I need you to make sure Bates is ready to move in the *Chupacabra* at a momet's notice, and organise a couple of trucks as close to the ground as you can get them – ideally at the very toes of the Spartan Officer. Bowlegs, I charge you to come report back to me, hopefully to find me lifting the Seskie.'

He gave Barrie a hug, then one to the astonished Bowlegs, as an excuse to hold his child close for what he realised might be the last time. He had been explicit in delegating the return trip to his bondsman, to get Tristan out of the Zuteca and keep him out.

Although the lad's footballing abilities had not come into the calculation, Sir Tristram realised that dispatch of the three cut his squad to the bone. He was not impressed to have John

Ivanhoe confirm his defection to the Young Faithfuls for the second half.

'I mean, that was what we agreed, Tram. And with all due respect, even I can't make bricks from straw. The service to me in that first half was woeful. I won't embarrass the City when I score or when the game is won, you can count on me for that.'

'That's mighty big of you, John.' Already turning his back, Sir Tristram added 'Let's just hope PV doesn't outscore you.'

While the two Knights spoke, Yellow Cloud was addressing the Indian stand, without a microphone or even raising his voice. He used a mixture of verbal and sign language, neither intelligible to other races but seemingly understood by all the Indians from their diverse tribes. He brought them in their tens of thousunds to their knees, heads bowed to the terrace sloping away beneath them. He brought them back to their feet, all arms raised to the heavens. Then he brought from them a chilling war cry, loud enough to make the volume of fans' support through the first half sound like no more than the piping of a penny whistle.

Little Doe stood a step behind Chief Yellow Cloud, following him and mirroring the crowd's actions. As the noise of the massed banks abated, the two remaining Blood City Indians presented themselves to their captain. 'We are ready to play the second half, Sir Tristram.' Their determination was palpable – determination he realised the team desperately needed.

'All right boys, listen up.' He addressed the whole squad. 'Yellow Cloud will come in left midfield between Little Doe and Cowboy on the wing. We'll have a whole Westerners' left side then, playing along the Indian stand – give them something to cheer.' He had a word of encouragement for each of his other players too, Chutney coming on at right back with Jakob and Sir Tristram himself as centre backs while Pink Viking moved up front beside Brittanus.

'Glad to see you consoling Schwartz there, Jake,' he said as they lined up for the kick-off. 'I couldn't make any promises, but I'll try to give him a run-out before the end. We may need him on the pitch when it's all over.'

'I wasn't consoling him. I was tasking him.'

'With what?'

'Once may be an accident, but if that horn comes into play again, whether on me or any City player, I told him to shoot to kill. First Viking Attacker, then Viking Defender – it's his helmet now, after all.'

Whether from a 'collegial' decision or his own choice, Tommy O'Reilly did not take the field again after the interval. Atilla dropped from midfield to right back beside his brother Hun, with Zito and Coluna completing a conventional back four. Scarface, a Pirate who played with a treasure chest under his right arm and a dagger between his teeth, came in on the right of midfield beside Suarez and Augusto.

Up front the Young Faithfuls now had a twin spearhead of Viking Attacker and John Ivanhoe. Almost comically mismatched in height, they were nevertheless a perfect striking partnership, as the number of goals between them in the Cibolan league testified. Más had made way for Ivanhoe, with Ferdinand staying at outside right.

The Tuareg winger's fortunes changed, now facing a Little Doe invigorated by the huge applause every time he came near the ball and a sense of injustice at the death of his chief, protector and friend. Viking Attacker kept well away from that side of the field, matching up with Jakob O'Reilly towards the right side of the City defence while Tristram watched Ivanhoe.

Yellow Cloud was also seeing a lot of the ball, running with it to good effect on occasion but not really linking up with his forward line. Neither he nor Oscar were natural midfielders, while the fresh legs of Scarface, added to the wiles of Suarez and the energy of Augusto, were pushing Septimus deeper than he needed to be to make an impact. With Yellow Cloud more often crowding into Cowboy's space than seeking to give him a run down the wing, Pink Viking and Brittanus could have echoed Ivanhoe's first-half complaint about being starved of service.

The vastly experienced Young Faithfuls were happy to manage the match towards victory, looking more likely to add to their single-goal lead than surrender it. Sterling work had already been required from Ian in goal, Jakob and Tristram more than once when the vice-captain spoke up midway through the half.

'Tram, they're choking us to death here. Let me go into the midfield – we need to win more ball there. Let's get Yellow Cloud further forward where he can end his runs with a shot rather than a failed pass.'

'And leave me to cope with VA and John both? I'd rather go in midfield myself, Jake, but you're right. We need to change something. You're the better player. Let's give it a throw.'

Although predominantly left-footed, Yellow Cloud's true and preferred position was on the right wing, where he was more than pleased to move – taking, of course, the massive encouragement of the crowd with him. Cutting in from the wing and fending off Coluna, he hit a rocket that would have ended up closer to the corner flag than the net.

Would have. Pink Viking intervened. He stooped slightly to take the rising ball full on his forehead, using the pace of it to direct it past a motionless Chory into the back of the net: 2-2. The crowd went wild for the scorer as much as for Yellow Cloud's assist, each player claiming a full portion of credit for the equaliser.

Yellow Cloud had been constantly in forward gear. He therefore surprised everyone, having once again skipped past Coluna, by making a deliberate pass rather than shooting – a backward pass, at that. Perhaps only Little Doe could have called to him for the ball with any hope of receiving it. In a passage of play full of wonders, he added to them by being in the inside-right channel in the first place, then by smashing the ball into the roof of the net with his unfancied right foot. Blood City were 3-2 ahead with less than five minnits to play.

14

On the Spot

Needing an equaliser, it was the Young Faithfuls' turn to switch to three at the back, the mountainous Hun between Zito and Coluna, moving Atilla forward to help unlock the Blood defence as well as add his aerial power at set pieces. They brought on the Army's Cossack star, Little Boris for Ferdinand, switching the focus of their wing play from right to left.

Chutney was game but no match for a tough, speedy current international like Little Boris. Jakob, almost spent, had reverted to centre-back. He was there to block with his chest, from close range, a cross Boris had sent over Chutney, already gone to ground. It was a bonus that the ball ricocheted out of play off the Cossack's rifle. Goal kick.

'Almost there, Swallow. Take your time over this then try to find Oscar wide right.'

'You got it.'

They were interrupted by Viking Defender's whistle. 'Take a booking for time-wasting if you have to, Ian.'

Sir Tristram did not like the referee's intervention. Although the ball had clearly come off his vice's chest, was he going to say it had been a handball and rob them in the dying segunds? 'What's the problem, Vida? It was ball to chest, nowhere near his arm.'

'Thank you, captain. I'm glad you agree with me. So give the ball back to Boris for the corner instead of trying to run the clock down. You'll not deny them their last chance.'

'What corner?' Jakob was right in the ref's face.' It came off him. It's our goal kick.'

There was no budging the big Viking. When he realised that, Jakob booted the ball in frustration high towards the video screen, as Tommy had Albert's head what seemed a very long time ago. He was booked with his back already turned to the ref. 'No sweat, Jakob, it could have been worse. That may even have been an honest mistake.' Sir Tristram tried to calm and refocus him as they prepared to defend the corner, after which the whistle must surely go.

The Young Faithfuls were not multiple champions for nothing. Boris slipped the corner short to Suarez, who cut an angled pass across the ground into the box. Jakob, Pink Viking and the other City players, all back defending, had expected a high ball aimed at Hun or Viking Attacker on the far post, or even at Chory, doing a frantic war dance on the penalty spot. Sir Tristram saw John Ivanhoe's run, but the little striker was faster. He was always faster. He skewed the ball back across his own body, just beating Swallow's desperate, clawing dive. It hit the post, ran as if on a rail across the whole white of the goal line before reaching the other post and opting to turn left rather than right, into the net: 3-3.

As Scarface rushed to retrieve the ball in the hope of one more assault for an outright winner, Ivanhoe brushed aside the congratulations of the other Young Faithfuls in the box. It was his turn to speak to Sir Tristram as he passed him on his way back to the centre square. 'Sorry, Tram. It's my nature.'

Despite Scarface's haste, there was no time for any further action. Viking Defender blew the final whistle. City had been that close.

Sick to the stomach, Sir Tristram knew he had to help his soldiers overcome similar feelings and go again for extra time. He was gathering them to him in the goalmouth when he saw Tristan haring from the sidelines towards them.

'What happened? I said Bowlegs was the one to return.'

'I know, but I'm a faster runner. And I can't drive, so it was better for him and Barrie to stay with the trucks. We saw Slasher too – everything sorted. I can come on for extra time if you need me, Dad.'

'I might well. Wait a minnit. What's that ape saying now?'

Viking Defender, helmeted and miked up again, was bellowing to the crowd, his face occupying the whole of the giant screen. 'Some excitement there at the death, a stunning leveller from the great Ivanhoe. We're going to keep things right at that pitch with penalty kicks at the Vladi end.'

Sir Tristram just beat Coluna to Viking Defender, who had swiftly rid himself of the microphone. He tried to keep the anger from his voice, to still the pounding of his heart from his race to the middle.

'What's going on, Videf? What are you playing at? It's extra time now.'

'Extra time? I thought penalties.'

'Penalties come after extra time – that was the rules. You tell him, Martin.'

'I just announced penalties.'

'Well, you'll have to unannounce them.'

Now it was Viking Defender who spoke slowly to the two captains, as if to a couple of dullards. 'I thought penalties. I know the rules – who do you think made them? I *have* to do nothing at your bidding, Sir Tristram. I am the Deputy Vizor – Deputy to a different Vizor than when the sun rose.'

'And why at the Vladi end? Why do we have to face the Pirate hordes?'

'Does it really make a difference which end?' The referee spoke softly now, with a grin.

Sir Tristram realised it did not. Once he had given up the broader argument, he was only indulging his own vanity by trying to win the lesser one. Although he would certainly not have acted from such motives, Viking Defender might have done City a favour, sparing them extra time the Young Faithfuls would have entered with the momentum in their favour.

'No, it doesn't make one scrap of difference,' he grinned back. 'You're the referee' – the only title he would acknowledge him. He shook Martin's hand wordlessly, wondering if Coluna was also thinking that their next interaction might be a fight to the death.

John Ivanhoe was standing in front of him with the ball in his hands.

'Let me take the first, Sir Tristram, as I would for the City back in the dey.'

'It's all "the City" now, is it, wee man? Bit too late. Guilty conscience?' Pink Viking enquired.

'Not at all.' John was not in the least intimidated by the putative new Grand Vizor of the Last Ground. Was he mimicking him as he spoke of himself in the third person? 'Ivanhoe is even-handed. I shall take the first penalty for Blood City, then the first for the Young Faithfuls. And score both. I look forward to seeing your own effort, PV.'

Although he could be a spectacular volleyer, scoring some remarkable goals from mid-air, Pink Viking was not known for his dead-ball skills any more than for his quick wit and rapid repartee. He turned away, as if disdaining further discussion.

The pitch was smaller for the penalties. Syhigh's troops made a controlled cession of the west end of the pitch as far as the 'D' of the penalty area, while the less passive Indians spilled into an unmarked bulge of similar size at the centre line. The Army maintained a wall there too, with a double cordon of soldiers tramping their heavy boots on the paint of the centre square. Within that the two historic football teams stood, sat or even lay in some cases. There were a few instances of cross-city camaraderie – Augusto and Jakob, Oscar with his father Más, handshakes to each of the Blood City players from an unspeaking but seemingly relaxed Tommy O'Reilly – before they reformed into their separate squads. From these individuals would be ejected like shells, to find their target or not.

There was no exchange of courtesies between the two starting keepers, the Indian Chory and Cavalryman Swallow. John Ivanhoe beat them both (of course), pausing between shots only to change his shirt. Rather than returning to the centre, he left the field. Blood City number 9 shirt in one hand, Young Faithfuls' in the other, he resisted all the fans' pleas to be thrown either, muscling his way through the Indians to the dressing rooms beyond. He left the teams level on penalties, 1-1.

'My shirt is number 2. I'll take this one.' Jakob O'Reilly stepped forward.

Again, Sir Tristram was not going to argue. He sensed from the big Arab's stillness the pressure mounting in him for some explosive act. Let him relieve that pressure, even if he missed.

He did not miss. Neither did Viking Attacker, to bring the Young Faithfuls back on terms, at 2-2.

Sir Septimus was a dead-ball specialist, relishing the chance that corners, free kicks around the box, even throw-ins at times, gave him to go serenely about his business without the promiscuous jostling of the opposition. He had not had a good game; nevertheless, his sense of duty was strong, his pride undiminished.

As Sir Septimus strolled towards the spot, Sir Tristram wondered if, in their 500 matches together, usually as midfield partners, he had ever really got close to the aloof Roman. There seemed a distance even between Septimus and his fellow legionary Brittanus, like the little bit of personal space the Blood City number 10 always seemed able to conjure in even the most congested midfield.

That self-possession, that separateness, would not go amiss here and now. While the crowd had watched both Ivanhoe penalties in the respectful silence due a master craftsman at his work, they had been markedly rowdier during Jakob's run-up than that of Viking Attacker. There were many competing cross-currents – Yofas against the City, Blood against Casablanca, Pirates and the rest, Vikings and Arabs within the Pirate nation; the Knights had fewer supporters than any other faction in the ground.

Any fellow Indian loyalty Chory might have enjoyed was forfeit, not so much by his mixed race as by the reverence and affection in which they held the fallen White Eagle, and – by extension – his team. Sir Tristram was grateful for the way this had been roused by Yellow Cloud, and even more grateful for his and Little Doe's contributions to the match. Feeling they had been running on pure adrenaline, he had no plans to use them as cool penalty kickers.

Chory was also hopped up to an extraordinary extent, prowling the touchline even when Swallow was the one facing up to shots, quite unable to stand still. John Ivanhoe had beat the keepers without either getting a touch, but an athletic dive had seen Chory's fingertips scorched by Jakob's piledriver. Now he sprang with equal elasticity to the other side. Sir Septimus tickled the ball into the middle of the net, a foot above the ground where Chory had just been standing. As they crossed, the next shooter, the opposing number 10 Suarez, brushed hands with him. Sir Tristram did not quite dare a hug, but knuckled his own forehead in respect. 'Steel marballs, Sep.'

Anxious about his own players' efforts since Ivanhoe had left the field, Sir Tristram had not, so far, thought any of the Young Faithfuls would fail. Suarez kept up the pressure by converting their third kick, sending Ian Swallow the wrong way but at least doing him the courtesy of striking the ball firmly into the opposite corner of the net.

No one was approaching him as confidently as his early kickers had, as Barrie Knight surely would have were he not waiting at their getaway vehicles. Bowlegs too, who might not have put himself forward but would have found, in a nomination from his master, all the confidence he needed to score. Pink Viking was, for once, backward in coming forward. Maybe he was waiting to be begged – a satisfaction Sir Tristram would never give him.

'Number 4 – I guess that's me, as Jakob said a few minnits back. Unless there are volunteers we'll go by squad number from here on in.' Although he did not make a point of looking at their massive number 5, Pink Viking could not have failed to hear as all the other soldiers did.

Sir Tristram felt even happier to have a superstar behind him after his own spot-kick. He hit the ball true and hard; it was a matter of the tiniest margins that saw it smash against the underside of the crossbar off Chory's head rather than burst the roof of the net. It bounced back right to his feet, Chory still spread-eagled on the line. This time he did burst the roof of the net. Goal, but only in a normal matchtime penalty. In shoot-outs it was one shot and out.

Atilla was merciless. He put the Young Faithfuls ahead for the first time, 4-3. The next penalty for Blood City could not be a matchwinner, but it had to be scored to keep them in the game at all. Even then, if the Young Faithfuls scored *their* next, they won the Seskie. If the sides were still tied after five attempts each, they would continue on a sudden-death basis, the winners the first to be ahead with an equal number of kicks taken by each team.

Those were the rules.

Viking Defender had the mic in his paw again. 'So that's 4-3 to the Young Faithfuls, following that miss by Blood City captain Sir Tristram.'

Was there a relish in the way he had named the only shooter to have failed so far? Sir Tristram did not blame him – only himself. He had been bred to feel born to lead. Any anxiety he had felt about the dey's outcome had been at the potential loss of life he foresaw; not his own but those of his soldiers and, most of all, his dearest child. His efforts had failed to get Tristan safely away from the Zuteca. Against that, a missed penalty should not matter so much, perhaps. Yet it did.

He had not heeded the rest of Viking Defender's speech. He was rudely jostled back to the situation in hand by Jakob's beard in his face, the Arab rattling his captain's shirt.

'Did you not hear, Tram? They've moved the bluddy goalposts again. If we're level after five it's not sudden death but the fight to the death. Unless the Yofa champion is from the clan O'Reilly, I stand ready to represent Blood City. I will not let our team down. Not that—I didn't mean—'

'I know you didn't, Jake, but others will. With reason. I feel only too keenly I did let Blood City down. If the fight to the death is my way to redemption, I shall welcome it.'

'There'll be no fight to the death, not even a sniff at one, unless someone sticks our next penalty away,' boomed Pink Viking. 'Tell me, captain, is it to be me or does your pretty pup have a better claim, as he's insisting to the four winds? Won't let the ball go, but I'll make his ears sing if you want me to take it.'

There was Tristan behind the giant Viking, looking close to tears but clutching the football tight to his breast. Sir Tristram addressed him roughly: 'Give the ball to PV. I have already disgraced our family sufficiently.'

'And you think I would disgrace it further?' The voice quavered at the start but then steadied with further sharp questions. 'Is that it? Was it just a joke to name me in the squad? Who loves you more than I? Love and trust me in return. Let me take the last penalty, captain. Father.'

He would not have been swayed by the passion in Tristan's eyes had he not seen something else in Pink Viking's. Not fear, but certainly doubt. The great PV looked as if he did not fancy himself on the spot-kick. Maybe it was political, knowing he could not win the match outright, only lose it – a shrewd calculation of the odds in some people's books. Sir Tristram was reading a different tale. He could not support such a leader, on the field or elsewhere.

'PV, if you are prepared to stand aside, I am ready to give the lad a shot.'

Pink Viking spread his hands in front of him, palms up, a gesture caught on the big screen, as he had surely purposed. 'You are captain. I accept your decision. Go ahead, sweet cheeks, and good luck.'

'The lad deserves a worthy opponent to test his nerve. Chory seems to have been knocked even more senseless by Sir Tristram's shot, and has saved not a one yet, except that by sheer fluke. I shall replace him in the goals,' the all-red Yashin proclaimed. He put a paternal arm around Tristan's shoulders as they walked between the soldiers guarding the corral gate.

The crowd had grown restive at the pause in action following Viking Defender's announcement. He took the mic again to announce that Yashin would be replacing the injured Chory, who was in fact perfectly recovered from what had only been a blow to his blank face. At last he sat down cross-legged away from the action, facing a corner flag.

Viking Defender announced that the final penalty-taker for Blood City would be Tristan, of the line Galahad. Yellow Cloud addressed the Indian host, which raised a mighty ululation in support of the striker. The Pirates behind the Vladi goal tried to match it with a cacophony of boos, a vain effort even before Yashin quietened them with an imperious raised fist.

Not until Yashin and Tristan were almost at the D did Sir Tristram realise what was going to happen. He heard again, understanding only now, the words 'Who loves you more than I?' Busting though the surprised Tommies, he ran to catch them, cawing the boy's name. 'Viya, I thank you again for the honour you do me and my stock. I do not claim I could beat you myself from the spot. Nevertheless, will you let me offer a word of counsel to my boy while you take your place on the line?'

'Of course. I will attend to that crybaby first.' Yashin raised his chin in the direction of Chory and went over to administer comfort or reproof.

'My child, there is perhaps no entirely welcome way to die – certainly not at your age. There are, however, good and bad ways. Do not condemn me to a bad death by missing this penalty on purpose.'

'But Dad—'

'Not a word. Listen to your daddy. You may miss, Yashin may save it – there is no disgrace in that. The disgrace is if you think to fail so as to save me from a fight to the death. I shall know, believe me. And I shall kill myself before you turn around. Remember Bowlegs' training on how to take penalties.'

Tristan was weeping as he disengaged himself from his father's long embrace. Tristania dried his face with a furious sweep of her left fist. Remember Bowlegs' training.

He had spent more time under the rough tutelage of his father's bondsman than in any shulroom. Often just following him around in his daily chores, slowing them no doubt in the ways Bowlegs always found for him to help. 'Put your finger there, boy...hold this steady...measure this off.' He had thought the soldier as keen as he was on their footballing breaks, not realising Bowlegs might sometimes have preferred to sit down and rest. They were not allowed to play on the main pitch at Camelot, but it was there he had been walked around the goal one matchdey.

'You see the framework here behind the goal with net draped on it, bits from the ground to where the posts meet the bar at either end, lifting like a long swan's neck then ducking as if it's going to peck at the join? That whole thing is called the stanchion. Here, come up.' He hoisted the boy onto his shoulders. 'Now, you see the curve where the white swan begins to flatten out? Chuck it under its neck there, right there.' He adjusted the pudgy little paw. 'That's the sweet spot. You find that spot and hit it hard enough, not even Yashin, not even Yashin the Great will be able to save it.'

For yeers after, the stanchion had been an imaginary point in the air between pullies for goalposts, or a white chalk cross on an outhouse wall – with Bowlegs, with friends like Christian, or with nobody at all in the place of Yashin. Now Tristan was laying the ball on the spot to face that very soldier. There were proper stanchions, fresh-painted, gleaming white.

'Either will do,' Bowlegs had answered his earnest query, 'but for some reason most soldiers feel more comfortable diving to their right. If you can slot it to their left and find the mark, so much the better.

'Never change your mind, though. Go right or go left – don't think one then do the other.'

Yashin was no longer styled the Red Cobra, for the speed with which a fist, arm or even leg would spring to divert a ball from the danger zone. Tristan had seen his lack of mobility in the Army game and the ceremonious early stage of the Seskie. Still, those stanchions looked awfully narrow, awfully distant.

The stadium was perfectly quiet. In a way he would have preferred noise, even boos. The freedom to focus on his own thoughts made it clear what an unruly, squabbling mob they were: don't scuff it; you're shooting for your father's life; just slam it down the middle; in ten segunds Yashin will be bouncing that ball off your head, just like Sigi's. He tried to drown them by repeating two sentences under his breath, turn and turn about. Hit it true. Hit the stanchion.

The Pirates behind the goal remained silent after he had taken the shot. He stood in disbelief. Then the Indians' noise started as Sir Tristam grabbed him from behind.

'I missed the stanchion, Dad.'

'A near miss can be a perfect hit, Son. That was a lovely penalty, just inside the post, rippled the net. No keeper in any world, in any time, would have got anywhere near it.'

'Even I might have struggled to keep it out.' Ian Swallow was thumping his back. 'You've kept us alive, Tris. Super goal. Let's see if I can do my bit now.'

Back in the centre square there were more hugs, an attempted kiss from Pink Viking, before they were distracted by an apparent quarrel among the Young Faithfuls.

'Should not I, the Grand Vizor, take the final, winning penalty, ending the Seskie as I began it?'

'I hear you, Tommy.' Suarez, having already dispatched a penalty, was not arguing for himself. 'All I'm saying is, you're a defender. With all due respect, I've never seen you take a pen. Why not let Ferdinand or Más have it?'

'So the honour of the winning shot would go to the Tuaregs,' Zito observed.

'I will take it,' the Hun rumbled after some prompting from his half-brother Atilla, who continued on his behalf. 'That would be fitting too. Tommy and Hun made a great centre-back pairing. It would be passing the bat onto the next generation, and avoid this fussing between you Arab tribes.'

'And mean that Vikings take three of the five penalties,' Más pointed out.

'Never mind.' Tommy O'Reilly raised his hands and the others were silent. 'I will not be accused of glory-hunting, whether for myself or my kinfolk. Let Hun take it.'

As Viking Defender announced the Young Faithfuls' number 6 to take the dey's last spot-kick, Suarez continued to mutter to Zito: 'I've never seen Hun take a penalty either.' Tommy only smiled.

Recognising the giant defender's strength in the air, Cibolans would joke for yeers to come: 'Hun had better tried to head it in.'

That, in the way of jokes, was slightly unfair, not just on Hun but Ian. The man-mountain may not have hit the ball in the exact direction he was planning, crashing to the ground as his feet somehow tangled themselves in his approach. That meant there was no advance notice of where it was heading, with considerable force and speed. Ian dived at full stretch – to his left – to fingertip it around the post in the direction of Yashin and Chory, watching with arms linked.

The penalty shoot-out had finished level: 4-4.

Before taking to his billy-club mic again, Viking Defender called the captains to him at a spot between the penalty area and the centre square, signalling impatiently for the picture on the screen to move away from them. There was no preamble.

'Sir Tristram, name your champion.'

'None but I. It would be dishonourable to name another. I shall stand for Blood City.'

'And Martin, we've already—'

'I feel the same way. As captain, I shall represent the Young Faithfuls.'

Viking Defender gave him a hard look then stalked away without a further word.

'Football could not separate these two historic teams. Penalties could not separate them. Only death will separate them. We shall now move the action to the centre square, in which no ref will be needed to ensure fair play. My role will be only to keep each soldier's second and their medical attendants, the only others allowed in the ring, from interfering in the battle. The choice of weapons is free, except no loaded firearms.

'The designated champion for Blood City is their captain…Sir Tristram of Camelot, of the line Galahad.

'And for the Young Faithfuls the champion is the Grand Vizor…'

15

The Grappling Game

'…Tommy O'Reilly.

'The two champions have five minnits to elect their seconds and medical attendants, make their peace with the world one of them must leave, to prepare for death or glory, to…well, so, five minnits and the fight will begin.'

It began earlier than that. Sir Tristram and Coluna had been left standing awkwardly side by side. If Sir Tristram was surprised to hear Tommy O'Reilly suddenly announced as his opponent, Coluna was galvanised. He at once began to move towards the centre square, through the Army cordon then between the knots of players to get closer to Viking Defender. It was only when he came to the abrupt end of his speech that Coluna, as if in some strange deference to the power of the mic, began to draw his sword. He spoke without amplification, but loud enough for all on the field of play and the nearest ranks in the stands to hear.

'I am betrayed. Silence is not agreement. I am captain of the Young Faithfuls and will live as such.'

He was preparing to attack Viking Defender with his raised sword when Viking Attacker halted the advance with his spear, thrusting it with the same deadly accuracy of his finishing between Martin's breastplate and helmet, piercing his throat. 'Die as such then – like all who challenge Viking power.'

As incapable of speech as a fish Martin, gaffed, wriggled on the point of the spear, raising his left hand to its haft but unable to lift the sword to hack at it as the strength bled from his right. When the weapon dropped to the soft turf, the son with whom he had not exchanged a word in fifty yeers made his own charge.

François might have had a chance against Viking Attacker, whose war-lance was still buried in Martin Coluna, but that his limping, lopsided gait was not built for speed any more than elegance. Yashin intercepted him with a swing of his axe into the meat of Frankie's armed shoulder, then a second which took his head clean off. Father and son died within segunds of each other.

'So it's axe work, is it?' Chutney yelled, his own shoulder-high to confront Yashin, who also faced Septimus and Brittanus. Although guns were of little use in such a tight-packed scrum, the Blood City Westerners stood ready to weigh in with their Knight colleagues, while Hun, Atilla and Yofa Pirates were gathering behind Yashin. The O'Reillys – Jakob and Schwartz from Blood, Zito and Augusto from Casablanca – had instinctively coalesced around Tommy. He snatched the mic from his Deputy Vizor, frozen with Pink Viking beside him, to bellow in a voice fit to deafen those around him, and the crowd too when it resulted in a fierce screech of feedback.

'Stop! This is my land. No more bloodletting unless on my say-so. Vida, you and I shall speak on the death of our captain. You assured me he was apprised of my wish to champion the Young Faithfuls. That wish is my duty now. Sir Tristram and I will decide the Seskie. Then I shall make further dispositions.'

Sir Tristram supported Tommy's intervention by planting himself at the head of his own soldiers and telling them to lower their arms. Wondering if Chutney would obey, he risked turning his back on the best mate of Sir François – whose title was fair-earned at last – to address the Grand Vizor.

'As to the further dispositions, I would expect no less self-confidence from the great fighter Tommy O'Reilly. For my part, I shall not die before seeing justice for the death of my own teammate. That is my pledge.'

A semblance of order was restored as the bodies of Martin and François Coluna, closer in death than ever in life, were carried from the field. Sir Tristram had not thought to name his medical attendant (the role an archaic courtesy anyway in a fight to the death), more exercised as to who would be his second.

'Sir Tristram, I can understand if you would prefer one of your own as second. If Barrie were here, I would press him forward myself. As your vice, I humbly offer my services. I shall ensure your body is treated with all honours, subject only to the safe escape of Tommy himself. And I shall do my supreme best to protect and carry Tristan safe home.'

'Was ever a second so sanguine of his principal's chances, Jake? The job is yours if you can contrive me a momet to speak in peace to your kinsman before we wage war.'

'If Dvid allows, it shall be done.'

Sir Tristram's heart caught when he saw his child, standing before him with the battered old briefcase Chutney had given his pal as a joke before they left Blood. 'Looks like my dey for subbing, Dad. With Frankie gone I don't suppose you have anyone else in mind to act as your cutman.'

'And are you as skilled in that field as at penalty kicks, Tris?'

'As much as Sir François was.'

Sir Tristram put his hands on the new medico's shoulders. 'The sponge would have to be real magic to help at this stage of the game. I would rather you were outside the Zuteca as I ordered. Since you are here, there is no one I would have closer, blood of my heart. I have every intention of leaving here with you, but if I should be…detained…heed your teammates. Barrie knows he is to take you as his ward. You can count on Bowlegs as if he were your own limbs, and on our fellow Knights, of course. On the other Blood City numbered soldiers too. Jakob is one born to lead, whose orders I expect you to follow, second only to Barrie's. If the situation descends into total chaos, you could do worse than cleave to Ian Swallow.'

The Knight bit through the top of his right index finger so he could sketch a red cross on Tristan's forehead. 'Carry on the line, my dear Tristania – that above all.'

Tommy had kept his small support team in the family. There was no sign of any medical equipment on Augusto, unless you cared to count the bloodletting capability of his scimitar. Zito as second was talking to Viking Defender, now again fully helmeted and horned.

'That dangerous fool' —Jake characterised the Deputy Vizor— 'will be lucky to survive the dey, though luck is one blessing he seems to have. He wanted to listen in as you and Tommy talked! He has no doubt made his way more by backstairs snooping and low stooping than any merit of arms. You have a couple of minnits, Tram. Uncle Tommy granted at once your request to parley.'

Sir Tristram spoke in close to the big O'Reilly, hand over his mouth in case the giant screen should fix on them. He had heard there was a magic in its eye that could broadcast even unheard words if it only saw the moving mouth.

'Tommy, I would not have you go deceived to your death. Know this. Viking Defender is naming Pink Viking as Grand Vizor, on the purported authority of Henry Morgan. Know also that was not Morgan's choice. He would have you out of Zanzibar dead or alive – dead it must be now – but not to name that soldier in your stead.'

'Good of you to tell me,' Tommy said, as if at the courtesy of having a slippery patch of turf pointed out to him. 'For telling me that you are not as sure of besting me as I am that I shall kill you. Otherwise, why even bother warning me?'

'I tell you because it is the right thing to do. My self-belief will become plain as your own soon enough. In one of us it must be misplaced. Dvidspeed, Tommy.'

He offered his knuckles. Rather than match the knightly salute in kind, O'Reilly bowed his head onto them.

Viking Defender insisted on patting Sir Tristram down, though the Knight had never in his life carried a firearm. He would enter battle as he always did, with his single-bladed axe, light and manoeuvrable. He considered discarding his sword, thinking he would have little opportunity to unsheathe, let alone use it, yet something made him want to go to war in full fig, including the dirk on the other side of his belt and spurs on his boots which might take a cheeky Arab eye out. He had his shield strapped to his back, knowing he would be in desperate straits should he have to scrabble for that.

'Win this and you can save us all a weight of trouble, Sir Tristram, so I wish you luck. You might even be allowed to leave with the Seskie. Except I don't think you have a prayer against Tommy.'

'If I am overmatched, Videf, consider yourself. His subordinate for a lifetime, to overtop him in a dey? For all you may need them, you have no prayers of mine.'

These pleasantries over, he watched Viking Defender take the rifle slung over O'Reilly's shoulder, to break and check it for ammunition. The Pirate wore a criss-cross of bandoliers stuffed full of bullets along with the rifle into the square. Perhaps it was a comfort thing, since the only legitimate way to use the gun would be as a club. He already had a staff for that, weighted and spiked at either end. Inside the soft folds of his thobe, Sir Tristram knew many hard and sharp edges could be concealed. Tommy was likely to take the field with a dagger in one hand or between his teeth.

They were of an age, the two soldiers. Sir Tristram had a height advantage, while Tommy outweighed and outmuscled him. Before the Cibolan football league, Tommy and the Indian keeper Tory had been the world's most famous wrestlers, fighting each other many times in exhibition matches to the best of three falls or submissions, or a knockout. If it came to grappling on the Zuteca turf, Sir Tristram was surely lost.

There was a four-deep cordon of Army all along three sides of the centre square. Two rows faced inwards, arms linked to mark out the fighting space. Back-to-back with them were two more, the worst placed in the ground for seeing the action, which they would have to judge from the reactions of the crowd almost on top of them.

On the fourth side, the inwards ranks completed the square while the outwards ones formed a rough semi-circle reaching almost to the touchline at its halfway point. The interior of the D was marshalled by Myhigh Syhigh himself with hand-picked troopers. These separated the Blood City and Young Faithfuls parties, ready also to reinforce the outer ranks of soldiers anywhere around the perimeter. The orders of soldiers directly facing the crowd were to restrain it with good-humoured banter rather than fisticuffs. The second rank was authorised to shoot on sight any spectator offering violence to their squadmates.

'I don't say we have much chance of making our way through such a crush,' the CIC confided cheerfully to Reaney in the VIS area, 'but the troops like to believe we have a contingency plan that doesn't leave them at the mercy of a howling mob. If you have to assume command, try to get to the touchline with as many of the footballers as possible. Above all, save the winner of the single combat. Whether it's Tommy or Tristram as dies, there'll be a lot of seriously hacked-off fans.'

The crowd went quiet as Viking Defender sent the seconds and medical attendants to their respective corners. From somewhere he had equipped himself with an ancient flintlock pistol.

'When I fire this beauty, the fight to decide the Seskie will begin. When I fire a second time, it will be over. Either because one of our heroes has fallen dead, or because I have had to kill one myself for a serious infringement of the rules, which would include disrespect of my authority as referee.'

It was too late to worry if they were at risk of further treachery from the Grand Vizor. Sir Tristram did not fear his own death by antique bullet. As the brutish Viking had said, a victory for the Knight might well save him some bother. If the ref shot Tommy – well, it would only be his end by another means. Sir Tristram hoped rather to spare his opponent against a promise to accompany him from the field, but first there was the small matter of gaining the upper hand with leisure enough to make the offer.

There was no expectation from anyone in the Zuteca – least of all the fighters themselves – of a long struggle. While the absence of firearms would prolong it beyond a segund or two, the presence of other killing tools made it unlikely to last more than a few minnnits. The ages of the two combatants had diminished their stamina for a lengthy brawl, while their experience furnished them with a variety of tried and tested death strokes.

Tommy was already almost at a crouch as they began to circle each other. Both knew that a mad rush towards a lethal blow, effective enough to dispatch opponents who were already afeard, would be suicide. Sir Tristram realised the Arab's stance was designed to encourage a downward strike rather than a horizontal swing through the air. If you did not split your opponent like kindling on the way down, or at least lop off a limb, you risked giving him the advantage with your blade buried in the ground.

The only danger Sir Tristram faced from a distance was a hurled dagger. While it might not pierce his chain mail shirt, other areas of his body were more exposed. Even if it made contact blunt end first, with the force at which Tommy was capable of throwing it he could be knocked fatally off balance.

Sir Tristram drew first blood. Seeking to add the support of whichever neutrals there might be in the heaving crowd to that of the Knights – the Indians too for the captain of White Eagle – he took the fight to the Grand Vizor. By a series of half-swings of his axe, he forced the Arab to retreat. He knew he could cut through the staff Tommy held horizontally at waist height in front of him, except at its metallised ends.

As he backed up, Tommy slipped. Sir Tristram rushed in with a full swing. Too late he realised he had fallen to a feint, Tommy ducking nimbly under the blade and at the same time seeking to trip the Knight, carried forward by his own momentum. He lifted his foot just in time, bringing the spurs raking down Tommy's calf and ankle, dyeing the ripped leg of the thobe a darker red.

Although he yelped in either pain or frustration, Tommy was not seriously hurt. On his lower axis he was able to spin more quickly to attack Sir Tristram from the rear as he careered towards the Army rank serving as the ropes of their makeshift ring. The Knight's half-turn was enough to save him from the disabling danger of the staff's maced end aimed at his ribs. Its spikes embedded themselves instead in the leather shield on his back, propelling him towards the opponent's corner. Zito and Augusto moved smartly, fairly, out of his path.

It was Tommy's turn to be unbalanced, genuinely so this time, by his grip on the swinging staff. Rather than let go, he drove at it, snapping it in half against his hip. The end still in Sir Tristram's back cleared out a few soldiers' teeth as he struggled to get himself back into free space.

Tommy, poised like a sprinter in his blocks, body-charged Sir Tristram, exposing his own back to a downward blow as he struck him in the midriff. Though winded, the Blood City captain had every intention of delivering that blow, until the Arab's head swarmed up his red-crossed jerkin, catching him viciously under the chin. A fist in the guts followed.

As Sir Tristram had swung his axe only a pass earlier, it was Tommy's turn to helicopter, whirling the Knight, gripped neck and crotch, above his head before dumping him from height, flat on his back in the centre of the ring, the head bouncing up as if in a brief nod of acknowledgement at the technique. Tommy slammed his own body crosswise on top, a surefire pin and fall in any wrestling match. A fall was not enough in this one.

Sir Tristram somehow still had both hands on his axe, but it was away behind his head, his arms in any case pinned by Tommy's meaty right forearm. In his left hand was a dagger pricking from below at the Knight's already abused chin.

'The Seskie is the Young Faithfuls' and mine, Sir Tristram. Your life is mine alone. Would you have me spare it for use in my service?'

He had not been stabbed, yet there was no part of Sir Tristram's body that did not hurt. His mouth was full of blood from biting his tongue at the Arab's headbutt. 'You have bested me, but I'll not beg. I recognise my life is in your hands.'

'Good enough.' Tommy cut Sir Tristram's throat.

16

Battle of the Zuteca

Tommy O'Reilly rose to hold the blooded dagger and broken staff aloft. As one fight ended, many others broke out in the Pirate section of the crowd. A low hum rose from the Indians, an oddly plaintive sound, as if seeking direction and comfort.

'Ho, Vida, not a word of congratulation? Fire that old blunderbuss into the air and give me the mic to address my people.'

The Deputy Vizor's hesitation in complying was his last act. Tommy unceremoniously rammed his dagger upwards into the Viking's heart. Dropping the staff, he relieved him of both gun and mic before the dying fingers could stiffen around them. He used the butt of the pistol to shove him to the ground, like

Sir Tristram flat on his back, the bejewelled haft of Tommy's dagger pointing skywards, its blade entirely buried.

Tommy fired the ceremonial gun into the air himself, though the crowd had already been muted by the toppling of Viking Defender. 'People of Zanzibar, guests from all the proud lands and seas of Cibola, hear me. It was the referee who broke the rules, broke his word of allegiance to me. That he kept his word so many yeers earned him a quick death. Until this dey I did not know he had betrayed me, and also Prince Albert. I may never be able to explain my decisive actions against him to King Henry, though here in view of you all, of the giant eye' —though the eye was closed— 'I offer to speak to Henry privately on this matter, as one ruler to another.

'I owe my enlightenment in large measure to my brave opponent, Sir Tristram...'

The crowd saw a distraught Tristan crouched over the body. He had taken the sponge from Frankie's old briefcase, without hope in its magical properties, to make his father presentable in death. Going first to wipe the blood from his face, he was glad he did not have to close the eyes, then nonplussed when they opened as the water hit his mouth.

'He spared me,' Sir Tristram croaked. 'Dvaeba, he spared me.'

Someone better versed in the killing arts than Tristan would have expected a greater profusion of blood from a fatally slashed throat. With the most delicate touch, Tommy had drawn a bloody arc practically from ear to ear without piercing any of the vital arteries below, which would have seen the life force flow out in a few heartbeats. Sir Tristram would forever bear the scar of a hanged man, but he would bear it in the world of the living.

'Sir Tristram came here on a mission,' Tommy had continued. 'He did not deserve to die because the team he led failed to lift the Seskie. I won our mano a mano and his life is mine. Nevertheless, I shall not impose on him the post of Deputy Vizor. I shall offer him it.'

There were cheers from all sectors of the Zuteca as Sir Tristram lurched to his feet, helped by Tristan, who had improvised a dressing with a kerchief knotted tightly round his father's neck. Not everyone was cheering, though; within the cordoned VIS area Yashin, Viking Attacker and Pink Viking were haranguing Syhigh, who stood between them and the centre square. Behind him was Reaney, hand on the flap of his pistol's holster. Behind the Vikings hulked A-Og.

'How many more murders will you allow that soldier to perpetrate in full public view, Grand Vizor or nay?' demanded Yashin. 'My nephew Pink Viking stands ready to assume that role in O'Reilly's stead, as dictated by Morgan himself.'

'Sir Tristram said he had evidence to the contrary that stayed my hand.'

'What evidence?' boomed the prospective Grand Vizor. 'And of what worth? Did you not see Tristram and Tommy snogging before the fight? It is they who are clearly in cahoots. Already the king's brother and a senior officer of the crown have died. Step into that ring and restore order.'

Tommy had embraced the risen Sir Tristram. No such resuscitation could be expected for Viking Defender. He was attended in the rites of death by Atilla, calmest of his tribe off the field as well as on it.

The Grand Vizor once more took up the mic. 'I will ask General Myhigh Syhigh, commander-in-chief of the Cibolan Independent Army, to present the Sesquicentenario trophy. I receive it in honour of two warriors fallen here, felled rather by Viking cowardice and treachery: White Eagle and Martin Coluna, great heroes and leaders both.'

The Seskie was solid gold. A product of Morrocan craftsmen, it had been brought from his home city with pride by the CIC himself. The ingot listing all the teams of the Cibolan league was topped by a football on which their world was mapped out. The Ogs had pledged to replicate the meticulous, ornate scrollwork exactly with their own arts, to engrave the winner's name on the plinth between final whistle and presentation. E-Og had been charged with this task in the VIS area itself, where the trophy now stood under Army guard on a sturdy oak table.

'You're not seriously going to hand the Seskie to that criminal or his kin? Let Hun receive it. I do not seek the honour for myself.' Yashin grabbed Syhigh's sleeve.

'Take your hand off me, sir. Only one thing is clear. Tommy's single-combat victory won the Seskie for the Young Faithfuls. I will present him with the trophy. Only then will I tell him he is under arrest. Only then will the disgraceful violence during and after the match be fully investigated.' His pale eyes fixed coldly on Viking Attacker.

Yashin pushed the general's arm away in disgust by way of releasing his sleeve, turning back to his supporters without troubling to lower his voice. 'Vitack, gather our loyalists close. It looks like we shall have to do our own wet work.'

Syhigh was more careful to keep his orders confidential. 'Sergeant Reaney, take an acting commission as captain, which I shall be happy to confirm when the dust settles on this dey – unless we ourselves are dust by then. I leave you in command of the VIS while I go and do the honours. Allow me a detail of six soldiers to watch the trophy – some dodgy types around here, you know.'

As he prepared for action, whether it should be a feel-good victory presentation or something rather warmer, the CIC seemed in good humour. 'Limdenberger, grab the Seskie. I suppose I can trust you not to drop the bluddy thing.' The Army keeper, in the VIS enclosure with other internationals and very important soldiers from all the Cibolan nations, would be the only one to spot the Oggish error in blazoning the trophy winners as the Young Faitfuls. He would not live long enough to point out the mistake to anyone else.

'People of the Last Ground,' Syhigh began when Tommy O'Reilly ceded him the mic. 'You have seen a spectacle by turns lamentable, enthralling, tragic and, perhaps to some of you, inspiring. It has been far more than a football match, though I will ask you as you leave the stadium to keep in mind only the beautiful game. Do not add to the violence we have already seen.

'I shall now ask the winning Young Faithfuls to gather behind the Grand Vizor, whose regret I echo that Martin Coluna is not the one to receive their trophy.'

The Young Faithfuls hardly presented the aspect of a team united as they assembled in the ring. Immediately behind

Tommy were two huddles: Yashin, Viking Attacker, Hun and Atilla on the one hand; Zito, Augusto and the Tuaregs Ferdinand, Más and Suarez on the other. Chory was hopping around behind them, Scarface lurking, while Little Boris, the limping Ortega and the wheelchaired Frenchie could probably not even see the presentation through the throng of bodies ahead of them.

There was no recognition for the losers. Sir Tristram was still struggling to believe he was alive, albeit defeated. Tristan was too happy at the resurrection of his father to be unduly upset at the football result. Jakob was very still. The remainder of the squad in the stadium, unsummoned, stayed in the VIS area: Yellow Cloud and Little Doe, Cowboy, Ian Swallow, Brittanus Septimus and Chutney, the Arabs Schwartz and Oscar. John Ivanhoe, scorer for both teams, was to be found with neither. Pink Viking had not needed an invitation to follow Syhigh into the centre square, accompanied by the gigantic A-Og and the only slightly smaller E-Og.

'We will receive the Sesquicentenario gold with a dignity to match the Young Faithfuls' proud history, before we resolve any problems between ourselves,' Tommy O'Reilly ordered the simmering groups of Vikings and Arabs. 'Do not disgrace our colours.'

There was a massive roar from the crowd as Tommy lifted the trophy high above his head with a great Arab war-whoop. The three Blood City players nearest him did not have to cheer. Jakob was tight-lipped, unmoving. Tristan followed his father's lead in clapping politely at the presentation and subsequent pass-the-parcel, each Yofa having his own chance to raise the

Seskie to the fans and the skies, usually after or before putting a full-mouthed kiss on it. The old campaigner Tristram did not watch the golden prize's progress. He was close enough to hear the exchange between the CIC and Pirate.

'Tommy O'Reilly, Grand Vizor of Zanzibar, it gives me no pleasure to arrest you on charges of treasonable revolt and murder. I do assure you of my personal involvement in the investigation of these grave matters, to ensure a true report is presented to the king.'

'You would lead me from here in chains?'

'If you are prepared to give me your parole to cooperate and leave peaceably, you may do so at my side. If not, I will have you cuffed.'

While Tommy's enquiry had appeared almost mild, Syhigh's reply upset him. 'You will have me cuffed? Why not harnessed and collared, leashed like a lady's pet to trot behind you? No one who serves the king is innocent. Whatever report is presented will matter not a tittle if I am his prisoner.'

'Grand Vizor, Tommy, I do ask—'

'Now you ask. You who would "have me cuffed". I do my own cuffing.'

The general was big, a head taller than Tommy, which exposed his jaw to the uppercut that knocked him unconscious to the turf. Without haste, his rage slaked by the blow, Tommy turned for a final look at the Seskie, now jigging with the renegade Chory. 'Zito, Suarez, I leave you to defend the pot of gold until we meet again in the city by the sea. Jakob, follow me. Come you too, Sir Tristram' —an almost imperceptible pause— 'if you will.'

'I will,' the Knight answered at once. 'Tristan, close to me till we are again among our own soldiers.'

Although they had just seen their general poleaxed, none of his immediate escort had the gumption to confront the Grand Vizor as he strode past them; neither did the narrow corridor to the VIS close on the small band.

Captain Reaney was more resolute. He stood behind the overturned table that had held the Seskie, his pistol with the rifles and sub-machine guns of half a dozen other Army soldiers pointing in the same general direction: at Tommy. Behind them the outer cordon was now struggling to keep the crowd at bay, both ranks with weapons drawn.

'Grand Vizor, I judge not on the larger issues but must detain you for the assault on the CIC I just witnessed with my own eyes. If you will not submit to restraints being imposed by my troops, I shall order them to open fire. I would not like to say how many deaths that might bring about.'

Tommy was amused. 'Another one who would have me cuffed. Stand aside, soldier, or I guarantee whatever the number it will include your own.'

There was already a substantial crackle of gunfire around the ground, though the fighting was mainly hand to hand. So it was between the Pirates in the improvised ring, where the Arabs were unwilling to let Yashin lead the Vikings in pursuit of Tommy. The two tribes were having at it with a vengeance, though Pink Viking stood aside between the two Ogs, whom nobody was yet at the pitch of madness to risk provoking.

Revived by an Army MO somewhat better resourced than poor Sir François, General Syhigh's hand cupping his busted jaw gave him a pensive air. His wits had been only briefly scrambled by the sucker punch. Ignoring the melee around him, he had two troopers hoist his bulky frame onto their shoulders, the better to bawl his orders.

'That's the chap, Reaney. You have my full authority to shoot at your own judgement, but preferably restrain the fugitives without bloodshed. I want further words face to face with the Grand Vizor. Hold the line, we'll be with you in a jiffy.'

Reaney seemed well up to the arguably greater challenge of holding his nerve, the urbane, verbose ADC persona shucked off to reveal the disciplined and trained fighting soldier. Sir Tristram quickly decided any appeal to his former allegiance as a Blood City player would be a waste of breath.

The City squad had instinctively moved towards their captain, then paused at Reaney's challenge. They formed a loose semicircle in front of Yellow Cloud. The three Knights and Little Doe faced the Army with their shields (probably otiose against high-velocity bullets) while Cowboy and Oscar stood, Schwartz crouched and Ian lay ready to return fire.

The chief began to dance and chant, again with the curiously hypnotic effect on the multitude of Indians down from the stand. The CIC was the first to spot the danger. 'Reano, take out that yellowhammer, or they'll drown us all.'

Whether or not he heard Syhigh, struggling through the already dense press of soldiers in the centre square, the tone of Yellow Cloud's invocation changed, as did his posture. He moved towards the line of soldiers. He parted Little Doe and Brittanus without a word to either, removing them from the line of fire to his own body. He raised both hands above his head, firing off the rifle held in one of them with a final ululation echoing Tommy's takbir.

Syhigh just had time to regret his order, realising the Blood City winger was inviting martyrdom, before Reaney carried it out. He blew the top off Yellow Cloud's head, clouding the air above it with feathers which would come to be prized as holy relics.

The cordon of soldiers could not hold. For every Indian they shot down another ten were upon them, some with guns but most finding knives or tomahawks equally effective. Whatever Yellow Cloud's message to them had been, they were become an irresistible force – though not a mindless one. They did not kill for the sake of killing, attacking and bringing down only soldiers who stuck to their guns and tried to use them. Not all did. Many threw up their empty hands, many crouched or curled to the ground hoping the stampede would blow over, leaving them somehow still alive. While some tried to effect a disciplined retreat to regroup under new orders – Reaney was waving his red cap above the parapet of the oak table – others just ran.

The crowd pressure was not limited to the dressing room side. Pirates, Knights and other Westerners as well as Indians from all round the stadium were drawn to the pagga in the centre square. Many completely lost their heads, some literally, as the fighting intensified.

Syhigh's shattered jaw focused his mind cruelly on the urge to bring O'Reilly into custody. He had a clear strategy in mind. All Army, uniformed or not, should form an arrowhead as if fired from the giant screen, aiming towards the halfway line outside the dressing rooms. Unlike Yellow Cloud, he had no way of communicating the pictures in his head to the scattered masses. He could only hope his brighter, braver officers would reach a similar conclusion, enabling him to drive a wedge in pursuit of Tommy.

The corridor between the ring and the VIS area had disappeared as the Army cordons disintegrated under violent pressure of numbers. Within the VIS, the firestorm that followed the shooting of Yellow Cloud had claimed the lives of his long-time wing rival Cowboy and the gallant Brittanus, as well as those of four Army, every bullet from the Blood City marksmen finding a billet. The deadly exchange was brief because the space between the opposing groups was suddenly a heaving mass of fans, blocking their view of each other and making it almost impossible to manage a rifle. Not so a pencil; incredibly, some of the current generation of football stars, including Sinbad and Greenman, rather than drawing their guns were scribbling autographs in thick knots of geeks and obsessives.

The Blood City survivors were at last reunited with their captain who, without time to count them all, hoped against hope that one or two were only obscured from his sight by the crush. The diversion incited by Yellow Cloud had drawn Reaney's guns away from them, for which he knew the chief had paid the ultimate price. Trying to include as many of them as possible in a rallying scrum, one of his arms around Jakob and the other Tristan, he addressed them one last time. 'Help us get Tommy outside – that's our mission now. Rendezvous at the Spartan Officer, where Barrie and Bowlegs should be waiting with transport.'

'We'll do our best, Sir Tristram, but I have a piece of work here first,' Chutney demurred.

'It gladdens me to see our cousin Tommy, yet I too must first seek out my father and uncles,' Oscar added.

'Go with my blessing, then. You all deserved better leadership of me. Your efforts merited the Seskie.'

Sir Chutney's mission was already almost upon him, in the person of Yashin. Little Doe fairly snarled at the sight of Viking Attacker. Slightly behind them was Pink Viking, flanked by the two Ogs.

It took three of them to bring down Viking Attacker – no coward, despite Tommy's imputation. Sir Septimus approached him dagger drawn and shield high, wary of the great spear that had already killed that dey and seemed to find its own way through the crowd. The Berserker Oscar, whether seriously seeking to engage the two Vikings or merely blast a way to his elders in the ring, rushed full tilt, firing his rifle from the hip and with cutlass raised vertically in front of him. Chutney was looking at last to begin with Yashin the axe work he had proposed earlier.

Unwilling to leave his teammates to fight alone, for the odds would be heavily against them should Pink Viking and the Ogs bestir themselves, Sir Tristram followed Jakob towards the battle. 'Ian, Schwartz, Tristan, keep on moving towards the exit with Tommy.'

'All respect, cap'n, you need to keep movin' too. Din't you just say gettin' Tommy out was the big job now?' He allowed himself to be tugged back by Ian Swallow, who added, 'The boys will be along.'

Not all of them would. Oscar burst through to the ring and was lost to view. Sir Septimus perished in battle at close quarters with Viking Attacker, on whose broad back Little Doe managed to leap, grabbing a fistful of black beard. Unable to shake him free, the Young Faithfuls striker fell purposely backwards, trying to crush his adversary. Little Doe had gotten out from under too many pintos in his time to fall prey to that trick, slipping round to straddle Attacker, goading hand still at the beard. 'Look in the eye of Little Doe and hear my curse before you hear no more.' Spitting in the Viking's face, he stabbed through the left ear into the brain.

As with his football, Sir Chutney's bravery and tenacity took him further as a fighter than his skill. Despite being winged already by a bullet from the charging Oscar, Yashin knew too much for him. He put Chutney down, before being himself overwhelmed by Jakob, a blur of movement with a scimitar in each hand. Turning to the Knight, Jakob lifted his visor. 'Sir François is avenged, my friend – you played your part.'

Chutney really did his best to thank Jakob. All that came from his mouth was blood.

Jakob O'Reilly and Little Doe, the full-back partners in that historic Blood City team, glowered at their centre half, unmoved between the two Ogs. Pink Viking did not seem upset at the death of two kinsmen who had been seeking to elevate him to executive power in Zanzibar.

'I will not go against my teammates, and I would advise you not to raise so much as an eyebrow against me. A-Og is organising, as we speak, complete shutdown of the Zuteca. You may go tell Tommy and Trissie they cannot escape. They will be brought to account by the Army with our support, and may before long have to look to me for mercy.'

'The lion does not fear the hyena, for all the power in his jaws. Let the big lunk fiddle with the buttons on that chestpad to his heart's delight – if he manages to block all the exits from the ground it will be the first Og trick I've seen come off since arriving in Zanzibar. See you in Casablanca when we raise the O'Reilly banner, PV. Teammates no more, then.'

The Arab and Indian exchanged urgent words as they slipped back into the crush, to negotiate the now sodden terrain, humped with dead and dying soldiers. They passed again Reaney, his troop depleted by death and desertions. Now with his back to the overturned table so as not to be mashed from behind against it, he had his remaining soldiers fix their bayonets. His only thought was to present an organised fighting body in support of the CIC, who was making progress towards him with his own followers in the broad slipstream of the Vikings and Ogs.

Although nobody offered them violence, even the personal authority of the Grand Vizor did not speed his escape. It did not help that the diminutive Schwartz had insisted on leading their way to protect his pa-brother. For all he was as dangerous as a rattlesnake, his similar closeness to the ground was not best suited to clear a way for others. Sir Tristram, following Tommy with Ian bringing up the rear, would have liked to take Tristan by the hand, but would not shame the lad by doing so.

As they made their own way, Little Doe had been passing hurried messages to other Indians, so that when they caught up with Sir Tristram they had a substantial escort, with an even broader feathered tail behind them. 'Tommy, Tram, they say the Ogs are going to lock down the Zuteca' Jakob yelled. 'Whatever that means, we need to move a bit quicker. Little Doe's people will help.'

'I regret my lack of White Eagle's dignity, or Yellow Cloud's eloquence, but I will do my best.'

'We must not expose more of your people to the risk of death. Army and Og weapons are too heavy for them to fight.'

'They will not fight. Better said, we will not fight, for I stay with them. I promise only to gain you as much time as we can.'

As they spoke, Indians were clearing a narrow channel ahead of them, a friendly gauntlet of back-slaps rather than blows which they ran to reach, at last, the touchline: a foot-baller's sprint of no more than five segunds from the centre spot had taken them more minnits than Sir Tristram could compute. He continued to remonstrate with Little Doe.

'If the Ogs deploy their anti-personnel bombs they could kill you by the thousund, make a boneyard of the stadium. You can do nothing to stop them.'

'I can be one among my people. If we survive, I look forward to seeing you again in Busted Jaw to talk of this dey. If not, no better tomb for Little Doe than one where White Eagle rests. You must go and bear witness, or remain trapped in here.'

Realising further debate was not only futile but dan-gerous, the Blood City skipper embraced his number 3, as did

Tristan, Jakob and Ian. While Little Doe turned back to the pitch, the others followed Schwartz and Tommy to the welcome indoor shade of the almost deserted dressing-room complex.

'Stand down, soldier, it's my show now.' Syhigh had caught up with Pink Viking and the Ogs to join Reaney's force with his own band of men. 'We cannot control that madness in the middle. I presented the Seskie to the Young Faithfuls, but it will be a temptation to every rogue and cutpurse in the ground to make off with it – if someone hasn't already. Will you be closing down all sides of the Zuteca, A-Og?' He gestured in the direction of the giant screen, blank for some time now and pocked with random bulletholes.

The Og leader's paws went to his chest. 'I can attempt it. I was focused on the Spartan side.'

Syhigh leaned down to Reaney. 'They told me the Zuteca was in lockdown, so it's only a matter of time before we find the fugitives. Are we sure they're right?'

'I'll not swear by ETechnolOGy, sir. I only hope the process can be reversed if they've already sneaked out and we find ourselves stuck in.'

The Army faced an immediate barrier beyond Reaney's table on their way to the dressing rooms. They were confronted by a solid wall of Indians, arms linked like the Army cordons earlier, but 30 or 40 ranks deep rather than two. They stood in complete silence, as one body.

'A-Og, can you blast us a way through?'

'We have the weapons, PV, but it would entail enormous loss of life.' The Og leader was looking at Syhigh, who caught his appeal.

'Is there any other way through? If the exits are blocked, they cannot escape us, and I would rather not add to the carnage.'

'Any hope of reasoning with them, getting them to stand aside?'

'A typical technician's suggestion, E-Og. Do they look to you susceptible to reason, or threat?' Pink Viking's tone was peevish. 'And who do we talk to? I can't see Little Doe – or rather, I can see about thirty of him.'

'PV is right,' Syhigh conceded. 'This ridiculous replica shirt business – no tellings how many people are wearing the Blood City 3. Little Doe himself I don't see in the front row. We could hardly direct our snipers to take him out even if we wanted to.'

'General, E-Og and I, with P-Og and K-Og already on their way, can use our personal force fields, not turned up to lethal levels but impossible for Zunis to breach. We could clear a way through with, at most, a double file of your soldiers under its shelter. It would be slower but, beyond a shock for anyone throwing themselves at the field, nobody would get hurt.'

As the Indian wall looked on impassively, on its other side Tommy O'Reilly and Sir Tristram were considering their next steps with the luxury of room to breathe and some separation from the sound of battle.

'How will this lockdown work, Tommy?'

'Something like the portcullis at Camelot – large grilles coming down automatically at each of the gates where fans come in and out.'

'And I don't suppose the spaces in the grating would be big enough for us to squeeze through?'

'There are no spaces. If it looks like a conventional grille, that's only a visual aid to stop people banging their noddles needlessly. It's a solid force field. I only hope it doesn't reach far enough below the complex to compromise my own escape route.'

'Your what?' Ian did not care how rude his interruption sounded.

Tommy continued to address Sir Tristram. 'I was not always as secure in power as in recent yeers – at least until *very* recent' he added grimly. 'I have more than one underground slip-away. The one here predates construction of the Zuteca in its current form.'

'And the Ogs or Army top brass won't know about it?'

'The last soldier to know about it is still digesting my dagger out there. Make haste – it starts in the ref's room.'

'And where does it end?' asked Tristan.

'What? Outside the stadium of course, boy. Let's go.'

'It comes up about three varsts from here, on the road to Morumbi,' Tommy corrected Sir Tristram's assumption.

'We can't go, then. See? I knew, Dad. That would leave Barrie stranded outside, not knowing what's happened to us.'

'Surely you can return for them?' Tommy was growing impatient. 'Were you not planning to leave by the port anyway?'

'You knew that?'

'Of course. It is my business to know everything in Zanzibar.'

'Things have changed in Zanzibar, Tommy. We will

have more chance with motorised transport. Let us pick you up on the road. Give us a landmark. If Slasher was to frustrate us, perhaps he will still obey you and take us to safety.'

'On the downslope from Hangman's Hill, marking the boundary between St Michael and St George. Head up the stairs and take any of the fans' gates – if you still can.'

'Come on, Dad, we can't abandon him.' Tristan was already springing up the steps three at a time, not only much newer than his father but not fatigued by a football match and a fight to the death. Ian was off straight after him, then Sir Tristram, with no time for farewells to the three O'Reillys.

Most of the concessionaires in the great internal ring of the Zuteca had already shuttered their stands, knowing there was little scope for further business but plenty for dog's abuse, rising to assault and robbery after a big match. A score of corridors led off from it, like scything blades affixed to a chariot wheel.

Tristan hesitated only long enough to ensure the others could see which exit he took. Entering the corridor, Sir Tristram saw a grille slowly coming down from the ceiling. Ahead of him Ian found the energy to shout, 'Wait, Tris, wait, we'll never make it.'

Tristan did make it. With a duck of his shoulders and a half-roll he was through. With his most important dive of the dey, Ian Swallow managed to get his arms and head under the guillotine, Tristan grabbing his hands to pull and help him wriggle forward. He was almost there when his trailing right leg went into spasm between two bars, the apparently empty space between them already administering a warning shock.

Luckily his cavalry boot was not a tight fit. As Sir Tristram arrived panting, he saw the sole of Ian's sockless foot, scarred and striped, on the other side as the grille started to drive the boot through the floor.

With Ian struggling to his feet after pulling off his other boot, Tristan faced his father. He tried to reach through the grate to him, learning from touch what he had just seen as the thin air jolted him backwards. 'I have to warn Barrie, Dad – and Bowlegs. You understand.'

'I do not, but you have my blessing. Ian knows our Plan B: first link up with Tommy and the others outside town.'

'And with you, Dad. The others and you. Don't give up now. Go find Tommy and make your way out with him.'

'Get you gone first, both of you. Any delay can only make things worse.'

What had at the time felt like a body blow, the half-time summons to the referee's quarters, meant Sir Tristram now knew where to look for the O'Reillys. He found nobody there. He sat down on the bench under the peg for the official's civvie gear (Viking Defender had not bothered to change for the match), ready to face whatever charges the Army or a new Grand Vizor might trump up against him. As his breathing quietened, he leaned his head back against the wall and closed his eyes.

Outside the Zuteca a number of screens had been improvised, including one projection on the enormous shield of the Spartan Officer. The crowd had grown increasingly restive since they went dark just as the mortal combat was to begin, able to hear the hullabaloo and gunfire inside the stadium without knowing if it signified anything more than exuberant celebrations by the winning fans. Knots of Army were more intent on holding a porcupine formation, bayonets and barrels pointing in all directions, than intervening in brawls.

Although it was Tristan who had seen where the lorries were parked, the Spartan Officer was prominent enough for Ian to lead their way towards it, with his sharper elbows and readiness to use his rifle butt to clear a way as necessary.

'Tris, I only see one truck, and it don't look like it's goin' anywhere very fast.'

They found Barrie Knight, marooned in a sea of spectators, in the driving seat of an Army surplus vehicle similar to the one in which most of the Blood City squad had entered Piedra. A centurion and blue Knight occupied the bench beside him, while the bed of the truck – its canvas roof no longer more than a few tatters around the edges – was crammed with soldiers of all Houses, some passed out, others still looking stupidly up at the Officer's blank shield.

Barrie sprang down to greet Tristan with a bear hug, thumping his back with a hand he then extended to greet Ian. 'I thought we were here for the night. Where is Sir Tristram and the others?'

'Not coming yet, but he lives. We'll explain on the way – need to get gone. Where's Bowlegs and the other lorry?'

'Someone had to wait here for you to find us. I could see the press was getting too great for a quick way out, so I pulled rank and had him move it a few streets away while I watched the second half. The idea was he could take the key players on ahead as necessary.'

'I guess we're all key now, and few enough to fit in one truck. Let's go to him.'

On the point of sinking into a much-needed but unsought sleep, Sir Tristram heard a clunk from what seemed almost inside his head. On his feet with the alertness of an experienced fighter, he rushed through the next door into the referee's ensuite. He saw at once the shower had a false floor, because the oversized head of Schwartz O'Reilly was glaring out from it, behind his rifle. Seeing the intruder was Sir Tristram, he pulled back the gun. Then he pulled back his head to let the trapdoor fall.

17

Road to Casablanca

Sir Tristram only just got his steel-capped boot into the closing gap. He needed all his strength to lift it to the point where the door's own weight carried it crashing backwards to the floor. He would have kicked Schwartz off the narrow ladder he was descending, had he not feared knocking him onto the two more important O'Reillys in the darkness below.

By the time Sir Tristram reached the foot of the ladder, Jakob had produced light from a sconced flambeau. He was the first to enquire about Tristan.

'They got through.' Jakob had not mentioned Swallow. 'I was too slow to make it with them, as I nearly was to join you now.' He looked hard at an unabashed Schwartz.

Tommy's escape route was luckily beneath Piedra's sewage system rather than within it. The pipes were not entirely watertight nor, indeed, proof against some leakage of slippery solids. None of the soldiers had a dainty nose, and Sir Tristram soon stopped thinking about what his feet were squelching in, putting aside regret for lack of that extra turn of speed which would have seen him now in fresh air with Tristan and Ian.

'We were betrayed by Slasher, then?' He resumed the earlier conversation with Tommy as they followed Jakob. Schwartz brought up the rear – with the other sewer rats for company, the Knight thought uncharitably.

'His cousin is Sambo.'

'It may be as well that we never planned to sail with Bates. If you are sure his loyalty is more towards you than the Vikings, the *Chupacabra* might still serve, if we could only reach it. The mass of Army and Ogs will surely be all over Piedra now, especially the port.'

'Although I still feel this is my land, I accept power may already be usurped. We must get to Casablanca. If that means marching head high through Piedra and Pedrilla to see who will rally to their Grand Vizor, I am ready to do it. If you never planned to use Bates, perhaps you have another idea?'

That was about as close as O'Reilly would come to asking for help, Sir Tristram sensed. 'If we were leaving in triumph with your full consent and in full company, the main port with Bates and the *Chupacabra* would have been the logical departure point. We are not in full company' —he dared not let himself dwell on how many of his squad were gone— 'nor in triumph. Swallow helped me arrange with an

Indian fisherman to take us through the forest and to sea from Morumbi Cove—'

'I give Syhigh much credit. He will no sooner secure the port than realise there is one other way off the Last Ground.'

'I agree. Especially as he will know we arrived by that route. I think it better, not risk-free. We would still have to negotiate the Army control post at the edge of the forest.'

'Jakob, what do you think?'

'We must get back to the mainland. The way to Morumbi will be faster and safer even if we have to footslog it – better yet if our teammates bring transport. Will they be able to do so?'

'I can only pray. My son is with them.'

Myhigh Syhigh had overruled Pink Viking to follow the Ogs' slower, but less destructive, path through the Indians, who offered no aggression but no cooperation either. Reaching the players' tunnel at last, he set Reaney to comb the ground floor in case Tommy and his small band were holed up there, while leading the bulk of his soldiers upstairs to the fans' exits.

The CIC himself led a party to check out exit W19, with E-Og in support and to maintain contact with A-Og, who followed Pink Viking to W17. The force field barrier was working at Syhigh's gate, he confirmed by having a workshy private touch the grille, recoiling from the shock to provide a brief amusement for his mates. They were quickly called to W17, where Pink Viking pointed out a mangled boot, scuffed heel on their side, pullstraps and piping peeping out on the other, along with its intact, discarded pair. 'No sign of its owner' —he stated the obvious— 'so we can assume Swallow has flown.'

'Yes indeed. What we don't know is whether he was first or last in line.'

Relying on old-style Army comms, a breathless conscript came running to them. 'Sirs, the Sarge – I mean, Captain Reaney – says to come down. We've found something.'

Two minnits later they were all looking at the big dark hole in the ref's facilities, where Sir Tristram had not been able to replace the trapdoor.

'One flew vlad, one flew west...' mused Syhigh.

Bowlegs had the manservant's enviable capacity to take his sleep whenever and wherever a half-chance presented itself. Woken by Barrie Knight rapping steel-knuckled on the driver's window, he had to be reassured that Sir Tristram was alive and without serious injury before being persuaded to drive out of the city towards Morumbi rather than the port.

There was little motorised transport on Zanzibar, so they would have been able to make decent speed but for the parlous state of the highway and the need to watch out for debris or stray animals – pointed out forcibly to their driver by Barrie after a near miss with some great horned creature which ripped off their nearside wing mirror. The truck laboured at even modest elevations in the road. Unsure whether these would count as 'hills', and desperate not to overshoot their meeting-point, Tristan had his nose pressed to the windscreen.

'Do you think that could be it – the hangman's tree?' he asked about a huge oak coming up to the side of the road. Its branches extended far enough to scratch the truck's sides and tickle its roof. Various of them would comfortably bear a soldier's weight at neck-snapping height off the ground.

'Maybe it once was. That's probably the new version right ahead.'

Barrie was looking at a gibbet, stark in the truck's feeble headlights as the representations with which Tristan and his shulmates would draw Hangman on exceptionally boring deys. It stood out against the skyline at the very top of the hill, on a patch of green inside the roundabout with exits to left and right as well as straight ahead. A corpse hung upside down on it, kilt flapping where the head should have been, covering torso rather than thighs to expose filthy underpants. They had found the rest of Albert.

'Tris, concentrate. What does that sign say?'

'That's it – 'St George'. This must be the place. Go straight ahead, Bowlie, they said to meet them on the downslope. Take it slow.'

'How we'll find 'em I don't know. Night's as black as a Cowboy's...hat.' Bowlegs sacrificed alliteration to Tristan's sensibilities. He had to keep a foot half on the brake pedal to maintain a slow enough speed down the hill to satisfy his companions.

They had already regained level ground when Tristan saw a splash of unexpected colour floating in the air off at the passenger side.

'It's our cross – the red cross. That must be them. Pull over, Bowlie.'

'Are you sure?'

'Do it,' Knight ordered. 'Whether it's Sir Tristram or the soldier who stole his shirt, we have business here.'

Jakob had borrowed rather than stolen his captain's shirt, hanging it on the dull side of his scimitar and waving it to attract the attention of the passing vehicle. They had been confident enough of slipping away into the countryside if the truck had contained hostiles, though Jake realised Sir Tristram had not kept back the prudent distance agreed when he ran past him to join Barrie and Tristan in the road.

'Well done and well met – but you stepped down from the truck too quickly,' he chided Tristan. 'Now we are eight. Time still has its foot on our necks. The Grand Vizor agrees to take the road to Morumbi with us.

'Tristan's eyes are sharper than any of ours, as is Ian's shooting. Can I suggest they ride up front with my trusty Bowlegs' —the clap on the shoulder was all the reviver that soldier needed, having stationed himself as close to Sir Tristram as he could— 'while we take counsel on how best to get past the Army command post?'

'Make it so,' Tommy agreed.

Lieutenant Muntian was dead drunk when one of his soldiers, scarcely in better shape, brought him the field telephone. 'Syhigh? Come off it. Is this you, Nikita, trying to pull my plon—?' There was an oath at the other end of the line and a new voice. 'Reaney? So it's you playing— It *was* the CIC? Code Red? We're down to bare bones here, my friend. Offer the general my deepest apologies. The Homo? If we can't detain the fugitives, at least delay them…and make the great gun ready. Got it – coffee – I will. Yes, sir.

'You fool. Next time don't just shove it in my face without letting me know who's on the other end. How many souls have we got?'

'Four or five in any fit state. You were signing leave chitties like the PV does autographs, Munty—I mean, sir.' He realised from the officer's bleak look that military discipline was again the order of the dey after the party atmosphere of the Seskie.

'May be more delay than detain then. If they're coming in the Homo, at least they shouldn't be long. Don't stand there catching flies, Luis. You know, the Hover-Motor, the Grand Vizor's state vehicle, can literally fly over the ground, and big enough to hold – what? – forty soldiers. Set up the machine gun nests while I see what state the tank's in. What are you waiting for?'

'Is the Grand Vizor coming here? Sir?'

'I really hope not.'

Tommy O'Reilly had not visited in many yeers the security and customs post where taxes were levied in his name, and Barrie had bypassed it altogether with Tristan in the *Torvid*. While Sir Tristram had been preoccupied with the safety of his son, Jakob had taken a professional interest as they chatted over chai with Muntian, and was able to brief them on the barracks' dispositions.

'Do we even need to approach them in the truck? Didn't you say the road runs out pretty soon after the tollbooths, at the big tank?' Barrie asked.

'It does, but I'd rather use it as far as we can. Muntian said the area around the road was mined. Right, Jakob?'

'I thought he was joking about that.'

'We'd be beyond a joke if he wasn't,' Sir Tristram answered, thinking he would not mind sending Schwartz ahead as a pathfinder.

'I have heard enough. Have the driver pull over and I shall tell you all what we will do.' Tommy spoke decisively. Sir Tristram was relieved to follow orders for once rather than have to lead.

A weak yellow light spilled between the kiosks onto the road, which was blocked by a five-bar gate adapted from some old cattle crossing, with metal bars replacing wood.

'That's our first decision taken for us, then,' Barrie Knight said to Bowlegs in the cabin of the truck. 'Pull up short enough to get a run at it if we must, keep the engine running, leave the talking to me and be ready to put your foot down.'

As they drew to a halt, Muntian came out to meet them with two soldiers, still feeling the effects of his souse.

'Colonel Muntian?' Barrie held out a mailed fist. 'We have not met, as I was already in Piedra when Sir Tristram led the Blood City squad through here for the Seskie. I now bring his body back for burial at Camelot.'

Scanning the Russkie's features for suspicion, Barrie saw only a mixture of celebrity-struck awe and a monumental hangover, both expressions with which he was familiar enough. They had realised much would depend on the point at which live transmission from the Zuteca had ceased and what communications the border post had received since.

Muntian knew, because he was being asked to detain Tommy O'Reilly, that the Grand Vizor must have survived the fight to the death, which had been announced before the signal cut out. Which surely meant Sir Tristram must not have survived it? Nobody had mentioned Knights to him. His head hurt. 'But why through here? Why not through the port?'

'Colonel, do you have any idea of the chaos in Piedra at this point? We were told Pedrilla was closed.'

'And your clearance to leave Zanzibar?'

'Does a corpse need a passport? I'm sorry, colonel, if I sound unhelpful. We have paid a heavy toll in blood on this island, beyond even that of our dear captain. Please do not ask me for paperwork to leave it.'

'You will not mind if I inspect the back of the truck.'

'I would much rather you did not. That fine lad Tristan is keeping vigil with his father. I would not have him disturbed in that, or in sleep if he should have found it.'

'I understand. Nevertheless, I will look. Vanka, come with me. Drusha, stay here.' Not only was Muntian personally accountable to the CIC – that had been made very clear to him – but with his lack of manpower he would have to do the legwork himself. Although he had the machine pistol in his right hand, he was not envisaging any trouble from Knights. That would come if and when Tommy arrived, whom the Knights had every reason to hate. Apart from carrying out his orders to the letter by inspecting the bed of the vehicle, the Cossack had a genuine wish to offer his duty to the Blood City captain.

Ian Swallow's orders were simply to lead Tommy O'Reilly to Thunder Cloud and accompany him across the waters to the mainland. He crawled along the roadside dyke followed by Tommy and Jakob. They hoped to slip past the guard posts and reach the forest's edge, with or without the Knights in the vehicle. As they drew level with the blockhouse further away from it, Schwartz remained behind in the ditch to cover their rear should battle break out there.

Peering over the tailgate, Muntian saw a white, boyish face appear from a huddle of shadows in the well of the truck.

'I am deeply sorry for your loss.' The lieutenant awkwardly removed his shako. 'Please lower the backboard. I would like to pay my respects to your most distinguished father.'

'We do appreciate the gesture, colonel, but there is really no need. To be honest, we would rather no one else sees Sir Tristram until a professional has prepared him for the grave.'

'I am a soldier. I dare say I have seen worse. Lower the backboard. Vanka, shine a light in here, will you?' he called back as he and Barrie clambered into the truck, his own hands full with hat and gun.

Schwartz may not have heard the request. He did see the Cossack reach to his side, pull something from his tunic and point it into the wagon. He needed no more prompting to shoot the soldier dead, just as the torch came on.

Muntian turned sharply and was raising his machine pistol when Barrie grabbed at his arm. It discharged a burst of fire through the floor of the lorry by way of Knight's leg, collapsing him instantly. The lieutenant felt the corpse's grip at his throat, with no time for superstitious dread before a dirk through the ribs took his breath away.

The two of them, the dead and playing-dead, were hurled on top of the wounded Barrie as the vehicle lurched forward. Hearing the gunfire and seeing the soldier in front of him raise his sub-machine gun, Bowlegs had driven straight at him. He floored the accelerator as a blizzard of bullets came through the windscreen.

Ian was out of the ditch and into the road on the forest side when the lorry smashed through the barrier and full tilt into the blockhouse on the left. He dropped a soldier who came running out of the one nearer to him. Inside that, Luis, who had been anxious to see the Grand Vizor, did so without knowing it, as Tommy burst in with his rifle raised. The other gunner was equally unable to leave his post before Jakob was at his throat.

'Quick, Tris, we need to get out of here. The whole thing is liable to blow up,' Sir Tristram recovered quickly to tell his frozen son. He heaved Muntian off Barrie, not without a pang of regret for the essentially good-hearted officer, bending to scoop up his friend.

'Leave me, Alfred, I can't walk.'

That was evident from the unnatural angle at which the lower leg was extended, attached to the upper more by the suit of armour, pierced multiple times though it was, than the pulverised patella and exposed strips of ligament and tendon. Tristan tried to support the leg, at the same time holding Barrie's hand very tight. Schwartz might have been trying to help; he was told by Sir Tristram to keep his dviddam paws to himself.

Swallow confirmed with a quick glance there was no one left to kill in the spared blockhouse, before turning to the one in which the truck was half-buried. If anyone was trying to get out, they did not make it before a deafening explosion sent flames and smoke high into the moonless sky.

Sir Tristram lowered Barrie to the ground as gently as he could in the middle of the road, not from fatigue but so he could kneel in an act of homage that would have horrified Bowlegs. 'He was my bondsman since we were new.'

'There's no chance, Dad…?'

'None at all,' he answered, harsh in his own grief. 'He was most likely gone before the explosion.'

'That woke the neighbourhood, for sure,' said Ian. 'Anyone followin' us'll be pretty clear now they on the right track. I suggest we move, specially as we're gonna have to hit the forest on foot now.'

'Agreed. You lead the rest on while Tris and I try to scout up some medical supplies and maybe a stretcher for Barrie. We'll be along.'

'I will stay to help you,' Jakob insisted. 'I would offer Schwartz, except he would have to yoke any stretcher round his neck.'

'Thank you, Jakob, I appreciate the gesture, but no one is to stay with me.' Barrie's voice was still strong.

'We will not leave you,' Tristan cried.

'No, you will not leave me. I shall stay of my own will as our rearguard. If you can only help me to the tank, I shall do my best to disable it, or at the very least delay our pursuers bringing its fire to bear on you.'

'Come, Barrie, you can still make it with us.'

'Never to play football or cricket again? Even so, you do not know how much in my heart longs to come. It cannot be. It must not.'

Sir Tristram knew his friend would not budge once his mind was set. For all he and Tristan tried to handle him gently as they manoeuvred him through the tank's turret, Knight could not prevent the odd whimper of pain passing through his clenched teeth. Ian, in brief farewell, had passed him the prized flask he had last shared with Mbulu at the whipping post. 'I never thought I'd say this to a livin' soul, but you prob'ly need it more than me, pard.'

Although the Brittain's technology was of their own world rather than from the Ogs' planet Gog, it was too advanced for the three Knights, baffled by its control panel. 'Maybe I won't disable it after all.' Barrie tried to smile. 'I can at least fight. Draw my sword for me, dear.' As Tristan was doing so, trying to keep his eyes off the butchered leg, Sir Tristram passed Barrie his bloodied dirk. 'Take it. There is no shame in finding your quietus if the Army do not come or make you wait too long. Your place at High Table will always be honoured in Camelot.'

Jakob arrived feet first in the cockpit, with a big basket in the shape of a roosting hen, beaked and tail-feathered. He caught Tristan's less knightly farewell, locked in a mouth-to-mouth kiss with Barrie. Resolutely avoiding eye contact with Sir Tristram, he put the basket and its freight of hand grenades down within easy reach. 'Look what a fine clutch of speckled eggs I found' —his joviality more than a little forced— 'pull the pin on any one of them and it should be enough to spike this piece of crap. If you can reach the turret you might even be able to have an over at the Army openers.'

'Good spin, Jake. My bowling deys are over but I won't drop this dolly. Thank you.'

Syhigh and his soldiers were quickly closing the distance to the control post when they heard and saw the blockhouse explosion. 'At least Muntian and his Russkies are engaging them,' the CIC said. He sported a chinstrap bandage keeping his jaw roughly in place till surgery could replace the Og painkillers he was gobbling like chocolate drops.

'Hardly sounds as if the situation is under control,' Pink Viking retorted sourly. 'You know we need a body. Tommy O'Reilly disappeared is almost as dangerous as escaped. If they do get through your roadblock, what are our hopes of catching them?'

'From an Army point of view, not great. The Homo is only good over more or less level terrain. We can hopefully shell the forest from the tank, but that's a bit hit-and-miss.'

'And from the Og point of view, A-Og? I knew I should have asked you first.'

'It would be hard to find the Indian trails through the forest, let alone follow one with a large body of soldiers. Much will depend on how much of a start they have. We can clear our own way by fire, at the risk of destroying the whole forest.'

'The forest can go hang. If they get to Casablanca we could have a whole country in flames.'

Sir Tristram set a fast pace away from the tank, despite having to drag a stumbling, sobbing Tristan by one arm the first part of the way along the dirt track to the jungle. It petered out some distance still from the trees.

'Where now, Jake? Do you remember which way we came from the jungle to here?'

'We will not be taking the smugglers' trail – it is too well-known.' Thunder Cloud materialised between them, holding a rifle and wearing nothing but a loincloth. 'Take the other end of the rifle, hold onto each other and follow me.'

When they reached the others on the edge of the forest, their Indian guide draped a thick coil of rope over his shoulder and paid it out to them, for each to shoulder in turn at one of its knots. There was still plenty of rope left wrapped around the Indian's torso – he had been told to expect a bigger group – as he led them without further comment into the deeper darkness on a path only he could see.

They were glad of the rope when they discovered just how deep, how dark. Instructed to pull on it if they found themselves in trouble or sensed any danger, the six of them behind Thunder Cloud were headed by Ian and tailed by Schwartz. Tommy followed Ian, then came Tristan, Sir Tristram and Jakob.

While the Blood City captain could hardly see Tristan in front of him, the picture of that kiss with Barrie Knight was seared into his mind's eye. He only hoped he would get the chance to task his boon companion on it. There had been too many deaths already, each striking nearer and costing dearer since that of Nkulu the Zulu. He remembered saying in Whipping Square he was not the one fit to deliver a eulogy for that soldier. Who would praise the others, his own lost in search of the Seskie and Tommy: Vic Swallow and Malabar on the *Chupacabra*, leaving Ian as perhaps the only one able to tell who really murdered Nkulu; White Eagle, carried from the field of play in the Zuteca; François, dying in his claim at last to a son's right to avenge his father?

At least none of them had to endure the sight of the golden trophy being presented to the soldier two knots ahead of him in the jungle. Was Tommy's presence, offering still some hope of success in their wider, covert mission, really a justification for the others fallen? Yellow Cloud, without whose intervention they would never have escaped the Zuteca; Brittanus and Cowboy, mown down he knew, though he had not witnessed it – he could at least hope that Oscar and Little Doe were still above ground; Sir Septimus, slain by the Vikings; big-hearted Chutney too. They had all supported him to the end, if not always quite as unquestioningly as Bowlegs, who had driven himself without hesitation to a flaming death in service of Sir Tristram.

The darkness was broken by a great flash and simultaneous blast from behind them – surely Barrie Knight's funeral pyre. He stumbled into Tristan, who must have stopped. Putting his hands on his child's shoulders from behind, Sir Tristram whispered hoarsely, 'For all we loved him, we can do nothing more for Barrie now – except move on, so that his sacrifice is not in vain.'

There was no answer, but Tristan resumed his march. Sir Tristram kept his hands on the shoulders in front of him till he could bear their shaking no more.

They trekked on in darkness and silence until they felt a growing light behind them. Did the jungle grow a little thinner ahead too?

'The Ogs must be burning a way after us,' Jakob said behind him when the smell to accompany the light had become unmistakable. 'We can only hope the time Barrie bought us so dear will be enough.'

'He spared us the tank. One shell from that could have

taken us all out.' Sir Tristram felt the rope tighten ahead. Thunder Cloud was obviously trying to quicken their pace.

'Let's hope we can outrun them *and* any creatures they may stampede in terror of the fire. Who knows what beasts call this jungle home?'

The breeze blowing in from the sea saved the small band from suffocation by smoke from the clearage behind them. Nevertheless, Sir Tristram's lungs and legs were almost gone when they reached the forest's edge at Morumbi Cove, in the middle of its horseshoe. An unlit vessel sat low on the shoreline, almost a football field away. Ian was talking urgently to Thunder Cloud. 'Come on, cap'n, one last charge, the goal's ahead. I've told TC you'll see him right in Casablanca.'

'You can do that your—'

'No sir, they ain't far enough behind. I'll head off to one flank. Do you post Schwartz on the other. We can mebbe put 'em off rushin' you.'

'It makes sense,' Tommy agreed. 'Schwartz, head right, and when the smoke clears do your best to re-establish contact with Zito and the others.'

'Aw, shame.' Amazingly, Ian was grinning. 'I had visions of me and the wee feller steppin' out onto the beach at each other for a little game of last-man-living. Go ahead, Tris, lead your pa to safety. No time for goodbyes, and no need. Remember ole Ian's popped up to see you before when you least expected it.'

They ran in a ragged bunch to the boat, Ian heading barefoot to the left and Schwartz to the right as ordered, to seek cover in the edges of the woodland. They had barely reached it before another path to the beach appeared.

E-Og and G-Og were well into the swing of working as a team, the one clearing a flaming roadway, the other then dampening it sufficiently for the Army to pass along. Syhigh had let the soldiers under Reaney keep up with them, making as good a pace as he could behind with Pink Viking – apparently in no mad rush – and A-Og.

Reaney did not give the order for his two leading troopers to burst onto the beach, spraying fire at the five runners they could see. When they were felled by single bullets from either side, no order he gave could make others follow. 'E-Og, can you and your oppo smoke out the snipers for us?'

'Won't be so accurate at a distance, but we can splatter-paint the whole forest red if you like.'

'What are you waiting for, then? Let's put this horseshoe in the forge and fire it up.'

Unconcerned by any Zuni bullets that might bounce off their suits, the two Ogs followed roughly the same routes as Ian and Schwartz without troubling to track their footprints in the sand. Rather than make any effort to focus their fire, they sprayed in a huge arc, almost back to the point where they had themselves just emerged from the forest.

Sir Tristram knew as illusory the feeling that because his feet were splashing in water, he was safe. A couple of Indians, newer than Thunder Cloud, were helping him to boost and haul the others up the steps, over the side and onto the deck; a third brave stood at the tiller. The captain was last aboard of the Blood City Seskie squad of only three, plus Tommy O'Reilly, their bitter prize.

As the Indians manoeuvred their craft out into water deep enough for full throttle on its engines, the two Knights, father and child, looked back at Morumbi Cove, already a crescent of fire. They could not distinguish individuals among the troops, urged on by Pink Viking and firing again as they ran towards them. Always fighters, Jakob and Tommy were firing right back, crouched in the vessel's stern.

'Get down and hold fast to something' —Thunder Cloud ignored his own advice as he pushed them both— 'or go into the cabin. We're about to pick up speed.' Tristan turned and bent over as if to vomit, one hand at his stomach.

Suddenly fearful, Sir Tristram tried to shepherd the hunched figure down into the covered area. 'Will you go below?'

'Not yet. Let me see the stars and the moon.' He was right. During their time in the forest a waxing crescent moon had appeared, as if a pale reflection of the flaming forest below.

'What is it? Are you hit?' He gripped one arm as Tristan slowly lowered himself to the deck, sitting with his back to the perspex cabin wall.

'I am bleeding, Father.'

'Where are you hit? I see no wound.'

'Do not trouble. Mortal for Tristan, it marks only the beginning for Tristania, as a woman.'

She knew her father did not understand, but there was love in his eyes. That would be enough.

THE END

Afterword

From the Wisbechian, magazine of Wisbech Grammar School, December 1967 (Vol. XII, No. 4)

Under Form Contributions

First Forms

My Kingdom

When I was very small, I used to buy two plastic soldiers from Wisbech every day for about a year. I had a lot of them, but they were always fighting and killing each other. This situation went on for a long while until the people settled down in the land of Cibola. Although there is still fighting, the people are much happier now. Perhaps this is because, at last, they have a good, strong king.

Cibola had three kings including the present one. The first king's name was Frederick. Under him were two men of equal rank. One of them was the brother of Henry Morgan, the present king. Under Morgan's orders these three men and several other important people were killed. After this, Cibola was without a king and Morgan and his pirates terrorised the country. But, unknown to Morgan, the dead king had a son, who, after a while, succeeded him to the throne in an attempt to end the pirates' reign of terror. He was known at [*sic*] Frederick the second, but he was a weak king and only made matters worse. At last the people got tired of him and revolted, killing him, and leaving the throne empty again. After this, the whole country was sick of fighting so they elected Morgan as their king and that is the situation today.

The future looks bright for Cibola. The population is steadily increasing and they have a good king who looks like being on the throne for a long time.

D. Bailey

Connect with the Author

Find David G Bailey on Facebook at **bit.ly/D-G-B**

Lightning Source UK Ltd.
Milton Keynes UK
UKHW011111151021
392226UK00002B/50/J